CHASING CZARS

BOOK 3 of The CHASING CLEOPATRA Chronicles

TINA SLOAN

Chasing Czars: Book 3 of The Cleopatra Chronicles

For information about this title contact the publisher:
TATI KHAN Publishing
tinasloan@gmail.com

ISBN: 978-1-7330577-8-3 (softcover)
        978-1-7330577-9-0 (eBook)

Cover and Interior design: 1106 Design

To Hazel, the dancer; Mather, the athlete;
Field, the blue-eyed charmer; Renny, my incredible son;
Helen, the most wonderful daughter-in-law.

To Steve, the perfect husband for nearly fifty years,
and to the fun family puzzle, Meg, Marcus, Piper, John,
Cristina, Keely, Sandy, Celia, Ashlyn, Alexa, Genie, John, Jack,
Eliza, Gil, Martha, Hillary, and Lucy the "other grandmother."

To all my beloved friends, I thank you for reading my books,
listening to my Aging Tips, and even asking, "How's the writing
coming, Tina?" You know who you are. If you don't, call me!!!

To Nathan Vigneri for all his help and tech prowess
and Serena Turner for all her genius help

But especially for Nicole, the Bravest of the Brave,
I salute you

Prologue

Vera

Call me Vera. Like Ishmael. We have things in common—mostly a deep spiritual malaise.

Years ago, a devastating event linked my fate with a man who was equally affected. His constant presence comforted us. But as years passed, the man's marriage and children took him away. Still, every year, he never forgot to call on that day. And we were grateful.

My husband, Barnie, and I were inseparable, finding solace in our lovely estate adorned with towering evergreens and vibrant maples. We played golf and hiked. Barnie's prized stamp collections funded our love for travel. But our main passion was chess. It led us to global competitions and friendships, especially with a Russian couple, Anatoly and Ilse Rustikoff.

For over fifty years, Barnie and I shared a tremendous love till life's unpredictability struck. A brain aneurysm stole him away from me. He was pressing the "Power Off" button on the television remote. Oh, the irony.

I was shattered.

PROLOGUE – VERA

T HE MAN FROM OUR PAST, whom I hoped to share my grief with, was noticeably absent. I had even saved a seat for him next to me at the funeral, but not even a single petal arrived. He hadn't called on that day for several years either. My solitude overcame me, giving way to despair and anger, eventually fueling fantasies of retribution against him. These dark thoughts brought an adrenaline rush. This newfound purpose, Revenge Against Him, admittedly twisted, reignited a spark in my life.

I HAD TRAINED at The Royal Academy of Dramatic Arts in London, mingling with fellow thespians and later gracing stages in New York and London. Marriage to Barnie shifted my priorities; but our shared love for theater never waned, leading us to support repertory companies and mingle with actors. Two talented performers from a local production I saw a few weeks ago caught my attention, and seeing their potential, I enlisted them in my brand-new plan of psychological warfare. In tribute to Barnie's love for chess, I named them Kasparov and Carlsen for two of the world's greatest chess players, Garry Kasparov and Magnus Carlsen. As Pierre Teilhard de Chardin once said, *'Within every being and every event, there was a progressive expansion of a mysterious inner clarity which transfigured them.'* Revenge is my inner clarity, and it is transfiguring me. A visceral revenge for what was taken from me. Revenge for forgetting us. . . . But above all, a chilling revenge for her. Her, whom I talk to every day.
  Her.

St. Moritz, 2016

CLEO, 1

"To be a woman is a great adventure:
To drive men mad is an heroic thing."

BORIS PASTERNAK, DR. ZHIVAGO

I finished reading Zelli her new Unicorn book, *Uni's First Sleepover,* followed by *Eloise in Paris,* her favorite of all the Eloise's because Paris is where we live. Now, it is time for Nannie, ironically her real name, to put Zelli to sleep. I usually do the nighttime ritual, cocoa, and her favorite song, *"You Are My Sunshine."*

But tonight, I am going out, so Nannie will fill in. "Thank you, Nannie, and goodnight, mon petit chou chou," I kiss Zelli's nose. Since my father has always called me his "little cabbage," and I hate being a little cabbage, I am unsure why I bestowed my daughter with the same nickname. But she likes it, perhaps since she hears her grandfather use the name for me.

"Goodnight, Ma Mere." Zelli kisses me, hugs me, and tries to hold onto my beige cable knit sweater as I walk away to get ready. This makes me so happy. Her little face, a replica of mine except for her big blue eyes, which were a gift from her father, is my world. Having a child very late in life has been my greatest joy. She is my best friend, if it's possible for a four year old to be a grown adult's best friend. She jumps off the bed and runs to get the tiny bottle of Chanel No.5 that I gave her for Christmas, her most prized possession. She starts spritzing both of us on our wrists and behind our ears. I wear Endgame, but she already has her own perfume ideas.

"Ma Mere, behind my knees too, please!" Zelli smiles.

I can never say no to that smile. She gives me the perfume, and I spritz her knees on the front, back, and sides. Then she beams up at me, and we are both drenched in perfume. "Goodnight Zelli, I will come in and give you a kiss when I get home."

"Promise?"

"Yes, I promise."

"Can Endy sleep in my room so I won't be lonely?" she pouts. "Oh, Zelli, what an actress you are. But yes, she can if she will stay there. She likes to lurk around the front door, and I am always afraid she will walk out on us." Zelli looks terrified. I kiss her, "Just keep your door shut, and she can sleep in your room tonight." She laughs as she leaves, knowing she got her way with her cat. Then she starts performing cartwheels. One after another after another. I applaud heartily . . . As a child, I was never able to do cartwheels, backbends, splits, or even somersaults, so her agility thrills me.

Tonight I am not just going out but am going to the night-club Raven to catch up with friends I have known and skied with most of my life. Raven, which is a long walk from our hotel, is quite unpretentious. There are no signs, not even a visible door. It looks very sedate, but once you enter, the excitement is throbbing. People are overflowing. They are all gorgeous and brimming with health and the joy of being there.

Chomi, the owner, knew "everyone" from his many years as a concierge at the Badrutt Palace Hotel, so, naturally, when he opened Raven, "everyone" came. He made sure "everyone" only included those whom he thought would make it fun and flirtatious. And ever since, it has remained the go-to destination at night. I haven't seen these friends in a decade so, of course, it is really important to look stunning. How vain one is. Makes me smile at that reflex, but I really do want to look "fabulous."

I walk across the hotel's expansive living room carpet from Zelli's bedroom and into mine. Out come all the jewels and the furs—faux, of course—as well as my favorite sky-high Sarah Flint beige suede boots and matching suede vest with fur trim. I add pearls and diamonds on my throat and wrists and slide my mother's beautiful emerald ring onto my finger. The hotel's hairdresser, Julien Sabatier, makes house calls. Thankfully, he paid me a visit earlier, so my long dark hair is in perfect waves. And I am Zelli-spritzed with perfume.

Nothing starts until midnight, but for those that Chomi is fond of, there is dinner before the crowds come. I haven't seen Chomi in ten years, but he relayed to my father that he will be serving cheese fondue in my honor tonight.

Chomi and I became friends one day when I was a teenager, pouting in a pile of snow because my father had to leave for yet another business engagement. My half-sister Tree, who was to visit me, had to stay behind in New York after she came down with German measles. I was alone with my ever-present French tutor, Madame Saigal. Chomi walked by in his Badrutt Palace Hotel uniform on his way to work and sat next to me in the snow. I told him my horrid news, and he just listened as I let it all out. He then asked me to meet him on his break right back here at noon. When noon finally rolled around, Chomi arrived with snowshoes and told me about snow art.

"There's a man named Simon Beck, Mademoiselle Cleo. He was born fifty years ago, and he's the world's first snow artist.

Oui, Monsieur Beck has walked more than fifty miles in circles wearing snowshoes, He does this to create très grand snow drawings in Colorado. I try to be like Monsieur Beck, so I walk in my snowshoes every day.

Mademoiselle Cleopatra, do you know what we are going to do today? We are going to create a snow drawing of a gigantesque heart."

And off we went.

We stamped on the snow in an enormously broad field where they now play snow polo. We made hearts and circles stamping with our snowshoes, and it felt so good, stamping and stomping and stamping. I met Chomi at noon every day until my school break ended, and I became very accomplished at stamping designs. Chomi made me promise to just put on snowshoes and head out to make snow art whenever I was feeling angry or hurt. Every year, I send Chomi a new pair of snowshoes as a grateful thank you from the spoiled little girl that he transformed into a stamper.

A knock on my door, and in comes my father, Didier Gallier, who, in his seventies, reminds everyone of an aging James Bond.

"Bonsoir, mon chou chou," he bends over and kisses both of my cheeks. "You look beautiful, as always."

"Thank you, Daddy. Can I get you a drink while you wait for me to finish my makeup?"

"I'll hold off until we get to Raven," Didier says as he sits in an easy chair while I finish adding my mascara. "Are you excited to see all of your old friends? I saw Julio on the mountain earlier, and he is very much looking forward to seeing you . . ."

I offer Didier's reflection an amused smile, and he returns the gesture. He loves to extract little details about my personal life under the veil of the most innocent of questions.

"On second thought, I'd relish an ice water. May I get you one?"

I nod, and Didier crosses to the silver pitcher on the large marble table. My father has skied in St. Moritz all his life and brought me here almost every winter since I was three years old. I don't remember skiing with him as a child, but he insists he had me between his legs as we went down the bunny slopes. There are no photos, but then my father has always been a very secretive man. There are few photos of us anywhere, though I do have one of him that's at my house in Honolulu, where he's wearing a dark turtleneck with his cigarette dangling from his mouth, looking very much like a movie star. Always a cigarette dangling, though since Zelli was born, he doesn't smoke when he is near her. As I am his only child, Zelli is Didier's only grandchild, so the aristocratic Marquis title that he has will pass onto her after it goes to me. He shakes his head as he tells me it proves to be extremely useful at times.

Didier and I stroll along the snow-covered pavement on our way to Raven, looking out at the magical scene, which is reminiscent of a screensaver. Close to the hotel are all the shops and the spas and crepe eateries, and as we walk on, we pass other hotels and stores selling skis and bindings and parkas, goggles, and lift tickets. When we pass horses to give us a ride in their painted carriages, I hop in one. Didier glares at me for a split second and then follows suit. He no longer hops in—his age has begun to show in tiny ways. The carriage will take us the rest of the way to Raven.

"How's Zelli's skiing coming along?" Didier asks as he lights a cigarette.

"Oh, she loves her instructor, JoJo. But she's only four, Daddy."

"You were three when you started. Don't you love how you can ski anywhere, anytime? That comes from learning early. If you fall, it's funny, not scary. This is the age for her to learn, Cleopatra."

"Who knows, we may have the next Lindsey Vonn before she's able to read."

"Exactly," he laughs. "How exciting. And if she's like her mother, she can hardly wait to hit the slopes every morning." He pauses. ". . . Or maybe Zelli takes after her father?"

I start laughing at his not-so-subtle approach. I have revealed the identity of Zelli's father to Didier, but he has yet to meet him.

Didier is allergic to direct questions, always leaning on his endless charm to get the answers to the things that he must know. He has his ways—an international secret agency called The Business at his fingertips being one. My father and I enjoy playing our little games. We laugh. We have always had the same laugh. Ah, I love being back in St. Moritz with my father.

THE WONDER OF FAMILY GENERATIONS. Because of my father's long-standing loyal patronage in St. Moritz over the decades and his lasting friendship with Chomi, Raven serves wines from both of his vineyards, the one in France and the one in Algeria. Didier had his designer craft a special label for Club Raven, featuring beautiful black birds soaring high in the mountains above Corviglia. The name Raven is actually quite clever as it is the translation of the Italian word, "Corvi." Our favorite mountain here is Corviglia.

Even before we walk in the door, I fall into the arms of people I have missed terribly these past ten years while I was living in Honolulu, Dubai, and Paris.

"Cleopatra! Is it really you?!"

"How long has it been? Ten years? It can't have been that long, can it, Cleo?"

Hugging and kissing and holding hands. But then again, it feels like we just met for lunch yesterday to chat about our love lives and our travels and our jobs and families. The whole St. Moritz group is so close-knit, with appreciable intermarrying. When I was young, I dated several of the men whom my father told me would be here tonight, and I've known many of their wives for just as long. Ah, speaking of which, there are the smiling Trevor brothers across the dance floor flirting with one of my closest friends, Cindy Louise, who is such an enchantress and dressed perfectly, as always, in black. All of her ski clothes are jet-black as well. My friend Lady Eleanor comes up to say she has room for me in her cabana for the World Cup Finals of the Snow Polo tomorrow afternoon if I'd like to come. I do. She plays polo, so it will be exciting to hear her talk about the game and the players.

Lola, Raven's very own Catherine Deneuve, floats up to my father in one of her gauze creations that is absolutely breathtaking. Lola, whom he just met this season, seems to have stolen first place from the many women who enjoy his company. She is not the usual "type" he sees. She is more social than he is but he seems smitten, and she is so lovely.

Didier notices everything. "Lola, you might as well have been teaching that Austrian instructor you had on the black diamonds today . . . You have all the grace, and style, and finesse. Something that he quite lacks. Well, until he tripped you, and you let out that expletive! In Russian, no less. No finesse then!"

Lola floats closer to him as she smiles at me. She does look like Catherine Deneuve, and she totally engrosses my father with her wit. She says things to him no one else would dare say, and he just smiles. But I do notice she is always the one asking him to do things. She seems to initiate their time together. Not that he seems to mind at all.

All around us are tidbits of conversations . . .

"Luis, you went to the Snow Polo today. Who won? You don't know? How can you not—ah, of course, you weren't looking at the polo but at everyone around you."

"I gather they met in Argentina, where he was playing polo. He's playing tomorrow in the final, you know."

"Yes, all the polo players will be here tonight, and they are rather easy to pick out."

"Are those the pearls you got from your father when you turned sixteen, Cleo? Remember we both got them for our birthdays a day apart? We celebrated with corsages made of pink bubble gum. What fun we had," Anne grins. We lived near each other growing up in New York City and had such wonderful times.

My head is spinning. Since Zelli was born, I have only been to small dinners and occasional cocktail parties. I have not had so many friends under the same roof in a long, long time. I feel like I am twenty-one again. My father wanted me to get back into the social whirl, but I was only interested in Zelli and her friends' parents. Just then, Suzie, another friend from New York City, comes to say hello to Anne and me. Suzie, one of the most avid skiers in St. Moritz, and I ran into each other earlier today on the mountain.

"My, you have a gorgeous little girl, Cleopatra! What is her name?"

"Zelli," I smile proudly.

"Zelli. How divine. She looks just like you! Lucky girl."

But Zelli wasn't with me earlier today. How does Suzie know what Zelli looks like? She can see the confusion on my face.

"My daughter JoJo is ski bumming . . . She has been teaching Zelli's ski school class!"

"JoJo is your daughter! Zelli adores her and wants to have red hair just like her."

Suzie takes a sip of her diet Coke, which she loves.

"And who, dare I ask, is Zelli's father?"

"No, Suzie! You don't dare ask!" I smile.

Anne smiles broadly. Suzie, laughing, joins in, "Well, I tried since everyone said that only I could get his name out of you."
Anne looks over at her and grins at me,
"I already got it!"

JAKE, 1

Fresh powder. There's really nothing better. I've wanted to ski St. Moritz since I read all about it way back in the day on the pages of *Backcountry* magazine. The slopes are perfectly groomed, and the views make even Jackson Hole look like a dump. Here, it's a paradise for any sports enthusiast.

Snow starts to fall at precisely the same time that one other guy and I step onto the gondola. We're headed straight to the top. White powder swirls around the crystal-clear walls, and it feels like we're living inside a snow globe.

I came to St. Moritz to clear my head. I desperately needed some time away from the chaos that's awaiting me back in the Big Apple. My life over the past five years has been total and utter chaos.

It all started on that fateful family vacay to Honolulu . . . In no particular order, I fell out of love with the woman I thought might one day be my wife, met another woman with whom I'm still currently obsessed, helped save my family from a near-death experience on a helicopter, and witnessed a man fall to his death before he could carry out the deadliest terrorist attack on American soil since 9/11. Then, I discovered that my father, a.k.a. the guy I'd looked up to my entire life, was living a complete lie.

He wasn't just the corporate lawyer he'd purported to be. No, he was also an undercover CIA agent. Oh, also, the terrorist was not just pushed over a cliff; he was pushed over that cliff by that woman whom I'm still crazy about. My life changed more in those four days in Honolulu than it did in the twenty-six years that preceded them.

A few months after we got back to New York, my dad flexed a wee bit of nepotism and scored me an interview with one of the CIA's top recruiters. I passed the background check and aced the polygraph. And then, two years after that, I became a father. To recap, I escaped death, went through a major career and relationship change, found out about my father's secret identity, witnessed the death of one of the world's most lethal terrorists, and became a deadbeat dad.

Beyond my father, what really helped me get my size thirteen foot in the door at the CIA was Russia. As a lifelong diehard sports fan, I was obsessed with *Miracle on Ice* when I was a wee lad. Not only could I rattle off the entire Team USA roster, but all of the Russian players, too—including their positions and stats. Years later, when I was captain of the Middlebury Hockey Team, we played at a yearly tournament just outside St. Petersburg. They brought in a professor who taught us the basics so we could get by while we were over there, meaning we could get by ordering a beer or asking for directions. Then, a few years out of college, I dated this babe who was originally from Stalingrad. During the three years we were together, Natalia Nabatov and her family helped me sharpen my Russian fluency. Russian, a language that is not commonly spoken by today's American youth.

And the rest is history. For the next year and a half, I underwent rigorous training outside of Langley at—I kid you not—The CIA University. That name still sounds so fake. It's like something out of a kids' movie starring Bugs Bunny and the rest of the Looney Tunes gang.

"How you doin'?" I say to the other guy in the gondola. He's got on this dope all-white ski suit. His accessory game is on point too, a matching white hat and a white neck warmer that obscures most of his face. And, to top it all off, white gloves and boots. The only thing on his body that isn't white is the sleek pair of black and gold shades that I wish belonged to me. I flick my eyes over at the label. Bulgari. Of course. This guy definitely doesn't fuck with lame, pedestrian brands like Ray Bans or Maui Jims like the rest of us peasants.

White Ski Suit smiles and shoots me a curt nod. "Have you skied Corviglia before?"

Even his accent is cool, though I can't actually place it.

"First time," I say with intentional nonchalance.

"Ah. Well, then you are in for a treat," he smiles.

"You come here often?" Jesus, Jake. Get a grip. *Come here often?*

"Yes," he smiles knowingly.

Of course, he has. Guy's a pro. "Nice. I'm jealous."

I look back out at Corviglia. I sound basic, but the view really is awesome. Or at least what I can see of it . . . She's still a beaut, but damn, it's really starting to come down. As a kid, my parents took us on all sorts of ski trips out west—Vail, Park City, Aspen, Jackson Hole, you name it. It's not like money was no object, but Dad always did pretty well as a "lawyer," and so we were lucky to go on some pretty sweet trips. At a young age, Ricky and I fell in love with the slopes, and we've always been pretty competitive with each other. Matt, poor guy, still hates the snow and couldn't even make it down the bunny hills to save his life. He'd stay inside with my mom doing God knows what. Eventually, she felt bad that Matt was so miserable in the cold and so after Ricky and I graduated from college, we started vacationing to places with much warmer climates. You know, like Hawaii.

"My God. This snow is crazy, yes?" White Ski Suit asks.

I'm tempted to sound chill and pretend it's no biggie, but there's no denying that the blizzard has kicked it up several notches in just as many minutes. "I think we'll be okay though, right? Two young bucks like ourselves?" I laugh at my own dumb joke.

"Yes, you are right," White Ski Suit laughs back. "We'll be fine."

I can't wait to feel the crunch of the powder beneath my rad new Enforcer skis and the cold, crisp air as it whips past my cheeks. I'm embarrassed at how long it's been since I've even set foot inside a gondola.

St. Moritz has one of those incredible European, very luxe vibes that you only see in a Slim Aarons photo or a Bond movie. Actually, I think they actually did shoot Bond here, but it was one starring Roger Moore, so I'm not sure that even counts. I've heard about this one place here called The Evergreen Club about halfway down the mountain. It's all about the apres, and the only way you're granted an entrance is if you have a royal title or you're devastatingly good-looking. Take a guess which category your boy falls into. On one lazy Sunday, I went down an Instagram hole scrolling through photos of The Evergreen Club. It's definitely where all of the fabulous and famous flock to and tipped the scales in St. Moritz's favor when I was deciding between vacationing here or Verbier.

"This weather isn't exactly welcoming you with open arms . . ." White Ski Suit says.

"Nah, I'll be fine," I shrug, hoping to manifest that into reality.

"They should have told us that a whiteout might be coming in . . ."

"Maybe they didn't know? It came on pretty damn quick." A whiteout, Jesus.

"I imagine the ski patrol will come and retrieve everyone who's stuck."

"How long will that take, do you think?"

"Hours, probably. Usually, I just risk it and ski down myself. It's much better than wasting hours of your life stranded up on the mountain."

I nod, picturing myself with frozen eyebrows as I trod pathetically down the mountain.

"I would think they will close the gondolas if they haven't already."

"Yes. I wouldn't be surprised if we were the last ones to make it on . . ."

CLEO, 2

I am effortlessly switching between French and Italian, but I am teetering with this when I hear a bass voice with a touch of a Russian accent mixed into the Tower of Babel. He is speaking to my father who has made his way over to me with my usual "Purple for Her Eyes" concoction—a drink that only I am given whenever I am here to celebrate the purple eyes I inherited from my mother. I forgot what it is like to be coddled and charmed and to feel glamorous and fun again. My father is laughing with the handsomest man I have ever seen. That sounds just ridiculous but it is true.

"Cleopatra, this is Sergei Kominitz. Sergei and I skied together these past years while you were away in Hawaii and Dubai."

I catch something in my father's eye, and I'm not sure what he is trying to say to me.

He turns back to Sergei. "My daughter majored in Russian Literature at the Sorbonne. She speaks the language quite well. You will find she loves your country. Moscow and St. Petersburg lured her from Paris often, didn't they, mon chou?"

"Oh yes, they did. Very often," I smile at my father and then at Sergei as we shake hands.

"Ah. Well then, Cleopatra, perhaps you will tell me which city you prefer. Moscow or St Petersburg? And then tell me why." Sergei laughs, and I think I am in love. "This is a very serious test . . ."

His smile is genuine and perfect, as is he. Tall, at least six feet four, and fit, which I can see through his black turtleneck. His dark hair is long and wavy and thick, like a poet's. This is how easy falling in love is. And I have never done it quite like this before. Ridiculous, but exhilarating to feel this happiness coursing through me. It is swirling, and I am almost lightheaded, and it is not my "Purple for Her Eyes" drink. The gauntlet has been thrown.

"It is a good thing I love tests, Sergei . . ." I stop and think for a minute before launching into one of my favorite topics, Russia. Home to some of the world's greatest writers, musicians, palaces, playwrights, and dancers. My heart pounds and it is difficult for me to think clearly. It's a cliche, laughably so, but Sergei really has taken my breath away. His sharp features give him strength and like my father's, his tan and dark eyes give him a dangerous edge. All of the love songs are finally making sense to me as there is something in his presence that I feel I have known all my life. It sounds absurd, but I am almost shaking. Can one person change your life in one second?

"Well, I prefer Moscow, so I hope that's where you're from, Sergei?"

I speak in Russian and fairly adeptly, as I should, seeing how long I studied it. Interesting how we have developed so many different languages to listen to each other and how many are here in this room right now.

He smiles and nods for me to continue. I see my father slip away to join his friends and Lola in her silvery floating dress joins him, but he winks at me as he leaves. And again, that look.

"Ah, and the why of your test . . . I drowned in the immaculate decorative subway stations that were so deep underground."

Just like I am drowning in your dark eyes. "And the pink and blue, green, and yellow houses. I wanted to knock on their doors just to see who chose pink or yellow or who preferred green. I didn't, of course, as I do believe I was being followed . . ." I laugh since everyone is followed when they visit Russia. And under Putin, it is even more noticeable and more scary.

With just the slightest nod of Sergei's head, he acknowledges the well-known fact that the FSK, formerly the KGB, has foreigners followed and their hotel rooms bugged.

"But most of all, I loved the Novodevichy Cemetery. The aristocratic graveyard where so many of your writers and playwrights are buried—Chekhov, Gogol, among many others as I am sure you already know. And at Donskoy Cemetery, the grave of Solzhenitsyn and the great teacher of acting, Stanislavsky. But best of all, was visiting the grave of my favorite writer, Boris Pasternak, in Peredelkino just outside Moscow. Ah, to have been Lara and to have been loved like Zhivago loved her . . . Though I know Olga Ivinskaya was put in jail for being Pasternak's real-life Lara." I catch myself, I can't believe how long I have rambled on. Though the look on Sergei's face tells me that he is enjoying my ramble. "Ah, sorry! I am digressing, Sergei . . . But I believe I am finally done?"

He smiles but shakes his head no. "Sankt-Peterburg," Sergei says as he steps closer to me to let a waiter pass.

I tingle all over, and I think it passes on to him as well. He looks surprised.

"Sankt-Peterburg, yes, as I do need to pass this test. And what will be my reward for passing?"

Sergei looks at me. As far as I am concerned, he could just keep looking at me forever with those eyes, and that would be all the reward I could ever want. His attention is total, and everyone passing us can see this, too, as they keep walking past us instead of breaking in. I notice a few women eyeing Sergei who would love a chance to break in, but I am not giving them that chance. Not tonight, not ever.

"In Sankt-Peterburg, I was excited to visit Yusupov Palace where Rasputin was killed. I was doing a paper on him at the time. I wonder if you might be like Rasputin who hypnotized the Czarina Alexandra?" I laugh. And then, "You look puzzled at my choice."

"No, not puzzled. All of your talk makes me want to be buried near Pasternak. Perhaps you would come to visit me there . . ." He takes my glass, sips my purple drink and it is the sexiest thing.

"Sergei," I whisper as I move closer to him. The room is very noisy, and again, my breath leaves me. "If you enjoy the topic of cemeteries, you might appreciate what my mother Sandrine had me do for her after her death."

"Oh?" he smiles. And I have fallen even deeper in love.

"One of my mother's dying wishes was that I scatter her ashes all over the world from a very long list she left for me. She called it The Pilgrimage of Ashes."

"Quite a fascinating woman she must have been."

"She was. She had many husbands—my father Didier was her first—and many lovers, so I went to gorgeous restaurants all over Europe and America, where my first stop was the San Diego Zoo to sprinkle her ashes in the cage with the snow leopard. On to Disney World to ride *IT'S A SMALL WORLD*, and hotel suites from NYC to Rome and Mexico. It was a remarkable way of being buried while educating me about what she had done when she was alive. I scattered a tiny portion of her ashes in each place, climbing to 19,970 feet in Africa to scatter the last of her. She was truly 'nearer my God to thee' there.'"

Sergei laughs. He makes me feel as if he has enjoyed every word I have uttered. "Great concoction. What's it called?" he asks, handing me back my drink, nearly empty.

I demurely answer, "Purple for Her Eyes."

"I am building a ski resort and might need this drink to lure you there . . ."

"Really, where? Hopefully, near a cemetery, so I'd find it compelling to visit?"

"Sochi, on the Black Sea. And I will be sure to find a cemetery nearby to compel you to visit. Putin has built an immense palace near Sochi, so I imagine land will be free for a cemetery." Is he putting Putin down? No Russian would dare. Was that comment for me to pass to Didier? Just not sure what he meant.

"Will night skiing be part of your plan? I love to dress up and have dinner, then ski down to my hotel room past the flaming torches and plop into bed," I blurt out, desperate to distract myself from the tingles I am feeling all over. I sound so ridiculous.

"With your skis still on, Cleopatra?" he smiles and then adds, "My favorite insight from Club Raven is that after it closes at five-thirty in the morning, you are still expected to be on the slopes two-and-a-half hours later, at eight sharp. Just enough time to change your clothes and have some breakfast. Would a member be dropped from the Raven if he was not on the slopes in the morning? I imagine with your father's pedigree and your . . ." Sergei looks at me directly, ". . . incredible beauty, you will never be dropped." Then he leans over and whispers, "It is your dimples that enchant me the most."

Again, I feel my father watching us from across the room. Why? I still have no idea what I am to learn from this exceptionally charismatic, deadly, handsome man. Well, I have learned one thing. He likes my dimples.

"I will be at the funicular at eight . . . I don't want to be dropped!" I laugh. "Though no one is really dropped; it's de rigueur to show you can play all night and ski all day."

And he just smiles. He is so sure of himself that it thrills me.

This conversation has become so trite. I decided to see if I could catch him off guard, and so I asked, "What was the worst day of your life, Sergei?"

It's unnerving, but he's staring at me as though I am something he has been searching for his whole life. I sip the last drop of my drink.

Sergei puts his head down, his whole face changing. "The day I lost my young son when he fell through the ice at Lake Baikal."

And now there is really nothing to say.

An old friend comes up to us with open arms. "Oh, she is back! Our Cleopatra is back!"

"Hi, Julio," I stammer. My eyes remain on Sergei's and his stay on me.

"It looks like you could use a fresh drink . . ." And the Count takes my hand, bows to Sergei, and pulls me away with him. As we move toward the bar and away from Sergei, I turn back to him. He is not looking at me but at the painted beams on the ceiling as though he did not just give away his nightmare to a complete stranger. As Julio plies me with questions and babbles on long enough to catch me up on all of the gossip over the last ten years, I keep looking for Sergei above the crowd, but I can no longer see him.

AT EIGHT IN THE MORNING, after a sumptuous breakfast of waffles with tons of maple syrup, I drop Zelli off at ski school. She kisses me with a mouth sticky from all the syrup and I head to the funicular to go up the mountain. But Sergei is not there. Looking around at all of the other skiers I find myself praying he will come. Instead, I see a group of friends from Aspen.

"Cleopatra! Ski with us, will you?" I hesitate as Alison and her daughter Maya might be held back by me. They are fabulous skiers, and I am very rusty. But I agree.

The day looks perfect; the sun is out, and the snow is soft. As we head up the funicular, the views out over the valley look painted on. We agree to ski the moguls first and then hit the back bowls until lunch. Flying down the mountain and floating over the moguls, I keep wishing that he was here with me. He seems so dangerous and what woman isn't drawn to that? This type of adrenaline rush has not been with me since I killed Mohammed Abdul Rahman. I feel it in my blood, and though my Krav Maga sessions still feed me, they are not enough, and I need more, so much more. At last, the moguls give me the high that I crave, and suddenly, I'm laughing as my friends and I whiz down the mountain. The best of friends are often even more competitive than the bitterest of enemies, and so we push one another to ski even faster and more precisely. Everything else except the joy of skiing, weaving in and out as we dance down the diamonds, simply fades away. Oh, how I have missed this place.

Being a mother seems to have dimmed my desire for danger and fast runs and steep mountains. These past four years, just being with Zelli has been enough. Perhaps the time has come to awake from the slumber of motherhood and see if I can do some work for my father. That will bring on the adrenaline rush.

Alison, Maya, and I decide to take a breather, so we sit with others on the patio midway down the mountain. I see friends from Paris, Heidi and Jay. They are both dressed in mad ski outfits with black-and-white checks, which I gather are the "in" look here. I have on a navy Bogner with green trim that I've had since Willy, the founder, gave it to me years and years ago.

Heidi and Jay are catching the sun and sneaking a few cigarettes. "I saw you talking with Sergei Kominitz last night at

Raven, Cleo," Heidi smiles at me blowing a smoke ring. She's always smiling and always happy.

I snap out of my fog.

"Heard he is a huge fan of American baseball. He loves the St. Louis Cardinals. Since everyone thinks he was once KGB, I find that pretty interesting," Jay adds.

"Yes, he is interesting and I am guessing, complicated." I glance down at my watch. "Oh dear, I have to pick up my daughter. Alison, Maya, will you be skiing tomorrow? Eight o'clock at the funicular again? Heidi, Jay?"

I continue down to get Zelli for the SnowPolo World Cup final and I start musing about *him*. Oh God, I want to apologize for my question. But can I? After all, he did answer me honestly and so he must have wanted to tell me about his son. It would have been so easy to have laughed it off and mentioned a broken leg or a car crash or a broken heart, but instead, he told me the truth. And that so rarely happens.

I feel somebody close behind me. The slope is wide open so why would they choose to ski right behind me? I turn back with a big smile, figuring it's a friend who is mimicking my turns. Instead, I get a wink from an attractive man who then skis off way ahead. I see him stop off to the side, then use his ski pole in the snow as if the mountain wanted his autograph. I watch him ski off, taking the black diamonds backward. Backward down the black moguls. Quite a skier. When I reach where he had stopped, I stop and see the design of a crown in the snow. Hmmm. Strange but charming.

I smile when I ski down to JoJo, watching her teach Zelli a hockey stop. Zelli is hardly paying any attention and just giggling madly as a cute boy about her age throws snow in her face.

"Pretty darn good and pretty darn naughty at the same time . . ." JoJo laughs.

I try not to grin, but I am thrilled with this summation of Zelli.

"Hurry, mon chou," I urge Zelli as we walk down the plowed path leading to the frozen lake. She is taking detours to throw snowballs at me. The lake is covered with snow, and nearly three thousand ski-suited spectators are watching the final match, already well underway when we arrive. We have a place in the cabana next to the field courtesy of my friend Lady Eleanor, who is an extraordinary polo player. She pats the seat next to her for Zelli.

"Don't the horses get tired running in the snow, Maman?"

"They do, so each player has a new pony for each chukka."

"Chukka?" Zelli questions, having never heard such a strange word. Lady Eleanor takes over to explain what a chukka is.

"Yes, Zelli, a chukka is seven and a half minutes. And in high-goal polo, there are four chukkas per match. I like to say chukka, don't you? Chukka chukka chukka." Zelli laughs and joins her. "Chukka chukka chukka."

The explanation goes right over her little head, of course, but she loves that new word, chukka. She is wrapt with excitement watching the red polo ball as the mallet strikes it, the horses racing and turning on a dime and saying over and over chukka chukka chukka. We eat sandwiches from the buffet and Zelli has at least three hot chocolates, scooping on whipped cream to each one. She thinks she is invisible, so no one will notice. She hums chuka chuka chuka to the French national anthem. All in all, she is in paradise.

"I vote for the red team. I like how they are the same color as the ball," she says in between sips and more sips of cocoa, the cream now all over her face. I want to laugh at her, but she does not like to be laughed at. Well, neither do I.

"Okay, so Team Cartier in red is your team, and mine is the other. It is called Team Badrutt Palace, like our hotel."

We study the horses and players of our teams from the pamphlets Lady Eleanor gives us. Lady Eleanor knows all the players since she's a player herself. There is little she cannot do. And then I see *Him*. He is on my team, Badrutt Palace, looking as deadly handsome as he did last night at Raven. No wonder he wasn't on the lift at eight; he was preparing for this match. God, I can't take my eyes off him. He rides on the snow over the frozen lake, maneuvering his horse beautifully, like he has been doing this all his life. While I'm looking up his handicap, Sergei hits a perfect near-side backshot.

Zelli tugs on my arm. "Ma Mere, I have to go to the bathroom," she whispers.

"Okay, this way." I take her hand to lead her to the bathroom, but I look back at him for a few more seconds.

"Maman, please!" Zelli is jumping up and down impatiently. I didn't realize I had stopped in my tracks.

As we head back to the hotel when the match ends, I know nothing can stop me from skiing in the moonlight tonight. But I won't tell him I saw him play today. All I need now is Beethoven's *Ode to Joy*. My daughter, the Engadin Valley mountains, skiing, my friends, my father, and that man. Oh, that man.

VERA, 1

Many years ago, Barnie and I went to a chess tournament in Montenegro. Everyone on the street, in restaurants, and even at our chess tournament was talking about Blackphones. So, we listened.

"No one would ever know what you are saying."

"They cost a fortune ."

"This is the phone that both cocaine and arms dealers use."

Barnie and I bought two of them. Barnie read to me from the computer: "The software for Blackphones was pioneered by computer scientist and cryptographer Phil Zimmerman, who first hit it big in the world of security when he came out with PGP in 1991, the most popular email encryption software on the planet. Over twenty years later, Zimmerman's company, Silent Circle, launched Blackphone, a smartphone that's primary function is to protect users' privacy."

Besides traveling to chess tournaments, we loved traveling to museums. Our favorite museum trip was to see the original Lewis Chessmen pieces. We own a chess set of Lewis Chessmen pieces that are replicas of some of the world's most famous walrus ivory pieces. Funnily enough, Harry Potter played

Wizard's Chess with the Lewis Chessmen pieces in his first film, *Harry Potter and the Sorcerer's Stone*. I would have loved to have been in that movie playing Professor Minerva McGonagall, though no one could have done it as well as Maggie Smith.

Ah, well.

The little Lewis Chessmen have expressions on their faces that are priceless. The queen, with her hand on her face, looks spectacularly terrified. The rooks bite on their shields. These rook warriors fought in a frenzied, likely drug-induced trance and are called berserkers. I always thought the knights looked sad, but Barnie thought they looked willing and ready to head into battle.

We have one other chess set we love—the gold and silver Egyptian Chess Set. The board is a solid block of silver with intricate scarabs and hieroglyphics etched into each of the squares. Four golden sphinxes are affixed to each corner. It has no history like the Lewis Chessmen, but it is so very beautiful. It was Barnie's favorite board. Our dear friends in Russia, Anatoly and his wife Ilse, sent it to us when the disaster hit us. They hoped it would help us through our painful loss since the goddess of chess, Caissa, loved this board.

THESE CHESS BOARDS are the perfect battlefields for my actors Kasparov and Carlsen. Combined with my latest investment in the newest Blackphones, they serve as our intelligence vector in my war.

My war against *Him*.

CLEO, 3

I go out and buy a brand new coat. It's a long, thin but very warm shearling coat that, best of all, is so light I can easily ski in it. I have become a Barbie Doll. I think it must be what St. Moritz does to me, or perhaps it is just that man. That man, Sergei Kominitz.

Zelli is quite put out with me, as she has been the center of my world since the day she was born. She sits on the floor playing with her five dolls, all of whom are named Hazel and have dark hair and blue eyes just like her.

"What earrings and bracelets should I wear tonight?" I ask, hoping to jolt Zelli out of her mood. She ignores me for a little longer, completely entranced with the five Hazels.

Finally, Zelli looks up and smiles. She gets up from the comfy rug on the floor and picks out a pair of pink drop earrings with a ring of diamonds and, next to them, a bracelet that is gold with pink stones in it to match. Then she goes wild and puts all my jewelry down in a long row all over the bed. She picks the pink earrings up again and puts them on.

"I played with this boy in ski school today, ma Mere," Zelli smiles at her own reflection in the mirror.

"Did you? And what is this boy's name?"

"Marco," she giggles. "We kept falling down. It was so funny. I can't wait to go back to ski school with Marco tomorrow!"

Like mother, like daughter. I shudder, suddenly imagining my Zelli in thirteen years as she dresses up to meet Marco, who is no longer falling down but falling for her. They are the emissaries of the future.

Nannie comes in and applauds Zelli in her pink earrings. "Look at you, Zelli! You look like a little princess, don't you?"

That gets a big smile out of her. I am blessed that my half-sister Beebe referred us to the woman who raised her two sons and whose name really is Nannie.

"Look what I have!"

Nannie pulls out two presents, one for Zelli and one for me. "They were just brought up by the bellhop." We both rip the wrapping right off like we're deprived children. Inside are beautiful velvet slippers. Mine are green, and Zelli's are pink to match the earrings she still has on.

"Who sent them? I don't see a note."

Nannie just shakes her head, smiling.

"Obviously, you have an admirer." Looking down, I see a crest on the front of the slippers—one that looks very much like the crown that the attractive skier carved earlier today in the snow before he skied backward down the mountain.

Interesting, he knows I am at this hotel and have a daughter named Zelli. Should I be flattered, or should I worry?

"You know, Princess Zelli, I think it might be time for you to give the earrings back to your mother and come in for your supper." Our black cat Endy swishes in and plays with the wrapping paper we had just thrown all over the floor as we opened our presents. Zelli picks up some of the paper Endy is jumping in.

Zelli looks at me for approval that she is being tidy when Nannie chimes in again, "We have spaetzle for you tonight, and for dessert, you can have two petit fours . . . and if you eat it all, maybe watch cartoons for a bit. . . .”

After Zelli dashes out and then back in for a kiss goodnight, I start to wonder how long ago Sergei's son drowned under the ice. I'm guessing he won't be here tonight. Then I decide he will be. Then I fear he won't be. I am a teenager again.

I join some of the guests who are already on the gondola going up to the party. My friend Brenda, who was a famous ballerina in London, is here. She has four daughters, none of whom followed her into ballet but all of whom inherited her great looks. There is a steady stream of champagne and caviar and pretty faces and healthy people who look like they must have no nightmares. We all deliberate about the skiing conditions today like a group of golfers reviewing their eighteen holes or bridge players their cards or teachers their pupils or actors their performances.

As I'm stepping off the lift, jabbering away happily about my new coat to a woman I have never met but who was in Gorsuch earlier when I bought it, he appears.

“Your daughter resembles you,” he says.

So he is here, here early, and he saw Zelli at the polo match. The woman from Gorsuch turns and gives me a wave before she disappears forever into the sea of people.

“She didn't want your team to win,” I smile.

“Oh?” he smiles back.

“Yes, your uniform didn't match the red ball, and so I'm afraid you lost her.”

“But not you, Cleo?”

“Hard to lose me with that near-side backshot of yours.”

“Ah, I take it you have played polo or spent a lot of time with the players, Cleo?”

I laugh at him. And he teases me back when he hands me a Purple for Her Eyes drink.

"Did you bribe Chomi for the recipe? Even I don't know what he puts in it."

"And I'll never tell," Sergei smiles.

I have had lust with Jake, Zelli's father, and I have had love with Danny, and now I am having something so different with Sergei, and there is no name for it. I feel I am on a precipice. I am a tiny, spindly tree planted on a wild, windy slope with no other trees around for shelter. I have no roots, but strangely, I also have no fear. I think of Rasputin and the hypnotic power he had over the Russian Czarina Alexandra. And Rasputin, too, was dead under the ice after he was shot. Who is Sergei Kominitz? I want to see him in action.

"By the way, you'd probably be interested in something I treasure. It's a terracotta sculpture of polo players from China. It's from the Tang Dynasty era around 618–907. It was, as you might surmise, my mother's."

He just smiles.

"Shall we go see Nico?" Nico is our host who is great fun and very generous to others and to himself.

Sergei doesn't answer my question. He looks at me, just looks at me, and I feel utterly absurd, just the two of us standing there and not saying anything. So I do the most logical thing I can think of, and I kiss him. It's all I can do, and so I do it. I don't care if we are alone or not. I kiss him and he kisses me back, and that's all there is. Finally. Finally, that is all there is. When we let go of each other, he takes my skis and his skis from the ski rack and puts them over his shoulder. He carries them and our boots to the peak of the hill. He bends over to put my ski boots and skis on, which is ridiculously sexy, and then snaps his in, and off we go leaving my favorite Sarah Flint boots behind.

We are skiing quite fast in a dance that he is leading. It feels so free as we have the entire mountain to ourselves. Everyone else is at Nico's, enjoying salmon, caviar, champagne, and bellinis. About two-thirds of the way down, Sergei stops suddenly and pulls me into him. I am learning to say nothing and, oh, how I am loving it. Sergei stares at me as he puts his hands around my face and kisses me so deeply that my mouth hurts. Slowly, his strong hands move down my body. He unbuttons my coat and slides his hands around my waist, but I guide them up and I can feel how Sergei is thrilled by my wanting him so much.

I let him tear my clothes off. God, I want him so badly that I care about nothing else—not that we are on a ski slope, not that we have our skis on. One click and they are off. Three fast clips and the boots are gone too. He is as tormented as I am, lowering me down on my coat and taking me so fast. He has taken me, and I have taken him and it is the most perfect moment. He kisses me again and again. I never even noticed the snow or the cold, only his hands and mouth all over me and him inside me. We lie in the snow on my shearling coat, which is getting quite a baptism, and make love once again under the torches. It is still so frantic. If we could have waited, Sergei and I would have skied down and gone to a soft bed like two normal adults. But it seems we couldn't wait. It had to be now, and it had to be here on this snow-covered mountain. At this moment, we are so insane for one another that we have icy cold snow for our bed and each other for warmth. And it is perfect.

I look up at the stars, seeing their million-year-old light emanating down to us. And am content with how tiny and unimportant we are.

Sergei turns to look at me and runs one of his hands through my very tousled hair.

"Last night, you asked me a question, Cleo. And I answered you truthfully, and you heard me, so it became existent. In almost thirty years, I have spoken to no one else about my son's death.

And no one dares mention it to me." He turns to me. "Have you had a trauma that no one knows about, Cleopatra?"

My heart pounds, and I take his icy hands in mine. He stares at me when, finally, I open my mouth to tell him about my own past. "Besides my father, only one other person knows. Do you still want me to tell you?"

He nods.

"When I was very young and at my father's beach house in Algeria, I was brutally raped and nearly smothered by a close family friend." The trauma I had buried so deeply overwhelms me, and I start to shake the same way I did when I was so young and so destroyed. I tell Sergei all about that night and beyond. "It caused me to be frigid for so many years. I told one other man when we were together on Kilimanjaro. Coincidentally, the night I told him about my trauma was quite like this one—on a mountain and under the stars, but there was no lovemaking."

"What did Didier do? I don't imagine he let this 'friend' off easily."

"No. He killed him."

Sergei doesn't react. His unblinking dark eyes stay on mine. He knows what it is like to see life taken away from a man. There is that danger. I go on, "Or, rather, he gave the man an out to kill himself. He was one of my father's closest friends, my favorite, in fact, and so my father gave him that option."

Sergei pulls me closer. "I am sorry, Cleopatra."

"But I am here, and your son is not, Sergei."

"I have never cried for him . . . My son was so perfect. I know most parents think that of their child, but Dimitri really was. He was so trusting, so when my good friend let go of his hand, he never screamed. He was sure it was going to be alright. I am so sorry for young you too. But thank God, as you said, you are still here and that you have your lovely daughter. Is the man you told on Kilimanjaro the father of your daughter?"

"No."

He nods and says no more. I watch Sergei get dressed as I put my clothes and coat on. I bend over, sliding my feet into my boots and then my skis. Before he leaves, he stares at me, pulls something out of his jacket, and puts his hands around my neck. He salutes me as he snaps his skis on. He holds his hand out and says in Russian,

"*Byt' zhenshchinoy—bol'shoye priklyucheniye; Svodit' lyudey s uma—delo podvig.*"

It is from Dr. Zhivago, and I know the famous line well. "*To be a woman is a great adventure: To drive men mad is an heroic thing.*"

He starts to ski off and says over his shoulder, "Don't open it, Cleopatra. Wait for me to be with you."

What am I not to open?

And then he is gone. As I start to ski, I feel something pulling on my neck. I bring my hand up to my throat and feel the heavy strand of a necklace. Carefully taking it off, I move toward one of the torches for a better look. My eyes widen when I see an exquisite lavender Faberge egg on a thick silver strand necklace. Only the royal eggs were lavender. My mother loved Faberge eggs, so I have seen my fair share in museums, but this one is, by far, the most lovely. The egg has rows of tiny diamonds, pearls, and tiny lilies of the valley. My mother told me that there are always surprises hidden inside the eggs, but I am afraid to open it in the snow. That is what Sergei must have meant when he told me not to open it. I cover the egg with my white sweater and button up my shearling coat for safekeeping.

So much has happened. I need to try to understand it all. The snow has permeated me finally and I shiver uncontrollably as I ski back down to the Badrutt Palace Hotel. The well-groomed run on this magical mountain under the moonlight makes me feel as if I am in a fairy tale and that soon the evil villain will enter stage left and ruin everything.

When I get to my room at The Badrutt I find a letter from him on my pillow with a snowball that is melting all over. Well, I hadn't hoped for a snowball, but it does make me smile.

I tear open the letter. *What I want is to be witnessed exactly as I am, and somehow you do this. I spoke to you as to no one else and you didn't try to fix me. You went off when I told you of my son, and though you looked for me, you didn't come to fuss over me. And tonight, you didn't apologize for your question, you kissed me. And we were transported as we made love, not caring about the snow, not caring about anything except one another. I have had this egg for many years, and if I never see you again, I am glad you now have it. It belonged to the Tsarina Alexandra. I saw your purple eyes and knew you were the one I had been waiting for. When you asked about the worst day in my life, then I knew for sure. By passing this egg on to you, my pain has somehow lessened. Thank you for accepting this with no hyperbole. May the Fates allow us to see one another again, Cleopatra Gallier, my Lara.*

My fairy tale seems to be growing and expanding without a scary villain in sight. I look down at the Faberge Egg again, at this masterpiece, and wonder if it is all true or just a dream. I attempt to go to sleep holding the egg. Somehow, it is too much, so I leave it and walk out to leave a note for Nannie to please take Zelli to ski school at eight as I know I won't be able to sleep all night, but when I go to Zelli's room, and hold my precious child, I fall sound asleep next to her.

VERA, 2

Before they left, objective in hand, I had a lunch meeting with each of my pawns separately. First, with Kasparov, who is a genius of disguise. While we were lunching, he excused himself halfway through our club sandwiches. A few minutes later, an elderly gentleman who looked quite confused startled me when he sat at my table.

"Oh," I smile. "Sir, I am very sorry, but my friend is actually sitting there. He should be back any moment," I told him politely.

He proceeded to argue with me in a British accent for several minutes as I looked around for a waiter until he pulled his teeth out and chuckled. Even then, I still didn't know who he was.

"Vera," he took my hand finally. "It's me."

He is that good an actor. And he is to be the stalker. He can change so easily that he can be a different stalker all the time. "Vera, I am also a computer hacker. Thanks for the Russian code name you gave me. It makes me feel like one of the crazy Russian hackers you see on the news."

Then I had lunch with the actor, who is code-named Carlsen. He is not only a gifted actor, but he's quite elegant and handsome.

"Tell me about yourself. What do you enjoy most? Do you have a girlfriend, or I'm guessing many?"

He laughs, "Extreme skiing is my passion, as is acting—I have won skiing competitions in the Jackson Hole backcountry and Alaska where I traversed triple black diamonds—trails with exposure to uncontrollable falls along a steep, continuous pitch and high consequence terrain. I will send you videos of my ski competitions."

"Well, Carlsen, I'm a skier, so I know what you are talking about. I must say the thought of skiing along those high-pitched trails gives me chills. What's the hardest run in the world?"

Carlsen thought about his answer for no less than five seconds. "Ah. Well, the most famous one is probably the Streif in Kitzbuhel, Austria. It's got an eighty-five-degree gradient."

"Something tells me you must have skied it . . ." I smile again.

He nodded. "I competed in the Hahnenkamm ski weekend two years in a row. And with the money you are paying me, I can do it again this year," he said, beaming. "You should come see it. It's arguably the most exciting thing you will ever see. And as far as women in my life, there are several, and it is complicated, so I am glad I have a job that will keep me away from those 'complications' for a while."

A few weeks later, Kasparov and Carlsen came to my house for dinner to listen to the plans. When they arrived, I greeted them at the door with a Blackphone for each of them, explaining, "No one can track our calls, texts, or search history. Not even you, Kasparov, with your hacking skills. We can transfer and store files and most importantly to me, we can video chat through a virtual private network. Everything we do on our Blackphones is anonymous." Kasparov said, "Great, I have always wanted one. Already loving this job." Carlsen nodded and smiled. "Drama!"

I pour us all a glass of champagne "To celebrate the commencement of the game." We clink glasses, and I take them to my living room, where I have set up my two favorite chess boards.

I explain to them that I will be using one for each of them as they do their "scares," and unsurprisingly, Kasparov points to the Lewis Chessmen, which are fascinating like he is, and Carlsen points to the Egyptian chess set, which is beautiful like he is.

Again, we smile, more champagne clinking.

"Now, down to what you will do. The man I am trying to upset has hurt me badly, very badly, and I want to settle the score. I want to have him experience a bit of the pain and loss he has caused me. No one will be hurt but his stability needs to be shaken, and he needs to feel through his grown children a sense of powerlessness. I will give you a dossier on his children, and you will improvise how you can scare them. It has to be up to you in the moment which is why I chose actors. Actors have instincts, which is our greatest gift, and if we are open to them, we become chameleons in any situation. You have Blackphones, and you have access to offshore bank accounts in your names so you can buy airline tickets if they travel, clothes for disguises, and whatever else you want or need. If you need to hire someone else, I will trust your ability to do that, but my name never comes into this. I want your word on this."

VERA, 2

They both smile and nod. "This is going to be an Emmy-award performance," Kasparov says, and Carlsen grins, "It will be like skiing in the Hahnenkamm every day."

I am beyond thrilled. Nothing could have gone better. The pawns are ready for battle.

Let the fear begin.

JAKE, 2

At least our uphill journey is complete. We've finally made it to the top, and thank Christ for that because my claustrophobia has started to set in big time. As I step out of the gondola, White Ski Suit accidentally bumps into me.

"Je suis désolé,: he apologizes.

I'm distracted by a group of about thirty skiers, all huddled together nervously on our right. I can barely see them because of the storm, but I can see enough. "Are they . . . ?"

"Waiting for ski patrol, yes," White Ski Suit answers my question before I can get it out. He smiles. "Would you like to follow me?" he asks, evidently picking up on my anxiety. My anxiety, until this moment, that I thought I was suppressing quite convincingly. "Down the mountain, I mean. Just in case visibility becomes too difficult."

"Oh. Um," I glance over at all of the other skiers and weigh my odds. The whole lot of them, they look so nervous and scared. Like poor little lambs about to be sent off to the slaughter. But I'm not one of them. No way. Hi. I'm Jake Regan, CIA agent and superior athlete.

"I was on ski patrol for years. But if you'd like to wait up here, that's a safe option," he winks. I'm almost positive that's my first male-on-male wink action, but I don't hate it.

Screw it. You only live once, and all that other "grab life by the horns" BS. "Let's do it," I smile, throwing caution to the wind and praying that I don't totally eat shit.

"Excellent. Follow me," he says, snapping his white boots into his Oro Nero Classico, a pair of handcrafted Foil skis with a whopping $60,000 price tag. I know this as I looked at every ski before buying my Enforcer skis, which tested top of the list. I place one black glove three inches in front of my face. I can still see it, but that might only be because of the stark contrast between the white on black. I steel myself and follow my new friend as he starts gliding down the mountain. The white ski suit might be hella chic, but it sure as hell ain't ideal in a whiteout. He's only about six feet ahead, but my eyes have to strain in order to see him. He's clever, however. He starts whistling a song so that I can follow the sound of his voice. The more I listen to the song, the more I realize that it sounds vaguely familiar . . . The howling wind whips across my cheeks and enormous snowflakes stick to my goggles.

Wait a minute. I definitely know this song. *There's a fruit store on our street, it's run by a Greek. And he keeps good things to eat, But you should hear him speak!* Da fuq? How random . . . I haven't heard this song since I was in preschool. Dear old dad used to sing it to us when we were practically still in diapers.

"When you ask him anything, he never answers 'no,' he just 'yes's' you to death and takes your dough. He tells you yes, we have no bananas, we have a no-bananas today." The song is called, 'Yes, We Have No Bananas.' The brothers Regan used to adore this song. What little weirdos we were. We are making good headway and I imagine we are about a third of the way down the mountain.

Uh oh. White Ski Suit either has stopped whistling or he's skied too far ahead. I can't see or hear him anymore. Actually, I can't see squat anymore. Shit.

The howling wind howls past my raw, burning cheeks. If I ever manage to get off of this godforsaken mountain, my once-high cheekbones are going to look like sacks of crusty, old tomatoes. Snow continues to pile onto my goggles, forming a thick layer over the plastic. As I go to wipe them again, the maneuver affects my entire equilibrium and I lose my balance completely, almost nosediving over the top of my skies. At the last possible moment, I manage to catch myself and regain my balance.

Okay, screw this. I have to sit down. Now is not the time to be a hero, Jakey boy. Now's the time to figure out a way to get the hell off this mountain. I think I need help. I definitely need help. I pat my right pocket for my cell phone, but I don't feel it. Have my hands gone numb already? I stick my hand inside the pocket except there's nothing there. This doesn't make any sense. I know I put my phone in my right pocket, I always put my phone in my right pocket. That's where it lives.

No way. Could White Ski Suit have . . . ?

CLEO, 4

I am shaken from my sleep at about eleven when the phone rings. My eyes slowly open, and I move to the bedside table to answer it. Goodness, I am rather black and blue . . . I had woken up with Zelli for our breakfast in our room, and when Nannie took her to ski school, I went back to lie down for a few minutes, which was a few hours, I see.

"Good morning, mon chaton," my father's voice comes from the other end.

"Hi, Daddy."

"No skiing for you this fine morning?"

"No, I was up late on the mountain, so I am taking the morning off. But did you see Heidi and Jay or Alison and Maya? I was to meet all of them at eight at the funicular."

"I didn't." He pauses. "Cleopatra, I'd like to speak with you about something in person. Can I come by your room in about thirty minutes?"

I feel as if I am a teenager again, about to get scolded for staying out too late with my boyfriend. But this scolding, I am actually looking forward to. I just hope that my father isn't also my villain and that he isn't about to ruin this wonderful fairy tale.

Twenty-five minutes later, Didier is at my door. He heads straight for the silver coffee urn to help himself and me to Badrutt coffee. "I was with Sergei all morning on the mountain . . . Perfect conditions for back bowl skiing."

I don't take the bait, but I do take the coffee.

"Afterward, we went to his house so he could give me some papers that he asked me to pass onto you."

"House? He has a house? Here? A house? On the mountain? Where?"

"About one-third of the way down. It's fascinating. Truly exquisite. Lola bought the house next to his this year. I am surprised he hasn't shown it to you."

I am surprised as well. "What are the papers, Daddy?"

"I haven't looked at them," he tells me as he hands me an envelope.

As I open them, I can feel my father's eyes. He might not have looked at them, but this questioning glance that he is laying on me reveals a curiosity about their contents.

"Sergei gave me a Fabergé egg . . ."

If he were any less of a gentleman, he might have shown his surprise. Instead, he calmly asks, "A Fabergé egg?"

I point to the bedside table where I left Sergei's present, and Didier goes over to take a look. I am sure that my father, too, is thinking of my late mother and her love for Fabergé Eggs.

In the meantime, I read Sergei's papers. They show the Egg's provenance and its official gifting to me. He explains the importance of keeping these papers in a safe place and to use his name and call this number if ever I am questioned about it.

He has left. God, he has left. At the end of the letter, Sergei mentions that a storm is coming in and that he needs to be at a meeting early tomorrow in Moscow, so he's asked my father to give these papers to me. I look out the window. It is snowing, but not heavily. As I glance up the mountain, it does look much heavier there.

"You know . . ." Didier begins, still entranced by the Fabergé Egg. "Sergei is extremely wealthy . . ."

"Yes, you only have to look at him to guess that, Daddy."

"I didn't know what he meant when he told me to tell you that you should not open it. Like most Russian oligarchs, he has lots of secrets."

Didier dangles my glorious gift in the air. I can tell he is quite pleased for me. "And now, Cleopatra, you are a very wealthy woman."

I nod.

"Wear it, Cleopatra. No one would believe you have a Fabergé egg around your neck."

"I wish my mother was here to see it. She wouldn't believe it!"

"She would certainly try to steal it from you—maybe try to steal Sergei too!"

We both laugh. "What a coincidence that your middle name is Alexandra, just like the Empress whose gift this was. I can't take credit for that though. Alexandra was your mother's idea."

"Maybe it's fate," I smile.

"Yes, Sandrine must be doing cartwheels in her heavenly orbit right about now! You will keep it, I assume?"

I smile my yes.

"You know, he asked for your middle name for the documents, and when I told him 'Alexandra', he just nodded as if he always knew. It was quite strange . . ."

I have no answer for that either. I wonder when I will see Sergei again, and I am reminded of Rasputin's hold over Empress Alexandra. When you are not held tightly, you want to be, and he is sending me off with open arms but holding me with just that openness and yet telling me with the Fabergé Egg how important

I am to him. I will do as he asks and wait till he returns so we will find the secret gift inside together.

As I look out the window, I see that the snow has started to come down heavily. Sergei was right about the storm. How strange he has a house here and never mentioned it when we laid in the cold icy snow last night. He really does have lots of secrets.

I turn to my father. "We should probably go pick up Zelli from her class. I think we might be stranded here for a few more days before making our way back to Paris."

"Actually, I will be staying on for another week but will send you and Zelli back to Paris on my plane when this storm clears. I want to ski some more, and Lola is staying put at her house. I will ask to keep this suite for us in case we are stranded."

As I put the gilded egg back on, I feel Sergei's hands around me as I did on my neck last night. He will never be far away from me. I see him riding his polo pony, I see him putting on my skis at Nico's party, I see him tearing off my clothes on the mountain, and I hear him saying Pasternak's words to Lara in Russian. And I see him lowering his head as he told me of his son's death beneath the ice.

DIDIER, 1

It is now a total whiteout here in my beloved St. Moritz. Cleo and I picked Zelli up from ski school just a short while ago, and then Cleo left us to buy some toys for Zelli, which will surely come in handy if this storm lasts as long as they are predicting. Thank heaven we brought Endy on the plane, as Zelli will spend hours screaming and chasing her through every room until we all want to scream ourselves.

So, here, Zelli and I are at the bottom of the mountain in the lodge. It's cozy and warm, with just us and six other people. Zelli counted. Just like her mother, my granddaughter orders hot cocoa, a very thick chocolate cocoa. Zelli's cocoa has a lovely crown in the whipped cream, which she points out to me.

"Look, look! It's a crown, like on my slippers! Ma Mere and I both got slippers as a present with a crown on them. But we don't know who sent them."

The waiter brings my favorite apres ski beverage. A hot toddy. I ask him why I have no crown in mine. He looks at me strangely.

I point to Zelli's crown, and he just shrugs in confusion and walks off. I watch as Zelli sneaks a sip of my drink and then spits it out into her tiny mitten just as quickly. "Didi, my last name is the same as yours. I am Zelli Gallier. I have four Ls in my name and two Is and two Es."

My goodness, I do love her. She keeps me young by breathing new life into an otherwise aging man.

"And I have a middle name, but it doesn't have any Ls," she babbles on happily. "But sometimes, I forget what it is . . ."

I can tell that it's one of those times. I smile at her. Whenever I'm around Zelli, I cannot stop myself from smiling.

In the huge snowstorm, we set out for the hotel, which is close by. I take her tiny mittened hand in mine, feeling a pervasive protectiveness I have never felt before for anyone else, including Cleopatra.

As I walk through the revolving doors of Badrutt's Palace, the doorman greets us, then comes over and starts talking to Zelli in French.

"Viens avec moi, Zelli,"

We follow him over to a table where there's a coloring book. He tells her that it must have been left by another one of the guests and that she can have it. He then turns to me and mentions in a lower tone,

"You're going to want this for the snowstorm."

I agree. We both thank him for the book, and I tell Zelli to follow me. I always love to take a moment to admire Le Grand Hall. It's a vast room with high ceilings, rich wooden interiors, mismatched chintz armchairs, and usually a view of the slopes. But not today. To the left in the room is a beautiful painting of Raphael's Madonna, which Zelli and I always stop and admire. It is the start of our ritual, and the next stop in our ritual is a tiny secret door off to the right, which leads to a hothouse filled with moonflowers, orchids, and oddly enough, venus flytraps.

Then we head to the manager's office. Zelli always brings him a small Venus flytrap and giggles as he reprimands her.

And while he reprimands her, I survey the list of guests who have arrived the night before so that I have everyone's names at the ready when they inevitably come over to say hello. I spot a name on this list that will undoubtedly pique Cleo's interest.

"Shall we go find your mother, mon chaton?"

Zelli is my miniature shadow, dutifully following me. We walk through the lobby to the library, where Cleo is ensconced with her Fabergé egg on a large green sofa. I wonder what she will find inside the egg when she opens it.

I whisper in Cleo's ear that Jake Regan is here in St. Moritz and staying in this hotel.

She flinches. Her eyes drift out the large bay window which normally has an impressive view of the Swiss Alps. But today, it's as if a dense white blanket is covering the window.

"It's like an Agatha Christie mystery. And the plot has just thickened . . ."

Zelli asks us: "Who is Agatha Christie? Are we related to her?"

"No, mon chaton," I say. "Agatha Christie is a great writer of mystery novels. I'll read them to you when you're older. Let's go to our rooms."

The Royal Suite is on the top floor. The Hotel Badrutt always very generously gives it to me, but as I reiterate to Zelli constantly, alas, I am not a king. She insists on pushing the button to our floor as well as every other button on our ride up, even though I have asked her before not to do this. So, we stop on every floor.

"Zelli . . ." Cleopatra half admonishes her.

"What?" she says with all that four-year-old innocence.

We enter their suite, which consists of Zelli's room in pale blue with heavy pale-blue curtains and lots of stuffed animals, Cleo's room in ivory with thick curtains that match the white snow swirling outside, and Nanny's room in navy all off the main living room. Each room has chandeliers, thick rugs, and a kitchen where Nannie puts together Zelli and Cleo's breakfasts and dinners, all sent up from room service. My suite is across the long hallway. Cleopatra is staring out the window, no doubt thinking about Jake Regan, while I talk to the front desk on the house phone so I can update Cleo.

"Jake Regan is on the mountain, Cleo. Ski instructors think about thirty people are stranded. He was among the last to go up before the storm came in. He is on the camera that they have in every gondola getting on and again getting off at the top, though they can barely make anyone out at the top, and the person he is with seems to have not been caught on the cameras at the bottom. Shall we go down and look at the camera footage to make sure it's him?"

She nods, and we leave Zelli with Nannie and Endy, who is purring happily as Zelli hugs her. We head downstairs, though there is nothing at all to see except for Jake getting on the gondola and blurred photos of him getting off.

CLEO, 5

It's incredible how Jake should be back in my life after all this time. Several years ago, he left his job in finance and now works in the CIA, or The Agency, as it is referred to. I know all of this because, with a father like Didier, very few secrets are out of my reach. Jake opened me up, and he comes into my dreams now and then, but he is just a passing moment.

I am worried about him. Jake doesn't scare easily. However, I remember that flash of fear in his devastatingly blue eyes when I showed him the Banzai Pipeline. Mother Nature gave him a tremble then, and it is She who holds him in her icy grasp at this very moment. Jake has smarts and resourcefulness on his side, but the storm is not expected to abate until early tomorrow. Until then, the ski patrol is out searching for him and all the other lost poor souls.

For someone who says she doesn't care, I'm overwhelmed with how upset I find myself. After all, he is Zelli's father. I have taken to being Zelli's mother with such abandon and absorption that no man has been a part of my life again until now. She took all my time and my love. Now there is Sergei, whom I can't stop thinking of, and Jake, Zelli's father, who, once upon a time, I was totally absorbed by. How strange they should both come into my life at the same time.

Of course, the internet is not working. We are stranded but in a lovely warm room with sofas and a fireplace burning, comfy baths and beds and Jake is stranded in the cold. Oh, Jake. I am so glad Sergei got out when he did. I want to see him again and . . . ahh. Enough of this. Time to color in Zelli's new coloring book and play with her dolls that have her eyes, bright blue eyes, inherited from her father, Jake Regan.

But he has only seen her bright blue eyes once.

St. Moritz, 2016

JAKE, 3

My $1,850 Standard Expedition Canada Goose parka just paid for itself. There's a growing list of things I'm gonna do if I ever get the hell off this mountain, and I've just added buying Canada Goose stock to what I'm calling my "Things I'll Do if I Don't Die."

Like shooting my shot with the hot blond chick at Equinox. Hanging out with Ricky when I get back to New York. Getting to know my daughter.

After a lot of back and forth in my head about what to do next, I decide I'm better off taking my chances. I can't sit on my ass in the freezing cold forever. I'm a CIA agent for Christ's sake, and if I go slow enough, I should be fine. Option A: Strap my skis back on, and I can sidestep my way down. I'll look like the biggest loser that's ever lived, but no one can even see me all the way up here anyway. Option B: Carry my skis and walk. But that'll take even longer, and I want to spend about as much more time on this mountain as Julia probably did in Honolulu once she found out about Cleo and me.

My mode of transport is decided. As I strap my right boot back into one of my Enforcers, I vaguely feel as if a presence is near me.

57

JAKE, 3

What is it?

My mind wanders back to life off the mountain and the very reason why Dad suggested I come here to St. Moritz in the first place. Swell idea, Dad . . .

Most of the time, I love the thrill and the excitement of being a CIA agent—especially the work I'm involved in centering around the Russian oligarch, Anatoly Rustikoff. But heavy is the head that wears the crown, and ever since I started with the agency, I have hardly taken any time off. The joke's on me. This vacation is turning out to be about as relaxing as a colonoscopy.

Once my boots are buckled in, I slowly get to my feet. My legs feel like jello. I think my nerves are making me feel a presence nearby again. Hallucinating perhaps. Looking in every which way, I'm not even entirely sure which direction is down. I spit into the wind, and it's a good thing I did. I'd be skiing to the left had I not.

The snow beneath my skis is oddly reassuring. It reminds me that, yes, I'm still alive and getting closer to the bottom with every step I take. I wipe the snow off of my goggles for the nine-hundredth time. The snow crunches under the weight of my skis. My weary bones *creak* as I continue my long slog down the mountain. And my stomach growls, having had nothing inside of it since last night.

HOURS MUST'VE PASSED, and I still can't see a fucking thing. Now I know what my dad must have felt like for all those weeks when he was blind. I could tell that it was pure agony for him, but I don't think I really understood or appreciated how helpless you feel without your sight. Respect, Dad. But I'm still feeling a chill from something other than the temperature. That presence. Pretty weird.

I was never much of a poetry student. I know, shocking. Always been more of a numbers guy. But there is one poem by

Pablo Neruda that sticks out. Neruda said, *"Each one moved along, intoxicated by that boundless solitude, by that green and white silence. It was all the dazzling and secretive work of nature, and at the same time a growing threat of cold, snow, and pursuit."*

"Boundless solitude," "white silence," and a *"growing threat of cold, snow, and pursuit."* I wonder if it's fate. If I remembered those words to prepare for this very moment. Pablo had it way worse than I do—what with the poverty, persecution, and escaping the Nazis with all those terrified people he led over the mountains to escape to Chile.

Here's to me escaping this mountain.

JULIA 1

Oo la la, it's 6:00 a.m. in Gay Paree. Besides Whitney, I haven't seen many of my old classmates from the Sorbonne since I moved across the pond to New York almost ten years ago. God, has it really been that long? I can hardly contain my excitement as I swing open the curtains of The Four Seasons George V. I requested a room at the back of the hotel so that I could see the Seine from the comfort of my big, comfy king-sized bed. I gaze out at the river and then down at my slowly growing belly. A bit less than three months to go, nowhere near the finish line, but more than halfway. Ricky and I are both a little old-fashioned, so we've decided not to find out the baby's gender—partially because we don't want to throw one of those god-awful gender reveal parties. Even the name "gender reveal" sounds gauche. I'll just be grateful that our little bundle of joy comes out with ten fingers and ten toes, but my hunch is Ricky secretly wishes for a girl. I think it's sweet. Besides his own mother, he didn't grow up with any chicks in the house, so a change of pace would be nice for him.

Speaking of Ricky, he should be here soon. Sadly, we couldn't get on the same flight because he had to pull a late night at Slate yesterday. He hopped on a red-eye afterward that's scheduled to land at Charles de Gaulle in just under three hours, which actually worked in my favor. I love nothing more than having a luxurious hotel room all to myself. The fancy toiletries, the plush robes, the sumptuous eight-hundred-thread count sheets. I've already taken an indulgent bath in the gorgeous clawfoot tub.

Now that I'm bathed, I'm refreshed, and for once in the last months, I'm not suffering from crippling nausea. Life is grand. They call it morning sickness, but what no one really warns you about is that you actually feel terrible all the livelong day. But not today, Satan. Not today.

You know that feeling when everything's just coming up roses? You're doing well at work, getting good sleep, looking better than ever, eating delicious food, having great sex with your gorgeous husband, reading fabulous books, finally spending enough time with friends, and, to top it all off, expecting your first baby. And now, I'm in Paris, my favorite city in the whole wide world.

Paris, *je t'aime*.

Boy, did I need to get out of New York. First, it was a creepy guy at the gym. Every time I looked over my shoulder on my elliptical, this arsehole with dark hair wearing a T-shirt two sizes too small would be staring at me with his lecherous, beady little eyes. When I told Whitney over brunch back in New York, she just chalked it up to a very simple fact: creepy guys at the gym are like corny love songs in a Nicholas Sparks film. They're inevitable. So, I brushed it off.

But then, a few weeks ago, there was the curious incident of the dog walker on my morning commute. Every single day when I left for the office at 7:50 a.m. on the dot, lo and behold, this ominous-looking dog walker with scraggly hair would be stationed outside our neighbor's townhouse across the street. With tragically severe acne scars that I could spot from all the way across the street, the very look of this man reeked of a villain from a bad nineties thriller. Having about twelve dogs of all shapes and sizes in tow is part of his job description, but still. It just added to the creep factor. The whole thing just felt odd, mainly because he vanished off the face of the planet the following week. Then again, it's New York City. There are any number of weirdos coming and going, slithering around on every city block at any hour of the day. That's usually part of the reason why I love it.

The very last thing I consider myself is a tech buff. But I have seen about six hundred episodes of *Dateline*. When I called Ricky to tell him about the dog walker man, his phone rang once, twice, thrice. But then I heard something else entirely. These weird clicking sounds. Keith Morrison talks about wiretaps in every other episode, and those clicks only mean one thing: your phone's been bugged. But who? Or why?

I push down the past few weeks in New York, take a deep breath, and breathe in that pungent Parisian air. It's tinged with the smells of croissants baking, laundry drying, coffee brewing, and cigarette smoking. In the city, the Marlboros have often been replaced with Juuls and many New Yorkers have swapped out coffee for green tea and kombucha. But The City of Lights remains unchanged. As long as Parisians still enjoy it, to hell with good health. What a refreshing outlook.

I look down at the gold Cartier watch that belonged to my mother. It's almost two o'clock. Ricky texted me from JFK, giving me a heads-up that his flight was delayed because of the weather in New York. I've had a lump in my throat and a knot in my stomach ever since. Of course, I'm a very competent person, but is it such a crime to admit that I'd feel much better having my big, strong husband around? Because in NY, I always got odd feelings from people such as this dog walker who always wore these shoes, which appeared to be Belgian shoes? Couldn't be. It'd be like a homeless woman wearing Chanel. What was even more frightening was seeing those same shoes in the lobby yesterday while I was checking in. Whatever. Ricky's warmth is genuinely the only thing I want. But right now, I'm heading out for lunch to meet my best friend, Sarah, whom I roomed with at the Sorbonne.

JAKE, 4

I can barely lift my arms. I hurl my skis haphazardly into the deep snow by the entrance of the hotel. A classy joint like The Badrutt, I doubt anyone around here would swipe them—if they can even see them in the first place. Frankly, after the day I've had, I don't give a rat's ass if I ever lay eyes on those things again. It's warm, sunny beaches for this guy from here on out.

I walk into the lobby. Well, "walk" is a stretch. Hobble or limp is more like it.

"Monsieur Regan! Thank goodness you are alright!" the pint-sized concierge exclaims from across the marble lobby. Bad news travels fast.

"Hey . . ."

I have no clue what this little twerp's name is, but he hurries over to me as if I'm his long-lost brother. The warm reception is sweet. Suddenly, the emotions of such a dramatic afternoon surge through me all at once. I could have died up there. I *should* have died up there. Mother Nature is one tough broad.

My legs give out, and I crumble into the concierge's arm.

"Nina! Fetch Monsieur Regan a glass of water, *s'il vous plaît*!" He instructs a woman behind him that I don't see. "Here, why don't you take a seat, Monsieur Regan," he motions to a nearby pair of velvet chairs.

"Thank you . . ."

"Are you alright, Monsieur Regan?" he kneels next to the chair. "What happened up there? Ski patrol looked for you for hours. The man with you . . . he has not been found either?"

What happens next makes me wonder if I died on the mountain and had gone to heaven.

Cleopatra. Across the room, the elevator doors whir open, and the woman who turned my life upside down almost five years ago in Honolulu comes waltzing across the hotel lobby. She looks just as stunning in her ski gear as she did in a flimsy sundress. Better even.

"Here you are, Monsieur Regan," says a blond mademoiselle as she offers me a bottle of Swiss Alps water and a glass of ice. Maybe this really is heaven, Nina is Mother Mary, and the tiny concierge is the angel Gabriel.

I snap back to reality. "Oh. Uh, thanks. Thanks a lot."

Normally, a hot chick like Nina would have my full, undivided attention. But not around the ghost of Cleo. I'm dreading looking at my reflection in the mirror, which is not a thought I'm familiar with. My hair is drenched in snow and sweat. The fact that it's matted to my forehead is a nice touch. I can feel that my cheeks are chapped and windburned too. There's no way Cleo can see me like this. My reflexes take over and I duck behind a potted palm tree—why there are palm trees in the Alps during the dead of winter is beyond me.

But when I look up, Cleo isn't there. Excellent, I *am* hallucinating. I can't forget that presence I felt till the bottom of the mountain was in sight.

I stand up too quickly from the velvet chair. All of the blood rushes to my head. My vision is flecked with blurs and stars. I wobble to my left, then right. Then I sit back down.

"Monsieur Regan, are you alright?"

I muster an awkward laugh. "Yeah, just stood up too quickly. I'm sorry, I don't think I got your name?"

"Roger," he says after a moment. My guess is Roger probably isn't used to guests asking for his name. Though I see his nametag.

"Like Federer."

"Ah, yes. Switzerland's pride and joy," Roger smiles. "Drink your water, Monsieur Regan. You will feel better."

I chug the whole damn bottle before I try standing again. "Jake. Call me Jake."

Roger shoots me a nice smile. I bet that smile at least gets him in the door with the ladies. Something strikes me as I slowly start to get up out of the velvet. "How'd you even know I was caught in the whiteout?"

"At The Badrutt Palace, we are always watching . . ." he smiles.

Look, Rog. I'm really not in the mood to be screwed with. "No, but really . . ."

Roger senses my tone. "The cameras. There are cameras in all of the gondolas, Monsieur Regan."

Aha. "Jake," I remind him as I slowly make my way toward the elevators. It's a long way from my trademark Jake Regan strut but at least it's an improvement from when my sorry ass stumbled in here.

"Would you like me to send the doctor up? Just to make sure that you are alright?"

I'm about to nod. A doctor making a house call sounds like it's, well, just what the doctor ordered. Then I glance to my left into the old-fashioned tea room.

I wasn't hallucinating. My mind wasn't playing tricks on me.

It really is her.

Cleopatra.

Roger follows my eyeline. "Ah, Miss Gallier. Do you two know each other?"

Yeah, pal. In the biblical sense.

And before I know it, I'm standing at her table. Hovering above her like a real fool. She looks up at me as she brings a white mug filled with something hot to her lips and takes a sip. *O, that I were a glove upon that hand . . .*

"Cleo," is all I manage. My poor teeth are still chattering. I pray I'm not going to start stuttering.

She doesn't look surprised to see me. Hmm.

"Jake. Oh, Jake," she smiles.

And I crumble like a pile of mush. A totally strong and handsome pile of mush, but still.

"We'd be delighted to have you join us, Jake," the older man sitting next to Cleo says.

He looks strangely familiar. I know I've seen him before. But my brain has officially run out of juice.

He motions to some waiter in a black suit to pull up an extra chair.

"Oh, are you sure? I don't want to interrupt your tea." But I'm already sitting.

"Nonsense. You're family, aren't you?"

That's it. He's Cleopatra's father, and I've seen his face before in a photo at her house in Honolulu.

"And you know Zelli," Cleo touches the little girl's tiny shoulder.

I was so focused on Cleo that I hadn't even noticed the little girl sitting on her other side—*my* little girl.

I gulp. "Zelli. It's nice to see you."

The child smiles up at me. Clueless. She has inherited most of Cleo's features, dimples included, but those bright blue eyes are mine.

"Didier Gallier," her father sticks out his hand.

"Of course, Jake Regan. So nice to finally meet you." I shake Didier's hand. He has the firmest handshake.

"You as well. Jake." he asks, "Brandy?"

"God. Yes, please. That'll hit the spot after being stuck up on the mountain . . ."

Zelli lights up. "Are you the man on the mountain?"

"The man on the mountain? How did you know about that?" I'm looking at Zelli, but I'm asking Cleo.

"My grandfather! He knows everything," Zelli giggles.

Cleo puts a hand on my thigh, and I think I might blow a fuse. "How are you feeling, Jake? Eight hours, goodness."

"Oh, I'm fine. Actually, I was thinking about your friend Pele when I was up on the mountain . . ."

That gets a laugh out of Cleo. "Pele, the volcano goddess. I can't believe you remember her!"

"Does Pele, by chance, have a jealous sister?" I laugh back.

"Pele is my favorite goddess of all the goddesses!" says Zelli, her posture perfect.

"She does. Poliahu. Maybe Poliahu, the goddess of snow, was in love with you and that's why she kept you up on the mountain?"

"It felt more like she was mad . . ."

I just look at Cleo. It feels like we're speaking in code. After what I did, I don't blame her. I sip my brandy, nearly polishing off the entire glass.

"We're so glad you're safe. More brandy, Jake?" Didier motions to the same waiter in the black suit. First, white suit and now black suit.

"Yes, please have some more while you tell us about your adventure on the mountain . . ." Cleo is being so polite, talking to me as though I'm a guest on her Honolulu talk show.

JAKE, 4

The mysterious waiter in the black suit returns with another brandy.

"Where do you live when you are not in the snow on the mountain?" Zelli asks me with a twinkle.

That question nearly breaks my heart. Daughters are supposed to know who their fathers are. Daughters are supposed to know where their fathers live.

"Who, me?"

"Yes, you," she lets out another giggle.

"New York," I slur. Suddenly, I'm moving in slow motion. I've turned into Sleepy of the Seven Dwarfs.

"You must be absolutely exhausted, Jake," Cleo puts her hand on my thigh again. And I am.

My whole body feels like it's melting into the chair.

I try to swallow a yawn, not wanting to admit any defeat in front of anyone at this table. But the brandy, coupled with my exhaustion, has caught up with me.

"I am a little beat . . ." I try to stand, but there's no strength left in my legs.

And that's the last thing I remember.

CLEO, 6

I toy with the idea of going up to Jake's room and checking on him. He will still be knocked out from his mountain escape. The hotel sent a doctor to his room after the waiters Lucas and Stavie brought him up.

Outside, the snow is still falling. I have to wonder, how did Jake manage to get down the mountain? When we met, I could tell he was a remarkable athlete who made an effort to stay in shape. All you have to do is look at him. And now that he's working for one of the world's most elite agencies, I imagine that Jake has even more strength, stamina, and speed than he did on that bright, sunny day in Honolulu when our cars—and soon after, our bodies—crashed into each other. Jake was in my bed less than an hour after we saw each other for the first time.

I enter the marble lobby as the elevator door opens. The lobby is especially quiet tonight, even for this hour. Social butterflies who would usually be out and about are staying put at home, escaping the storm and getting cozy by a warm fire. As expected, the nighttime concierge is on duty. He's standing dutifully behind the large wooden front desk. I believe this one's name is Nicholas. Roger, the daytime concierge, knows my father better. Roger is never without a smile and he loves anyone with a title, and my father has a good one.

"Nicholas, is that right?" I put on a charming smile as I walk up to him.

He looks up at me, almost frightened by the sound of my voice piercing the silence that he was enjoying. But Nicholas quickly snaps out of it, and the corners of his mouth contort into a warm smile. "Miss Gallier, good evening."

"Good evening. My father, Marquis Gallier, says hello, by the way." This is one of the times my father's title comes in handy since the staff at Badrutt loves titles.

He beams. "Please send the Marquis my best. What may I do for you, Miss Gallier?"

Straight down to business. I love it. "Well, my father asked that I go check in on a friend of ours who was caught in the storm. Really, it's quite a miracle that he even made it down the mountain . . ."

"Monsieur Regan?"

"Yes. Is he alright, do you know?"

"I haven't heard a peep from him since after the doctor went up. No news is normally good news."

"Would you mind if I went up and checked myself? We are practically family, so it would just make my father, the Marquis, feel so much better knowing that I saw that he was alright with my own eyes."

Nicholas doesn't hesitate for even half a second before giving me another smile and handing over the key to Jake's room.

I quietly slip in. Someone, probably the doctor, left the light on in the bathroom, and it shines onto the bed just enough. There he is, sprawled across the large, king-sized bed, lying on his back with his mouth gaped open. That makes me smile. For such an attractive man when he is awake, I had forgotten what an unattractive man he is when asleep.

I tiptoe over to him. As I get closer, he terrifies me when he lets out a huge snore. I nearly scream. Well, the great Jake Regan is alive, and relief floods over my whole body. When he passed out after the brandy, I was concerned. I watch him deep in his sleep and notice that a few of his pillows have toppled off the bed and onto the floor. I lean down, pick them up, and spend an inordinate amount of time fluffing them back up for him. The maids must spend hours on these pillows just to make them look fresh.

Somehow, I had forgotten how much younger he is than I am, and in the soft light, he looks especially vulnerable and youthful. It's amazing how great a gap of fifteen years is. I gently prop both pillows behind his head. I creep back across the floor, and just as my hand is reaching for the doorknob, my eyes happen to land on his passport. I hesitate. Should I take a peek?

I do. And as I do, a small photo falls out of the pages and onto the floor. I pick it up and turn it over. It's Zelli. The photo I sent him when she was two years old. I had promised to send Jake a photo on each of her birthdays, but he had not answered. I had introduced Jake to his daughter when Zelli was two years old, just as he was leaving Honolulu to get on a plane back to DC—it was for his CIA training, though I pretended not to know.

"Say goodbye to Daddy, Zelli," I had prompted her. He just stared.

Jake called the moment he arrived in DC. "Why didn't you tell me, Cleo?" The pain and shock in his gravelly voice nearly destroyed me.

"After killing Jimbo, or rather Mohammed Abdul Rahman, I went to Dubai. A few months later, I went to a doctor as I was exhausted, and after some tests, he told me I was going to have a baby."

"Okay, but Cleo—".

I didn't blame him for being upset. "I know. I should have called you right away. But I was stunned, Jake. I thought I was too old! I wasn't even sure if I could carry it to full term, and I didn't want to burden you with all this when you were just beginning your new career. We all need a reason to keep going."

"What does that even mean?"

"It means if you are honest as to what your reason is to keep going, I think it will be your work."

"Yes, my work. But I love you. You know that. And . . . she does have my blue eyes."

"That is perfect for you to say," I laughed. "She has my blue eyes . . . Jake, I'm fifteen years older than you. You know I adore you," I paused, not wanting to hurt him.

"But you don't love me back, is that it?"

"It's not that simple, Jake. We have a beautiful child that will have us tangled together for the rest of our lives. But I want to live the way I want. All over the world. Paris, Algeria, Dubai, St. Moritz, Honolulu. And I want that for Zelli as well. She will hold you back when you meet someone to marry, and I certainly don't want to marry."

"But, Cleo—"

"Oh, Jake. Whenever you want to see her, I will make that happen. But if you are being as honest as I am, I think you will admit that your life is leading you to strange and wonderful places. Don't give that up. You have given me the greatest treasure, and I will be eternally grateful—not just for Zelli, but for you too. You saved my life in Anatoly Rustikoff's garden. I promise I will bring her to you whenever you want to see her. Anytime you want, we will hop on a plane and come to you."

But he never called to see her. He was either protecting himself or so overwhelmed. Or, he found someone else to share his life with.

Seeing that he carries this photo wherever he goes in the world shows me that he has never forgotten about her. I want to cry. It hurts my heart. It was so endearing of him to keep this photo with him all the time. He did care. But he could have called. He should have called.

JULIA 2

"Okay . . . So, what's the problem, Julia?" She cracks a smile. I feel like we are back in school in our room telling our secrets to each other. Nothing like an old friend.

I sip my tea. Then, finally, I blurt it out. "I feel like I'm going crazy!"

"Define crazy . . ."

"Well, for the past few weeks, I've had this sinking feeling that I'm . . . being followed."

"Really?"

"Really."

"By whom?"

"This man . . ."

Sarah takes a deep breath. I can see the gears turning and whirring inside of her head. She motions for the waiter and orders us another round. "Walk me through it," she humors me. "What exactly happened?"

I told her everything; About the guy at the gym, the dogwalker, the phone clicks, the dogwalker lookalike. Sarah listened as I rambled on, silently nodding the whole time without a hint of judgment or doubt in her big, brown eyes. It was so freeing, getting it all off my chest and laying everything—and I mean *everything*—out there. Sarah hung off of every word. She believed me. Not that Whitney or Ricky didn't. It's just that neither of them really had the complete picture. I was terrified of them thinking less of me.

And finally, I told Sarah what happened on the way here . . .

"I thought I was imagining things. That silly, little knocked-up Julia was suffering from a bad combination of jetlag, growing paranoia, and mom-brain. But every fiber in my being is screaming, begging me to trust my instincts for once in my damn life. Before I left the hotel, I had a sinking feeling that I was being watched. I can't describe it. The closest comparison I can think of is I felt like I was in a movie. I was the star of a film that someone was watching without my consent."

Sarah nodded while she had another bite of a croissant.

"There was a knock on my door, which was bizarre both because I hadn't ordered any room service and I'd only just arrived at the hotel, so there was no need for maid service. I threw a Q-tip in the bin, tightened my robe, and hurried over to the door. As I took a deep breath, I could feel my guard rising up, my drawbridge lifting."

"*Bonjour,* Madame Regan," the jovial man in a bellhop uniform greeted me.

"Bonjour," I smiled tightly. *"Comment puis-je t'aider?"*

The bellhop gestured to the rolling table next to him. *"Bienvenue aux Quatre Saisons. En guise de remerciement, nous serions ravis de vous offrir un petit déjeuner, gratuit,"* he lifted a large silver plate cap that revealed a smorgasbord of yummy-looking breakfast goodies.

My heart went a-flutter at the blueberry pancakes, crepes with fruit and cheese, eggs benedict, pain au chocolat, and toast with enough butter to give a bulimic high cholesterol.

I think I actually licked my lips. *"Pour moi?"*

"Oui, Madame. Puis-je?"

He had kind eyes. This man couldn't possibly be an ax murderer, I thought. What was he going to do anyway? Drown me in maple syrup?

"Merci," I smiled and opened the door for him.

"The bellhop wheeled the table inside, gave me a parting smile, and then left me alone with about five thousand carbs. I forgot to tip him, I was so overcome with the goodies."

"Then as I was walking over to meet you, Sarah I nearly collided with a cyclist. You called out to me, making me stop in my tracks. Said cyclist just so happened to be the bellhop. Coincidence? I think not. I could tell because he had the same black Belgian shoes with a bow missing on the left."

"Okay . . . I believe you, Jules. Totally, I do," Sarah admits after she's switched to wine. "But the Julia I know hoofed it all the way back to Carrefour in the sodding rain when the cashier forgot to charge you for a roll of toilet paper."

"So?"

"So, you're a bloody saint! Of all people, why do you think somebody would ever be after you?"

The million-dollar question.

JAKE, 5

I wake up groggy and foggy-headed. I try to lift my head off the pillows, but it feels like there's a one-hundred-pound anvil weighing it down. Jesus. What happened to me last night? I couldn't possibly have cleaned out my entire minibar . . . Could I? No, that was the old Jake. Party animal, Jake.

I glance over at the bedside table with one eye open. There's an orange pill bottle. Suddenly, yesterday comes flooding back. It all feels like a dream, but my aching body says otherwise.

I don't have my contacts in, so I can't read the prescription on the bottle yet. But it has to be in the hydrocodone or morphine family. My brain is cobbling together a memory of a doctor in my room last night. I stretch my arm toward the table and snatch the bottle. Vicodin. Nice. I pop two pills and swallow them dry.

I fumble around the bed for my phone. I need to talk to my dad.

No one will appreciate a good story where the big takeaway is how his son evaded death quite like Tripp Regan. I feel around until I find one of my phones tucked inside the fancy Porthault sheets.

Shit. Zero bars. Not only that, on the top right corner of my screen, three of the most horrifying letters in the English language: SOS. I fumble around for my other phone, my personal phone, but it's nowhere to be found. And then I remember. That Harry Houdini son of a bitch on the mountain. He stole my phone when he bumped into me when we were coming off the gondola. At least, I think he did. To what end, though? Judging by his spiffy clothes, the man sure didn't look like he was hard up for cash. Thank God I put my work phone in the safe before I hit the mountain, or I might be down two phones. But how did it get on my bed from the safe? Ironically, it might've been better if he stole my work phone because, in anyone else's hands, that thing is basically just a metal brick. The "geek squad" in the CIA encrypts each agent's phone with the utmost technological security that's not even on the market yet. The man would need my face, my thumb, my right eye, and three other multidigit codes in order to hack into it. It's unhackable.

I grab the landline. All I get is that damn *beep, beep, beep* when I try to get through to the outside world.

I turn to the window on my left and find that the snow is still coming down with all the force of a woman scorned. A shiver runs down my tired spine when I think about how cold and helpless I felt when I was in the eye of that very same storm just yesterday. That *was* yesterday, wasn't it?

In today's world, a snowstorm shouldn't completely knock out the mountain's cell towers. Maybe my man Roger knows what's up.

I shove the warm covers off of my body and swing my throbbing legs over the edge of my bed. I go to stand, but a blistering ache courses up from the tips of my toes all the way to the top of my head.

"Christ!" I sit right back on the bed—Change of plans. Sluggishly, I collapse back down on the bed and scoot closer to the far side back to the landline. I'm comically inching across the sheets, for once wishing I was lying on a twin mattress and not a king. And then, the strangest thing. I smell Cleo's perfume on this pillow.

Instantly, I'm transported back to her sprawling Tuscan house in Hawaii. Just picturing that house and everything Cleo and I did inside makes me hard. But the fantasy doesn't last. It never does because no matter which little sexcapade of ours I revisit, each memory of Cleo will now be forever tainted with a bittersweet ending. She doesn't want to be with me. Maybe she never did. I was just some young, hot guy who she wanted to have young, hot sex with. But the sweet side is that we have a daughter. Two years later, I still haven't gotten used to that word.

"Say goodbye to Daddy, Zelli."

I felt like a bomb detonated inside my head. That's how she chose to tell me. Right before I was boarding a nine-hour flight. Impeccable timing, Cleo.

I wanted to throw up, jump for joy, run in the opposite direction, and happily take the child with me back to DC all at once. It was my first out-of-body experience. Until the fatso standing behind me in the security line growled, I couldn't even move.

"You mind, buddy?" he'd said, gesturing to the growing chasm between me and the young gal several feet ahead.

"Oh. Sorry. Here, you go ahead," I grunted back and gestured for Mr. Fat Man to take my place in line.

I couldn't take my eyes off the woman that I love and our daughter standing beside her. *Our daughter.*

"Jake? Do you have anything you'd like to say?" Cleo asked.

"I—sorry. I'm . . . just. I'm, uh—"

"In shock?" Cleo smiled that incredible smile.

"You could say that," I blushed. "Why didn't you tell me?"

She looked down into the blue eyes of our little girl. "I suppose I was just being protective."

I understood that. But I couldn't help feeling frustrated at Cleo for springing this on me at the absolute last possible minute. "Well, I mean, obviously, I'd love to stay and get to know her, but I—I have to get back to DC or—"

"I know. This wasn't a test, Jake. I promise."

What I wouldn't have done to stay on that tropical island with Cleopatra, her smile, and Zelli.

Zelli. "It's a beautiful name. Zelli. Why did you choose that name?"

"You don't like it?"

"No, no, I do. I love it. I've just—I don't think I've ever heard it before."

"An old friend gave me the idea. And I just fell in love with it."

As I looked down at this tiny little human once again, I let another couple skip me. "I love it too."

"Well. You don't want to miss your flight."

Was she trying to get rid of me?

"Right. Yeah. Don't hate me, but I really do have to go."

"Never. You know where to find us . . ."

"You'll be in Honolulu for a while?"

"Probably not. But you're family. You can see her whenever you'd like."

I was trying to process this as quickly as I could, but it still wasn't fast enough. "Call you when I land?"

She just smiled and looked down at Zelli. "That sounds good. Doesn't it, Zelli?"

And that was it. I hadn't seen Cleo or my daughter again until last night. I blame myself, mostly. I realize now that I wasn't ready, and that's probably why Cleo waited so long to tell me. She knows me better than I give her credit for.

Now I really need to get hold of my dad. I'll leave out the part about Zelli for now. He'll be too focused on Cleo and how, of all people, I ran into her in St. Moritz. Of all the gin joints . . . They share some sort of weird history. That much, I know.

I lift the landline off the receiver again and dial "0." Good God, even this hurts.

"Bonjour!" says the chirpy voice on the other end.

"Hi, yeah. Is there any way to get an outside line?"

"Afraid not, Monsieur Regan. The storm knocked out all of the power lines. But they will restore them as soon as the blizzard stops."

I figured. "Okay, thanks," I sigh. "Could you please tell me if Cleo Gallier is staying in the hotel?"

My heart feels like it's going to beat out of my chest.

"Oui, Monsieur Regan. In fact, she is expecting your call. Would you like me to put you through?"

Oh, shit. "Sure, that'd be great."

"Very well, Monsieur Regan. One moment, s'il vous plaît."

I look down at my hand as the line rings. My fingers are shaking. Even though I saw Cleo just yesterday, it doesn't feel like that because my brain had turned to guacamole. I bet she and her father had a great laugh about how out of it I seemed. It's precisely the kind of perfect first impression I was hoping to make on my would-be father-in-law. He's probably thanking his lucky stars that his only daughter didn't end up with a chump like me.

"Bonjour?" she answers on the third ring.

"Cl-Cleo?" I stutter. Get your head out of your ass, Regan.

"Jake! There you are. How are you feeling?"

That enduring warmth of hers.

"Honestly? I've never been this sore in my entire life," I laugh, deciding not to lie. "I can hardly feel my arms and legs."

"I can imagine. You went through quite an ordeal up there," she laughs back.

We're both silent for a few seconds until I say, "I can't believe you're here. What are the odds?" I laugh again, nervously this time.

"It certainly is a very small world. I mean, my father has taken me to St. Moritz ever since I was a little girl. It's a tradition of ours."

Of course, it is. The Galliers aren't the type of family with ordinary traditions. Even our firmly upper-middle-class vacays to Aspen and Vail look pedestrian compared to St. Moritz.

"Nice. And um, speaking of little girls . . ." Well, that sounded creepy. "I mean, that was our little girl who was with you yesterday, right?"

"Zelli," is all she says.

"Zelli. Right, of course. I didn't know if my mind was playing tricks on me after being stuck on the mountain for so long," I force another laugh, hoping that'll bring some levity.

"No, Jake. That was her. Zelli is here." A very matter-of-fact tone this time.

"That's great. That's really great," I stall until finding the right words. "I'm here for a few more days. Do you think—I mean, only if it's okay with you, obviously. But do you think, um, that maybe I could, like, spend a little time with her while I'm here?"

CLEO 7

I am thrilled that today, Zelli and I will have lunch with her father, as her father, for the very first time. She met him as the man on the mountain but last night, I told her he is also her daddy.

"Maman, we should wear our matching ski outfits so Daddy knows you are my mommy," Zelli smiled over at me with a mouthful of peas at dinner.

She does make me laugh. "What a wonderful idea, Zelli. Though I am quite certain your father would recognize you with or without the matching ski suits."

She runs into my bedroom proudly modeling her orange and pink ski suit just as I'm spraying my wrists with my signature perfume, Endgame.

"Mommy, you're not dressed!" she accidentally drops one of her Hazel dolls on the floor. "Whoopsies."

"Oh, I was only waiting for you!" I bend down to retrieve the poor Hazel off the floor. "Don't you look pretty. Would you like a spritz of Mommy's perfume?"

She nods her head eagerly, just as I knew she would. I take Zelli's wrist and spray it twice with Endgame.

"Now we will smell the same too!"

A big smile lights up Zelli's little cherubic face. "I smell like you, Mommy! Do you think we should bring Endy to meet my daddy too?" "No, Zelli, Endy would probably run away and get lost. Better she stays in our rooms."

I kiss her on the forehead before crossing the room into my walk-in closet. "Okay, time for me to get dressed. I don't think it's possible for me to look as pretty as you do, though!"

When I asked Zelli yesterday where we should have lunch, her suggestion was—unsurprisingly—the lodge below the ski lifts. She adores that place, and even more, she adores preparations. The more complex, the better. Zelli asked if we could pick out a table ahead of time and decorate it for our "party" with her father.

"What a fabulous idea, Zelli! I am sure he will like that."

"Do you think he'll like me too? And will I like him? How come we only met him after he came off the mountain and not other times?"

And that's how it's gone since yesterday—an onslaught of questions and multiple trips to buy decorations through the hotel party planner.

"Can we get a cake too?"

"I'm sorry, Zelli, but we'll be late for lunch," I tell her as I zip up my candy-colored ski suit.

She pouts and sits on the floor with her legs splayed out in front. "But I love cake, and I know my Daddy will want cake."

I laugh at her ploy as I slide my boots on. "Next time, we will just have to think of cake earlier."

ZELLI AND I SPENT THE NEXT TWENTY MINUTES decorating the table. Balloons were tied to chairs, and sandwich and cookie platters on pink-and-orange paper plates were scattered around the table. Zelli put paper crowns at each of our three chairs—blue for Jake, pink for Zelli, and purple for me.

The festive atmosphere brought people over to wish Zelli a happy birthday.

"How old are you turning?" an older woman in a red parka asked Zelli.

"Oh, it's not my birthday. It's for my daddy."

The woman looks at me and laughs. "What a warm party you're giving him! He must love balloons."

Zelli hands me a bag of glitter that she wants opened. "Oh, I don't know him. I'm meeting him for the third time. But I don't remember the first time."

The woman looks at me again, her eyes wide with surprise. "I see! Well, I won't keep you any longer then. Enjoy!"

I hand the bag of glitter back. "Be careful with this, Zelli. We don't want to cover the entire lodge in glitter."

"I do, I do!" She starts sprinkling the table with gold. I suppose I set myself up for this one.

I smile and tickle Zelli's tummy. "Oh, I see. You want to eat glitter for lunch, is that it?"

That gets a big giggle out of Zelli. She just loves to be tickled. So I tickle her some more. "That's it, isn't it? You just want to eat glitter for lunch!"

"Maman, stop! That tickles!" She shrieks with glee. I have distracted her just enough to snatch the bag of glitter out of her tiny hands.

And then right on cue, I look up and see Jake cutting through the tables. He's wearing the same Canada Goose parka that he did on the day of the whiteout. I wonder if he did that so Zelli would recognize him. Zelli, who has moved on to the bag of balloons, doesn't see Jake coming our way.

I bend down and put both of my hands on her shoulders. "Zelli," I whisper. "There he is."

She gasps, and her little head snaps up. Her eyes follow my finger as I point it in Jake's direction.

"Do you see him? That's him. That's your daddy," I keep pointing.

Jake puts on a big, friendly smile and waves as he approaches our table.

Her eyes and mouth widened. "That's my daddy? The man on the mountain during the scary whiteout?" It sounds as if she thinks of Jake as a superhero.

"Can you believe it? Most other daddies would not have made it down the mountain. But yours did, Zelli. And now he is here with us, and he already loves you very, very much."

"Hey, Zelli!" Jake grins when he arrives.

Suddenly shy, Zelli buries her face in my legs. Jake gives me a questioning look, unsure how to handle it. I give him an encouraging nod.

"Don't you look pretty. I love how you and your mom are matching. You're like her Mini-Me," he laughs.

Nothing from Zelli. Her face stays buried in my legs.

Jake shrugs. "Did you put up all of these decorations, Zelli? Wow! I don't think I've ever seen so many balloons before!"

Ah, jackpot. That should get the attention of my little party planner. Our little party planner. Slowly, Zelli turns and shows Jake her face. She offers a slight smile and then a nod.

"What? No way. You put up all of these decorations all by yourself?"

She smiles and nods again, warming up to him.

"That's crazy! You're very grown up, Zelli. Your mom didn't lend a hand?"

Zelli just stares at Jake before she starts chuckling.

"What'd I say? What's so funny?!" Jake smiles.

"Lend a hand. No, Maman didn't lend me one of her hands. I already have two!" Zelli flashes her hands.

"Of course you do!" Jake is still smiling. "Sorry. It's just an expression and maybe not a very good one. I just meant, did your mother help you put up all of these awesome decorations?"

And we're off to the races. "Well, she helped me a little bit. But she was mostly just opening the bags and tying knots so the balloons wouldn't blow away."

I can tell that Jake is already in awe and unconditionally in love with this child, as am I. We lock eyes, and our matching smiles convey the same thing. Look at us. Look at how lucky we are to be chosen as her parents. Suddenly, I'm back in Honolulu again. I'm back on that winding dirt road where my yellow convertible smashed into Jake's Jeep Cherokee. I think of this day, this moment, often, so grateful that the universe–quite literally–dropped Jake into my path.

"Is that for me, do you think, Maman?" Zelli asks, jolting me out of my daydream.

She is looking at a present wrapped in a big pink bow.

JAKE 6

I have to say, the three of us make quite an attractive trio. The most beautiful woman, the most adorable girl, and the luckiest son of a bitch. Ha.

My eyes will forever roll whenever I hear someone use the cringy phrase: "My heart is exploding." I chalked it up to something that blushing brides, boozed-up grooms, or googly-eyed new parents used for their corny, emoji-splattered Instagram captions. You know the crowd. But looking across the table, the table that was decorated by my daughter and her mother, I finally understand what those losers mean.

I feel like a human firework. There's enough electricity coursing through my body to power a village. And so much adrenaline is pumping in my veins that I could moonwalk across the lodge.

"I have lots of dolls, you know," Zelli says proudly.

Shit. I glance over at Cleo. Not even one day on the job, and I've already screwed up. "Oh. I'm sorry, Zelli. We can always get you something else if—"

"No, I think I like her. I don't have any others with yellow hair," Zelli pats the doll's blond head.

Phew.

"Do you have a name for your new doll?" Cleo asks in her mom voice.

Zelli studies the doll. "Hmm. Hazel, probably."

Cleo leans her shoulder into mine. "Zelli names all of her dolls Hazel. It's quite an honor. Isn't that right?"

Zelli nods and licks her lips.

I dip my head closer to Cleo's. "Thanks for the tip."

I knew I couldn't show up to lunch empty-handed like some schmuck. Cleo graciously gave me the name of the toy store in town, and I hoofed it down to St. Moritz's version of Main Street and picked out a toy—my first real excursion after being caught in the whiteout only thirty-six hours earlier.

"Do you have any other daughters?"

I laugh. What a funny question from a four year old. "No, Zelli. It's just you, kid."

"Oh," she sighs, her voice tinged with surprising disappointment.

Silly me, I thought she'd want me all to herself. I glance over at Cleo, whom I'm relying on to be my Zelli whisperer.

"That's good, Zelli," says Cleo. "This way, you don't have to share!"

"I know . . ." Zelli puts her new doll on the table next to a pink plate of sugar cookies. "I just think it would be nice to have a sister or brother to play with."

I peer over at Cleo again. Not because I need her to interpret anything—I'm reading Zelli loud and clear. I look to Cleo to measure her reaction. I hope that doesn't hurt her feelings. I'm assuming getting pregnant at her age was tough enough. Most men would fall over themselves to knock Cleo up, but that might be out of the question for her. She rewards me with a little smile, but I can tell that stung a little. I put my hand on her thigh and give her an encouraging tap.

"Well, you know what, Zelli . . . My sister-in-law, Julia, is pregnant with a baby. So, you'll have a cousin to play with very soon!"

Zelli's little blue eyes light up.

"Julia's pregnant?" Cleo asks, her eyebrow raised.

"Yeah, she's like five months. And guess whose baby it is?" She waits for me to tell her.

"Ricky's."

Before Cleo can react, Zelli asks another question. "Is your sister having a girl baby or a boy baby?"

"Um, she actually doesn't know. They're going to wait to find out." I grab a brownie from one of the paper plates and break it into two halves. "And Julia's actually my sister-in-law, not my sister."

"That's for sure," Cleo laughs under her breath.

What a tangled web we weave.

"I hope Julia has a baby girl," Zelli says, cradling her doll in her arms.

"Zelli's other cousins are all boys. Both of my sisters, Beebe and Tree, had two boys each. We spent Christmas with them. Wasn't that fun, Zelli?"

Zelli turns to me. "They live in a castle like this hotel, which is a palace. It is like in my book, which I can show you, and it is so big, and the Christmas tree was this really big big big big tree."

LOL. My family is not like this one. Nary a castle in sight.

"And how exciting for Julia and Ricky."

"Yeah!" I lower my voice. "I mean, the whole thing's a little weird . . . But they're really happy. Actually, they're not too far from here."

"From St. Moritz?"

"Yeah, Julia had her tenth-year reunion or something in Paris, so little brother went along for the ride."

"Oh, that's right," Cleo sips her cocoa. "It was reunion week-end at the Sorbonne."

Dare I say I'm just a tad uncomfortable chatting about the ex-girlfriend that I cheated on with Cleo? Not that I regret it. But, still.

"Aren't you going to drink your hot cocoa? See my crown. I got one the other day with Didier. Mommy, you have one! Look. Do you have a crown, Daddy?"

My heart flutters. *Daddy.* I look up at Zelli, so full of love for this little mini-Cleo—until my heart free falls into my stomach.

That's when I see him again.

The man in the white ski suit, standing coolly, like a real jerk. He's fifty yards behind Zelli at the perimeter of the lodge. He removes his silver skis, which probably cost more than my first car, and stacks them on one of the racks. They aren't the ones he used on the mountain. He must have a storage room for his ski collection.

Even if I had been able to remember any of the man's distinguishable features, he's still too far away. Besides, his face is obscured by sunglasses, a matching white hat, and the collar of his coat. I hate him. What a dick.

Cleo turns to me. "Jake? Did we lose you?"

The white suit is waving to someone. A woman. Equally glamorous, in a chocolate brown ski suit and one of those poofy hats that the chick in *Dr. Zhivago* basically never took off. Could this be Mrs. White Ski, his deadly accomplice? She gives him a kiss on each cheek before resting her skis against his. A kiss on each cheek. Maybe they're European. Then again, when in Rome.

"Jake?" Cleo asks me again, more urgently. "What is it?"

"Sorry. I, uh. I . . . I thought I saw someone I went to college with."

Now they're on the move and walking toward us. Who does this asshole think he is? Somehow, he manages to pull off a strut even in his clunky, awkward ski boots. His arm is behind her back as they zigzag between round tables and wobbly people in clumsy boots.

"You went to college?" Zelli pipes in. "I don't want to go to college. I want to move back to Dubai and go to parties every day in the sand."

And I want to laugh. But I'm too distracted. I'm too caught up in Mr. White Ski Suit, only twenty yards away, canoodling with his possible accomplice. They find an empty table across from us on the outdoor patio and take a seat. They're laughing about something—Probably about how he almost got away with the murder of a wise beyond his years, hotshot CIA agent. I take a breath to calm my nerves. I need to focus on Zelli right now.

"Sorry about that, guys," I plastered on a smile. "I don't think it's him, after all."

"Oh, that's alright. I often think St. Moritz is one great big meeting place for lots of my old friends."

How chic. When I bump into my old buds, it's typically somewhere with the words "saloon" or "tavern" in the name. I look back over at Zelli. She's working on her third chocolate chip cookie. Something tells me "no" isn't a word she hears a lot.

"What about you, Zelli? Do you have a lot of friends here in St. Moritz?"

She nods proudly. "JoJo. She's my best friend."

I glance over at Mr. and Mrs. White Ski Suits. A waiter drops off two brown drinks at their table. I feel like the walls are closing in on me. But I have to keep my head in the game. I need to stay on Zelli.

"Lucky you that JoJo is also your ski instructor," Cleo twinkles. "But you have friends your own age too, don't you? What about—"

"Oh, and Maya. She's my best friend too."

"What about Marco?" The flirty way Cleo says 'Marco' implies there may be some preschool romance in the air. "Tell your father about Marco."

"Yes! Tell me everything there is to know about this Marco character."

Zelli brushes her doll's hair with her tiny fingers. "Oh, Marco's just a boy who likes to throw snow on me."

"Mm-hmm. And what are Marco's intentions?"

"To be determined," Cleo narrows her eyes in mock suspicion.

I look back over Zelli's shoulder. The White Ski Suits rise out of their seats, deep in conversation. Perhaps they're working out their next murder plot—death by snow plow.

But then, Cleo starts waving at them. "Look, Zelli. It's Didi!"

What the hell? The man in the white suit lifts his shades. It's Cleo's father. Didier. Didier is well into his seventies. He's an old geezer—a very spry, in shape, young-at-heart old geezer—but still, definitely born before the good guys won World War II. I didn't get a clear visual on the man in the white suit, but he wasn't even in the same ZIP code as seventy. Didier is taller, leaner too. False alarm. Or is it? My mind rewinds back to the whiteout and the aftermath from when I bumbled into the tea room. Didier was there looking relaxed and refreshed. I do some quick math, and it's possible he could make it down the mountain in time for a shower and shave before meeting his daughter and granddaughter for tea. It's possible if he's an expert skier who knows precisely how to maneuver those treacherous conditions. But that's a big, *big* if.

"Hello!" Didier waves two fingers as if he were an old-school movie star.

"Lola!" Zelli jumps out of her chair and into her arms.

"How did we not see you over here?" This Lola woman smiles. Her accent is charming. I can't tell what it is.

"We just had our daily hot toddy," Didier smiles as he gracefully slides off his gloves. Hot damn, he's debonair. Like a trimmer Mr. Belvedere or a way more ancient George Clooney. He is pure elegance.

Lola laughs. "This one went down quite smoothly."

I stand up from my chair, and Didier introduces me to Lola, a.k.a. not Mrs. White Ski Suit.

"Jake, I'd like you to meet a friend of mine. Lola de la Falaise. She's one of the finest skiers in all of St. Moritz."

"Jake Regan," I shake Lola's hand, then pause. "Zelli's father."

It sounds even weirder out loud than it does rattling around in my head.

"Didi!" Zelli jumps up and down at his feet with her arms in the air.

Cleo laughs and switches back into mom mode. "Zelli. Use your words."

"Will you please pick me up, Didi?" Zelli shines. As if saying no to this kid is even a remote possibility.

Didier looks down at his granddaughter and cracks an impossibly joyful smile.

Suddenly, looking at all of them, I'm overcome with a strange feeling. I wish my family were here too.

AFTER LUNCH, I TRY MY DAD AGAIN on his cell as I pace in front of the entrance to The Badrutt.

"Jake?"

"Hey, Dad."

"Jesus, Jake. There you are. Castillo told me about the storm. I've been trying to get a hold of you for the past two days." He sounds even more like Father Knows Best than usual.

"I know. Sorry. All of the power lines and the Wi-Fi have been completely knocked out."

"You're kidding. That's . . ."

"Primitive? Yeah, I know," I laugh, trying to get him to lighten up. "It was driving me crazy."

He lowers his voice, which tells me he's at home. "So, everything's fine then? Your mother has been worried."

"Shit. Okay, yeah, I'll text her after we hang up. I just—I literally didn't even have service until now."

"It's fine," he reassures me. "Just—well, you know how she gets. You'll be doing me a favor," he chuckles.

"I will, I will," then I pause, my snow boots crunching into the hard snow, which has now partially turned to ice. "There is one thing . . ."

"What is it?" his voice is low again.

I take a breath. "Just before the storm hit, I was with this guy in the gondola on the way up, right? And it's just the two of us, we're shooting the shit, going back and forth about how quickly the storm was rolling in. Blah, blah, blah. He tells me he's skied Corviglia a bunch, and by the time we get to the top—I mean, we were in a full-blown whiteout. So, this guy offers to basically guide me down the mountain. Neither of us wanted to wait for god knows how long for ski patrol, so I went along with it."

"Okay . . ." my father grumbles.

"Please, Dad. You would've done the exact same thing, Mr. I-Jump-Out-Of-Helicopters."

"Alright, alright. Cut to the chase."

"So, we start down the mountain and at this point, the visuals were basically nonexistent. I can barely see my own skis, let alone this guy. Then, he starts to sing, presumably so I can follow the sound of his voice," I pause for dramatic effect. "And you'll never guess what song he was singing."

"You're right, I won't. So just tell me."

"*Yes, We Have No Bananas.* That song you used to sing us when we were kids."

There's silence at the other end. "*Yes, We Have No Bananas?*"

"Isn't that crazy? I'd completely forgotten about that song. But anyway, I completely lose track of this guy. It takes me hours to get down the mountain, and—"

"Why didn't you try and call for help, Jake?"

"Well, Dad. That's the thing. My phone was gone."

"What do you mean 'gone?'"

"I mean, gone. I had it when I was in the gondola, and I didn't when I was on the mountain. So, somewhere in between—"

"Could it have fallen out of your pocket?"

"No, I'm good about that. I always zip it shut."

"You think this guy stole it?"

"That's the only explanation. I know I zipped it into my pocket. I remember doing it."

"You get a good look at this guy?"

"Negative. He had a hat, sunglasses, and a neck warmer."

"Please tell me it was your personal phone," he says warily.

"It was."

Again, there's silence at the other end. "Have you contacted security at the hotel yet? You need to locate this man."

"Yes, of course. There's nothing. No sign of this guy anywhere. I went down to the front desk, and they put me into a room with a couple of guys who do security, and they rolled the film again and again of me getting into the gondola, but he avoided the camera, and at the top, no one could see a thing from the camera."

"Alight, stand by. I'm going to get Singer on this. See if he can't infiltrate their security system," he pauses. "So, all you got is he was wearing a white ski suit? Height, skin, hair?"

"He was around my height, give or take. Six foot one, six foot two maybe. White guy. And I think his sideburns were brown."

"Copy that. Stand by."

And then, before I can even tell him about Cleopatra being here, his phone clicks off.

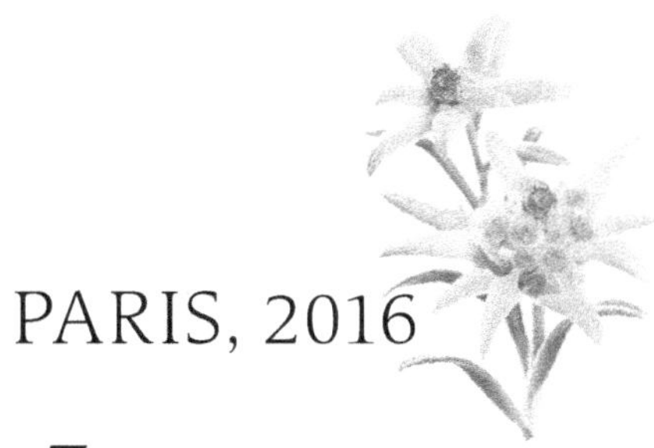

JULIA 3

Ricky's ringing phone jolts me out of my slumber. He releases his grip from around my belly and fishes it out of his pants pocket.

"Who is it?" I ask groggily.

"Jake. Wonder what he wants . . ."

I turn over to face my husband. "Isn't he skiing in St. Moritz?"

"Last I checked," he nods, his brow scrunched as he looks down at his phone.

"Well, answer it! He never calls."

"Hey, buddy. Yeah, touched down a few hours ago. How's the skiing?" Ricky looks over at me as he listens to his oldest brother. "Oh, what? Shit. A whiteout? No, I had no idea. I have a missed call from Mom, but I figured she was just being Mom and making sure I got in okay."

"What's going on?" I whisper.

Ricky puts his phone on speaker. "Julia's here too."

"Hey, Jake," I lean into the phone.

"Jake was caught in a whiteout yesterday while he was skiing."

"Oh my God. Jake, are you okay?"

"Hey, Jules . . . Yeah, I'm good. It was a little scary for a minute there, and I don't think my body has ever been this sore," he chuckles, sounding surprisingly upbeat. "But all's well that ends well, I guess."

"Dude. You sound pretty fucking perky for a guy who almost froze to death."

"I was going to say!" I chime in. "Maybe near death suits you."

That gets a little laugh out of Jake. "Well, that's actually why I'm calling . . ."

Ricky and I trade looks.

"Jules, I know you have your reunion. And, respect. But Zurich is only, like, an hour-long flight from Paris. And then, not gonna lie, kind of a long train to St. Moritz. But it's really pretty. Why don't . . . you guys swing by? The storm has totally passed."

My husband and I stare at each other. Now that we're halfway around the world from home, Jake wants to see us?

"Uh . . ." is all that comes out of Ricky's mouth at first.

"Wait. You want us to come to St. Moritz?" I'm still not sure I'm understanding him correctly.

"Like, now?" Ricky is fighting a losing battle with a smile. He hasn't outright admitted it, but I know Jake being so distant has hurt Ricky. He misses his big brother.

"Well, I'm not suggesting you hop on a plane, like, right this minute, but maybe tomorrow? Is that crazy?"

Kinda. Considering this is the same person who has avoided Ricky and me as if we have had leprosy for the past two years while we've been living less than three miles away . . . Something must be going on.

"Rick, you haven't been skiing in years. And after the baby comes, no offense, but good luck. And Jules, St. Moritz has some of the best shopping in the world!"

As if the only thing on women's minds is finding a cute new purse or pair of boots.

"Not that shopping is the only thing women care about . . ." He still knows me pretty well it seems.

". . . Are you sure everything's alright, Jake?"

There's silence on the other end of the phone.

"Actually, there's someone special I really want you guys to meet."

Ricky and I share another look. Finally, the smile on his face breaks free. My mouth drops open, thrilled that my brother-in-law has finally met his true match. "Go on . . ."

"Yes, tell us more!"

"Sorry . . . I think you're just going to have to come to St. Moritz to see for yourself."

I suspect Ricky's decision is already made. I wait for his reaction. He takes a breath, gives me a crooked smile, and shrugs. This is Ricky's way of saying "why not?" The truth is that Ricky would meet Jake on the moon if he asked him to. For the past two years, my poor teddy bear of a husband has been waiting for Jake's call, mourning their old relationship and how close they used to be once upon a time. There's no way Jake is still in love with me or anything like that. But I do think the whole brother-swapping situation was a bit . . . Ick. Maybe for us all.

If I'm being completely honest, relief washes over me. Jake has a girlfriend, and we can all be normal again.

St. Moritz it is.

"Excited, babe?" I hook my pinkie around Ricky's.

He's tip-tip-tapping away at his tray table as if he were Charlie Watts—which is not only driving me insane but probably the poor person seated in front of him too. Unlike most hungover people in the world, Ricky's energy the morning after knows no bounds. Me on the other hand, all I have the energy and brain capacity for is ordering something yummy from Seamless and finding something juicy to watch on Netflix. But seeing as I didn't have a drop of alcohol last night, I'm way better equipped to handle my ever-so-chipper husband this fine morning.

"Sorry," he laughs and takes the hint. Ricky returns his tray table to its upright position and peers over my shoulder out the window as we make our initial descent into Zurich.

I lean into Ricky. "Did you see there's an indoor pool?" I bring up my phone and show him a photo of the pool at The Steffani. "It kind of reminds me of the Roman baths. Just with electricity."

There weren't any rooms available at The Badrutt where Jake is staying, which came as a major relief to Ricky and me because we didn't exactly budget for a palace on this trip. St. Moritz is littered with hotels, and the price at The Steffani was right. The photos that I found online looked cozy and chic and the nail in the coffin for me was the free continental breakfast every morning. Say no more, fam.

Ricky cracks a smile. "Did you bring your suit?"

"I'm six months pregnant. What do you think?" I playfully swat him on the shoulder.

"Hey, I'm into this new you. I like a little meat on your bones," Ricky lowers his voice and smiles. "It's hot . . ."

"Yeah, I wonder why," I smile back and glance down at my boobs. I have had to buy all new bras.

"Well, that doesn't hurt," his voice still low. "But there's just something so sexy about the fact that our little part of me is growing inside of you."

"Gross," I laugh.

"What? Does that make me a creep? I meant it as a compliment!"

The captain interrupts this thrilling conversation when he comes over the loudspeaker. He makes his announcement in French first.

"Final descent, babe?"

I nod just before the captain goes through the exact same spiel, just in English this time.

"My big, buxom, beautiful babe," Ricky gives my cheek a kiss and my thigh a squeeze.

At least my changing, growing body doesn't faze my husband. My slim, strapping, sexy husband.

"Shut up," I laugh.

Forty minutes later, we're off the plane and through customs, sitting on the train, taking in the exquisite views of the Swiss countryside. Looking out at the mountains makes me want to scarf down a whole box of Lindor chocolates, strap on lederhosen, and go yodeling with Maria and the entire von Trapp gang.

Julie Andrews. And yes, I'm aware that technically *The Sound of Music* takes place in Austria, but the scenery looks identical. So there.

Ricky's ringing phone snaps me out of my Christopher Plummer fantasy.

"Jake," Ricky tells me before he picks up. "Hey, buddy! Yeah, should be there in a few hours. One sec," Ricky turns to me. "Jules, you good with Jake meeting us at the hotel after we drop our stuff? He'll show us around for a little before he and I hit the slopes."

"Uh," I think.

In all honesty, I was hoping to relax for a minute before meeting up with Jake. There's something about being squished into an airplane and now a train that makes me want to put up my hair and hop in a warm bubble bath with a Patricia Highsmith novel and a glass of wine. I look down at my watch. It's 10:47 a.m. "Um, sure. Can we say one forty-five?"

Ricky repeats that to Jake. "Great, see you then."

A little after one, our black cab pulls into our hotel.

"Welcome to The Steffani," the cute blond woman at the front desk greets us solicitously in perfect English.

"Man, do we look that American?" Ricky laughs. "Actually, my wife is a Brit from Gibraltar. But the same thing."

"Hardly the same . . ." I scoff.

Ricky's joke, however, lands with our new blond friend. "We're famously neutral here in Switzerland," she winks before getting down to brass tacks. "May I please get your name?"

Ricky grunts as he unloads his bag from off of his shoulder and onto the tile floor. "Regan, thank you."

I glance over my husband's broad shoulder and find what I'm looking for: a place to sit. "Babe, I'm just gonna," I gesture to the two beige lounge chairs across the room.

Even though I've only been standing for about ninety seconds, I'm still adjusting to lugging this extra weight around. I'm also finding it increasingly hard to stay on my feet for too long. I take a load off on one of the sumptuous upholstered chairs with a dark wood finish and open up my phone to see what's going on in the wild world of Instagram. Oh, that's a cute picture of us. Samantha posted a photo of our big, boisterous group at dinner last night. Ha. Everyone's eyes are suspiciously glassy-eyed. I hit the "like" button and comment with three heart emojis, the emoji I most overuse. How basic of me.

"Ready, babe?" he jangles a set of keys.

I plaster on the biggest smile I can and get to my feet. For real, this time.

After a brief elevator ride up to the third floor and a long waddle down the carpeted hall, Ricky and I have, at long last, made it to our room.

The cream-colored wooden floors are made of oak, and so are the bedside tables, armoire, and a matching panel above the queen bed. There's also a wooden chess set in the middle of the room, but the queen is not in the correct spot. Instead, she's standing unprotected in the row ahead of her pawns. Being the OCD freak that I am, I pick her up and move her back where she belongs.

Ricky looks around the room at all the wood. "I'm sensing a theme . . . You?"

"Woodland chic," I smile as I push him onto the bed. There's nothing like a good shag to take your mind off of the psychotic stalker that you've made up in your head. The sheets are all white except for a red and taupe-patterned quilt that's folded neatly at the foot of the bed. I run my fingers over it and almost gasp at how soft it is.

Ricky grabs my wrist, gently pulling me onto him, my roly-poly body toppling onto his. His hands run over my back and onto my bottom. And as if he knows precisely what's flashing across my mind, he says, "I told you, I love you in any shape, Julia."

"Are you sure?"

"Yes," he says as his fingers dig into my blimpy buttocks. "I love it," Ricky says breathlessly before he kisses me on the neck. I can feel him against my thigh.

No matter the time of day, Ricky is a big fan of christening a hotel room within minutes of dropping our bags—so his sudden, libidinous behavior doesn't surprise me. In fact, it relieves and thrills me. It makes me believe him when he says that my rounder, fuller figure actually turns him on. Hooray, my husband still finds me sexy. In one smooth motion, he rolls me over and lifts the Reformation maxidress that I can barely still squeeze into over my knees. His pants are halfway unzipped when there's a knock on our door.

"What the fuck?"

I glance down at my watch. It's barely 1:35 p.m. "Jake's early," I whisper.

"Jake?" Ricky calls out.

"Housekeeping!" a shrill, stifled voice shrieks back.

"Definitely, Jake," I groan, annoyed that he's gotten in the way of our afternoon delight.

Ricky reluctantly pries himself off of me and rolls off the bed haphazardly. "Coming," he calls out. "But not in the good way," Ricky says under his breath in my direction.

"Tell me about it," I pout as I pull my dress back down.

"To be continued later," Ricky tosses me a smile as he walks across the room toward the door.

"Babe, you might wanna," I gesture to his hair.

Moments later, the brothers Regan are bearhugging inside our little woodland chic room.

"I can't believe you're here!" Jake, dressed in ski pants and a parka, exclaims before his face is muffled in his brother's shoulder. His younger *and* taller brother's shoulder, thank you very much. "Flight was fine?"

"Totally fine. But forget about that. How are you feeling? Dude, a whiteout. Je-sus."

"I know. I'm still kinda processing . . . But plenty of time to catch you up on that later." Jake turns his sights on me next. "And look at you, Jules!"

"I know. I'm a *lot*," I wobble to my feet.

"Nah, you look great," Jake opens his arms. "Really. And thanks again for coming."

"Of course, so happy to be here," I give him a hug.

Jake turns to Ricky. "You ready to hit the slopes? Here, I brought you some stuff," he hands him a Badrutt Palace tote bag.

"You bet. Just gimme a sec," he takes the bag. "The question is, are *you* ready to hit the slopes?"

"Oh, yeah. I need to get back in the saddle, stat."

"Give me thirty secs," Ricky says as he closes the bathroom door behind him.

Jake turns toward me before there's even a chance for any awkward silence to creep in. "And because I'm stealing your husband away from you after stealing you away from Paris, I took the liberty of making you an appointment at one of St. Moritz's chicest hair salons."

Is he pulling my leg? This is the same man who didn't notice when I took a very ill-advised trip to my hairdresser a number of years ago and got balayage. I had seen a photo in *Vanity Fair* of Jessica Biel looking like a vision in her new balayage 'do. Serves me right for deluding myself into believing that what looks good on Jessica Biel would work on a pale British woman with naturally mousy hair.

"For real?"

"For real. And the appointment's in thirty minutes, girl, so we might want to shake a tail feather. It's just in town. Ricky and I will walk you there."

Jake looks like he's walking on air. Methinks it has a little something to do with his new "special someone . . ."

"Wow, thank you. I don't know what to say. That's such a thoughtful—and well, totally unexpected—treat."

"What is?" Ricky asks as he opens the bathroom door, having changed into Jake's ski stuff.

"Jake's arranged for me to have my hair done. Isn't that sweet?"

Ricky cracks a smile. "Did your, uh," he makes air quotes, "'special someone'" help you out with that by chance, J?"

"Nah. Shockingly, this was all me. You good to go, slowpoke?"

Ricky zips the parka and pulls a hat and gloves from the pockets. "Let's do it."

JAKE, 7

Flashes of white flicker across my brain like a recurring nightmare. Visions of alabaster nothingness closing in on me from every angle, as if I'm trapped inside a hellish upside-down snow globe, haunt me. It feels like it happened a zillion years ago and just yesterday. But it was three days ago. The gondola carries my brother and me closer and closer to the scene of the crime, and my chest gets tighter and tighter.

"I would've lost my shit."

I shrug. "Well, yeah. I did. Initially, at least. But I knew the only way I'd make it down was if I kept my cool." I glance over at our fellow skiers sharing the gondola with us. Half of me hopes I'll come face to face with the mysterious man in the white ski suit again, while the other half dreads that idea. My eyes scan the eager skiers and find the only person rocking a white ski suit. It's a woman who's about five foot nothing.

"Yeah, good point. You've always been pretty calm in a crisis, though. Nothing like our other brother," Ricky laughs.

"Oh, man," I chuckle. "Zero chance Matty would've made it down the mountain in one piece."

"Poor, sweet Matt. Zero chance he would've made it into the gondola in the first place."

"Bullshit!" I laugh. "Matt wouldn't have even made it to JFK to get on the plane to fly him here. Other than maybe the Bonneville Salt Flats, there's nothing he hates more than snow. Don't you remember? That's why Mom had us stop going on ski trips."

A pause. "Dude, what the hell are the Bonneville Salt Flats?"

"Some place in Utah. It's completely uninhabitable for plant life of any kind."

Ricky gives me a funny look. "How do you even know that?"

"Don't you know how smart I am, little brother?"

Ricky just laughs. "What'd Mom and Dad say about the whole thing? I'm surprised Mom didn't call me ten times on the verge of a mental breakdown. Beside herself that 'my Jake' almost didn't make it."

"Well, that's probably because I only told Dad. I asked him to keep it on the DL with Mom."

"Smart."

I flinch at the sound of a loud crack. Out of the corner of my eye, something white comes closer to me. When I turn toward it, I'm relieved to find that it's only that same pint-sized woman retrieving one of her ski poles after she dropped it on the floor.

"You okay?" Ricky love taps me on the elbow.

Of the three of us, Ricky has always been the most compassionate. Matt was born with the uncanny ability to hone in on little character ticks and quirks that most of the population miss by a mile. But Ricky, the baby, is different. Highly empathetic and sensitive to the needs of others, I've always chalked it up to a youngest child syndrome thing. He probably picked it up all those times I locked him in the basements with the lights turned off.

I did miss him. Our distance was my fault. I was avoiding Ricky for falling in love with the woman whose heart I'd sliced and diced into thousands of tiny pieces. I try not to think about how atrociously I'd treated Julia at the very end. If I sat down and really gave it the thought and consideration she deserved, I wouldn't be able to look her in the eye anymore. My stubbornness comes from my father's side. He can't apologize either. Ricky and I will go back to normal and pretend that these last two years didn't even happen. I doubt I'd offer Ricky the same grace if the shoe was on the other foot.

"Fine, yeah. Think I'm just a little jumpy," I force a laugh and look out the view from the gondola, avoiding the look that I know my brother is laying on me. It's fun to watch the skiers showing off for us. We're only a few football fields away from the drop-off. I take a deep breath, shoving down any negative thoughts.

Ricky takes a step closer to me. "Hey, it's still not too late to turn back around . . ."

"Actually, it kinda is."

"Only if you're above calling ski patrol and having them escort you down the mountain on one of their handy thingamajigs."

Ricky is wearing a blank poker face. Does my baby brother actually think I'm this big of a pussy?

Ever since the whiteout, my confidence has been shot.

"Are you . . . ?"

Finally, Ricky laughs. Damn, he sure took his sweet ass time getting to the punchline. "I'm messin' with ya, weirdo."

"Okay, you fucking better be," I punch him in the arm. "Because we're skiing down this mountain if it's the last thing I do."

I made it. I fucking made it down the mountain with flying colors, like I knew I would. It was a perfect run. My skis were moving and grooving from the moment I glided off that gondola, in flawless concert with the voluptuous curves of that beautiful, buxom babe of a mountain. Even Ricky, who's a prettier skier than me, was impressed by my performance. What can I say? The poor guy just couldn't keep up with his big bro.

Ricky, panting, yanks his goggles off as we ski leisurely back over to the gondola. "Well, I think it's safe to say your confidence is back and better than ever . . ."

That makes me laugh. "What do you mean?" But I know what he means.

"Dude. C'mon. You were one big ball of nerves on the way up."

"Who, moi?"

"Yeah, you, macho man," Ricky says as if he was Tony Manero. "Just because I haven't seen you in a while doesn't mean I don't still know you like the back of my hand."

I nod as we get in the short line for the chair lift. He's not wrong, but he's also not right.

Ricky nudges me with his shoulder. "Don't sweat it. I don't think you're, like, weak or anything. Most guys would never get back in the saddle. Let alone less than seventy-two hours later."

I force a laugh. Glancing over my shoulder, my eyes land on another person in a white ski suit. Oh, God. I squint and strain my neck, trying to get a closer look. The person turns and I spot a red and blue Canada Goose label. I can't remember who made White Ski Suit's white suit, but I know it wasn't Canada Goose.

"Jake? Earth to Jake?"

I turn to find Ricky standing at the lift.

"You coming?"

"Whoops, sorry. Thought I . . . saw someone I knew," I say as I join him in the line.

"Sure you're okay?"

Screw it. "Yeah, I'm fine. I just, uh, I don't know. Guess I didn't really . . . tell you the full story before."

He turns to me. "Okay. Well, do you want to tell me about it now?"

We are finally on the chair lift, which takes a bit longer than the gondola, but it's private. I take a deep breath. "So, okay. There was this guy. And it was only us in the gondola . . ."

Ricky just nods, letting me spin my yarn.

"We shot the shit a little, and by the time we got to the top, the weather was, well, um, not good. He said that he'd skied Corviglia his whole life and offered to let me follow him down. Long story short, I said sure. Anyway, we start doing our thing and I can barely see him. So, he starts humming so I could at least follow the sound of his voice, which I thought was pretty quick thinking on his behalf."

"Totally."

I pause. "Do you remember that dumb song Dad would sometimes sing to us before bed? I have no idea what it's called, but it's about bananas. 'We Have No Bananas' or some shit."

Ricky looks off, trying to conjure up the childhood memory until a smile lights up his face. "Oh, yeah . . . the banana song. Yeah, I think so. Matt was always singing it."

"Right."

Christ, Ricky starts to sing. *"Yes, we have no bananas, we have a no-bananas today."*

"Okay, good for you, dude. You remember the lyrics," I pat him on the back. "Anyway, I follow him until I can't hear him anymore. So, obviously, I'm like *fuck*. I'm alone now. Then I go for my phone, seeing if there's any chance I have a signal. But . . . it's gone. And you know me. I'm a crazy person when it comes to my phone. I'm positive my pocket was zipped." I look down at the mountain, concerned about my brother's reaction.

"Okay. So . . . I just want to make sure I'm following. You think maybe this guy in a white ski suit took it?" His tone is as delicate as can be.

"Maybe? I don't know. The whole thing is just . . . weird. The phone, the song. I just have a bad feeling. I don't have a clue if he made it down or if his body was found somewhere on the mountain or what."

"Right. And is there any reason why you think he'd want your phone or lure you down the mountain?"

Welp. For starters, little brother, because I'm in the mother fucking CIA. That's what I want to say, at least. But I just shrug and say, "No reason."

"Don't you think you'd know if he died though? Wouldn't there be some sort of report or memo sent to the guests?"

"Not necessarily . . ."

CLEO, 8

We are staying over for a few more days in St. Moritz. The skiing will be heavenly, and Jake would very much like to get to know Zelli more while he's here. I am thrilled with this idea. Zelli comes in and Nannie brings us our breakfast, just delivered from room service.

Zelli opens her french toast and I open my yogurt. Boring. We both have our dark chocolate cocoa frothed with homemade whipped cream. In the middle, there was another crown very reminiscent of the one the skier made on the mountain and the one on our slippers given to us anonymously. Zelli whoops with delight and tells me how she had also seen one the other day in her cocoa in the Lodge. It makes me wonder how in the world that skier managed to get that into our cocoa. Nannie looks over and mentions how she should get cocoa instead of her usual tea next time.

I wander over to the chessboard sitting in our living room. Interestingly, I see the Queen's Gambit opening set up. My father must have set it up for us to play today. Oddly, the queen is raised on what appears to be a 20 Franc gold coin, embossed on the side is the profile of a beautiful queen wearing a crown. Fitting.

CLEO, 8

SERGEI WILL BE BACK FROM MOSCOW TONIGHT, I hope. I'll admit it, that is the main reason for staying. I am besotted by him.

I arrive at Blonde, a tiny hair salon about the size of a cigar store but so chic with its bright blue doors. Blonde is always brimming with film stars and TV personalities—though "brimming" really only means five clients at once, tops, as it is that tiny. It's a really small, exclusive club.

I flashback to the morning so many years ago after my first night with Jake. Peach, my incredible make-up artist on my show *Close Encounters,* needed to make me look beautiful after a sleepless night spent with Jake. My visit to Jake the other night was very different. He was sleeping like a baby, and I watched him like a guardian angel, fluffing up his pillows and refilling his water glass. I'm just so grateful that he made it down the mountain. Ultimately, his episode on the mountain made me realize that I want Zelli to have a father as she grows up, and so I'm grateful for that realization as well. I only see Jake as the father of my daughter. Funny how you can have cared about someone and, several years later, have no feelings for him at all. All the lust left years ago, and I believe now that that's all that it really was. I had been frigid for years due to the rape when I was a child, and he woke me up. He is fifteen years younger, and what fun that wakeup was.

"Ah, *Cléopâtre! Content de te revoir!*" Gagoune, the owner and a close friend in Paris and here, greets me while she combs an elderly woman's long red hair. Perhaps her hair is a bit too long for her age.

"Bonjour, Gagoune. *C'est tellement merveilleux d'être de retour!*"

She looks over her shoulder. "*Villette, Madame Cléopâtre est là.*" Then she turns back to me and smiles. "*Je serai avec toi dès que Villette te lavera les cheveux.*"

"Merci, Gagoune," I say as Villette appears by my side.

Villette gestures with her hands toward the back of the salon. *"Par ici s'il vous plaît."*

Warm water pools over my head, and I take this moment in. This is my favorite part. Oh, I just love it when someone with strong hands washes my hair and massages my scalp. I would come to Blonde for only the head massages if they offered it as a service. I look up at Villette and offer her a pleased smile, letting her know that she has just swept me off to the gates of heaven with her magical touch. Villette, a smiling, diminutive older woman, has worked at Blonde for as long as I can remember. She does all of the washing and brings magazines to read and espressos to drink, making this whole experience just about perfect.

When she's through, Villette gently wraps a towel around my head and leads me to the chair where Gagoune will give me one of her famous blowouts. After several days on the mountain, the wind whipping through my hair, this blowout could not come at a better time. Skiing nourishes the soul, but it's not so fabulous for the hair.

From out of the corner of my eye, I notice a pretty girl sitting in the chair next to me reading a Vogue magazine. When I look over at her and smile, the pretty girl is already staring at me with her mouth gaped open.

"Oh my God, Cleo! It really is you!" And the pretty girl is on her feet. "It's Julia Regan!"

"Julia! Goodness!"

"It's so funny running into you! What a small world!"

For a moment, it's awkward. Neither of us knows if the occasion calls for a hug or not. To hug or not to hug, that is the question. But before I know it, Julia has made the decision for both of us and she wraps both of her arms around me.

"Julia! I can't believe it's you! You look stunning. You're—"

Glowing. Julia is absolutely glowing. Julia is glowing because now that she is standing and I am taking all of her in, I can see that she is quite pregnant. I had completely forgotten that Jake told me that at lunch.

"And you're having a baby! How wonderful, Julia! Congratulations!"

She leans in closer to me, so close that I can smell her sweet perfume. "I know . . . I married Ricky. Can you believe it?"

Love does win, after all. I want to tell her that Jake has already passed along this wonderful news but that might give away his surprise. "Oh! What fabulous news, Julia. I always knew he held a torch for you . . ."

"I know, after all of that, I suppose I ended up with the right Regan brother," she smiles. And I can tell that she has forgiven me for my affair with Jake. Forgiven, but perhaps not forgotten.

"Indeed you did. And what brings you to St. Moritz?"

"Well, actually, I was in Paris for my tenth-year reunion at the Sorbonne. But Ricky and I cut our trip short after Jake—oh, did you know he was here?"

"Yes, I ran into him the other day. He had just made it down the mountain during that horrible whiteout . . ."

"Right! Yes, exactly. He called Ricky, told us about the whiteout, and asked us to hop on a plane the next day. We were so close anyway, and neither of us has ever been to St. Moritz, so we figured why not?" she pauses. "How do you think he seems?"

"Oh, a bit shaken up, but perfectly fine given the circumstances."

Julia nods. "He and Ricky are taking a few runs on the mountain, so I came here to get pampered."

"Well, you've certainly come to the right place. Blonde is the very best. How long are you and Ricky in town?"

"Only a few days. Jake mentioned that there's a—" Julia pauses. "Wait, a minute. Oh my God. Are you the 'special someone?'"

"I beg your pardon?" I pretend to act like I have no idea what she's talking about.

"Well, part of the reason why Jake wanted Ricky and me to come here is because apparently . . ." Julia leans in closer and smiles conspiratorially. "There's a 'special someone' in his life that he'd like us to meet . . . so, are you that someone?"

You're getting warm, I think. "No, I'm not!" I laugh, and she laughs with me. "But I bet she is wonderful!"

My friend Celeste, a news reporter in Paris for BFM-TV, comes over with her hair in tin foil and her hands around a tiny espresso in its tiny china cup.

"Cléopâtre!" she squeals.

Our daughters are in preschool together, and Celeste is extolling in her fast French how lovely Zelli is. "*Votre fille Zelli est tellement adorable et ma fille l'a ratée pendant son absence. Ils jouent toute la journée à l'école, tu sais, Cléopâtre.*"

I am hoping Julia's French is not up to the speed of Celeste. Soon enough, she will know about Zelli, but Jake should be the one to tell her, not me, and certainly not a stranger. So I force the very biggest smile that I can muster and glance over to Julia to quickly change the subject. "Oh, Julia, meet my friend, Celeste. Should we have espressos like Celeste, Julia?"

"Um, sure!" says Julia. She really is so lovely and polite.

I ask Villette to kindly fetch us two espressos. Then I beckon to Gagoune and whisper very quietly in her ear. "Gagoune, can you please get to me right away?"

Without a word, Gagoune nods, picks up her hair-dryer, and, with a flick of her hand, turns it on and noisily gets to work. I love Gagoune. She is a magician, and the hair-dryer is her wand.

We have skied together for years and dine in Paris often. She is married but wanted to have a career of her own, so her husband bought her the chicest hair salon in Paris and it is now also in

St Moritz. She is the salon, and my favorite tidbit about her is that her grandmother was the face of the Statue of Liberty. But just as soon as I close my eyes to enjoy Gagoune's genius, Julia's voice jolts me out of my euphoria.

"Look who's here!" she shrieks.

My eyes open to find Ricky Regan in ski clothes standing in the doorway of Blonde. He's so tall that he practically has to duck to fit inside the tiny salon. Upon seeing me, he does a double take. "Whoa. Wait. Cleopatra?!"

From my chair, I simply wave at Ricky and blow him a kiss. There is hardly any room for normal-sized people to stand and hug in Blonde anyway.

"Can you believe the odds, Ricky?" Julia beams.

If anyone should be grateful for my affair with Jake, it is Ricky. From that very first night, I met the Regan family at The Outrigger Canoe Club, I could tell that Ricky was hopelessly in love with his brother's girlfriend. And he won her. I love the romance of it all. "Wait a second," Ricky turns to Julia. "Are you . . . ?"

Julia smirks and shakes her head. "Allegedly, not. But I'm not so sure I believe you, Cleo," she smiles.

"No, I promise. I am not Jake's special someone," I cut in with a smile as Gagoune shuts off the blow-dryer.

"I see you two have properly caught up," Ricky laughs.

"But of course. What else do you think happens in a hair salon?"

The two of them might as well be walking on air. "It's wonderful to see you married. You both look very happy," I smile again as Gagoune spritzes my hair with a touch of my favorite Caudalie spray.

Ricky shakes his head. "Nah, all smoke and mirrors . . ."

"Excuse you!" Julia laughs, her voice bouncing off the walls of Blonde. "How was the skiing?"

The woman sitting on the other side of me looks up from her book and shakes her head, annoyed by the disturbance.

Ricky answers, "Great. Jake kicked my ass."

"So, I guess he's back in the saddle?" Julia asks.

"Oh, yeah. Totally. Didn't miss a beat." It looks like he's about to say something else but then changes his mind.

"I hope you are all doing something fun tonight?" I ask, my voice low, hoping they will catch the hint.

"Oh, damn. Speaking of . . . I'm sorry, babe, but the concierge said Ecco's a no-go."

"Ah, bummer. But that's alright. We'll just head into town and let Jake lead the way."

My ears perk up. "You're trying to go to Ecco tonight?"

"Yeah, my friend at Slate wrote a rave review a few months ago. If I'd known we were coming, I would've coordinated better," Ricky tells me.

"Would you like me to . . . make the reservation? They know me quite well there," I offer.

Julia and Ricky share matching looks of reluctance. It's obvious that they would like me to make the call, but they are just far too polite to ask.

"Think of it as a late wedding present," I insist as I pick up my cell phone and dial the number to St. Moritz's most sought-after restaurant. "For three people, yes?"

Julia and Ricky trade looks.

"Assuming Jake will be joining you?"

"Yes, that's so nice of you, but really not necessary." She looks at Ricky. "Do you think the 'special someone' will come too?"

"No, he said tomorrow."

"Yeah, Cleo. You really don't have to—"

"*Bonjour, Louis. Oui! C'est Cleopatra. Ça va? Oui. Très intéressant . . .*"

Less than a minute later, I secured a 9:00 p.m. reservation for Julia, Ricky, and Jake.

Ricky laughs. "Sure, glad we ran into you!"

"Really! Thank you so much, Cleo!" Julia gushes.

"Au revoir," Gagoune smiles, and we kiss on both cheeks. She is one of my favorite women in the world.

"Comme toujours, merci. Tu es un vrai maître!" I thank Gagoune as I stand and gather my things. Gagoune has an account for me, so no money is ever exchanged between us.

Two other customers have arrived since Ricky entered, making the tiny space quite cramped.

"Cleo, I'll walk you out. It's a little crowded in here, especially for a big oaf like me. Babe, I'll just be outside reading my book." I glance down at the title. Good grief, it's a how-to baby book.

I kiss Julia once on each cheek before leaving through Blonde's blue door that Ricky is graciously holding open for me.

"So, you're still at Slate, Ricky?" I ask him as we spill onto the street. "I remember you telling me a bit about it when we were in Honolulu."

"Sure am, and I am covering 'odd culture,' which basically means stories about pandas mating in the Bronx Zoo, a haunted castle in Ireland. My latest story is about Station F in Paris."

"Really? I adore Station F."

"You do?" he turns to me.

I nod. "I live in Paris now. The bathrooms at Station F are worth the trip themselves . . ."

"Yes! Each stall is a total work of art, completely different from the next one."

"Yes. One is ultramodern, and I believe there is one that is a log cabin, and then there's my favorite—a sexy boudoir . . . Makes you want to use every single one!" I laugh.

"Have you been to the cafeteria?" Ricky asks. I'm writing about that, too, but really only from a tech standpoint."

"Yes. It is huge, and the fun for me is chatting with the young geniuses while they are having their lunch. Inventors of such brilliant things, it makes you want to be born again just so you can live their amazing lives. Listening to all of their ideas is insane."

Ricky laughs. "You would just waltz up to them and start up a conversation . . ."

"Oh, yes," I laugh. "Anyway, I am rambling on now. I hope you and Julia have a wonderful time tonight. And if I don't see you, enjoy the rest of your stay in St. Moritz." Even though I know I will see them again.

"You're sure you're not the special someone?" Ricky nudges me.

"I promise," I smile and wave goodbye.

Ricky laughs. He is so happy, like a balloon full of air heading toward the sky. To be in love is to live, and at that very opportune moment I get a text from Sergei.

Free to go to Ecco tonight at eight?

Ha! The very same restaurant where Jake, Ricky, and Julia will be dining. We will be well into our appetizers by the time they arrive . . . It is the most romantic restaurant in the world so, of course, Sergei would love it. That man. My polo-playing, Fabergé-egg-giving, glorious, handsome man will be with me tonight. I wave goodbye to Ricky on his bench and turn into Begum, my favorite shoe store, and try on a pair of fabulous black high-heeled boots. Sergei will love them.

2016

VERA, 3

My daughter Cindy Lowe went to the Olympics in 1984 in Sarajevo as a figure skater. She and her coach chose white like the ice for her skating outfit, and her long blond curls were pulled back with a diamond twine. She danced to "Clair de Lune" by Claude Debussy. Her routine included a triple salchow, a double lutz, all wrapped up with a combination spin as if she was tying a beautiful bow on top of her flawless performance. She won a very, very unexpected bronze medal. We were all beside ourselves when the National Anthem was played, and it seemed all of Ann Arbor, where we lived, had come over. Cindy was only fifteen years old, though she would turn sixteen two weeks later.

Her skating started one rainy day when we watched a documentary about Mystery, Alaska, where children skate before walking, the land being frozen much of the year. Cindy asked for skates halfway through the documentary and wanted lessons every day after. At age five, she did basic glides and wobbles, and mastered simple spins and her first baby jump, the bunny hop. By age seven, her skating teacher entered her in her first local skating contest, where she executed single jumps and a toe loop. Her teacher recognized her potential and suggested we invest in a professional figure skating coach and then a choreographer as her spins became faster. By age ten, her artistic side emerged, and she started winning regional contests with single and double jumps, graceful spirals, and crossovers. By age thirteen, she was entering national-level contests, with a combination of a double-toe loop to double loop. It was a significant milestone as triple jumps are rare at her young age. By the age of fourteen, she ended up qualifying for the Olympics! By this point, she had mastered the triple loop and double axel, which are moves usually mastered well beyond her years.

During her rehearsals and workouts for her Olympics in Sarajevo, Barnie and I were free to wander around. We bumped into Anatoly and Ilse Rustikoff, excellent chess players whom we knew from tournaments in Moscow. They were as thrilled to find chess competitors as we were. Anatoly was there to learn how the Olympics were run for the future when Russia would hold them. We played chess every morning, and afterward, they would join us to watch Cindy's rehearsals. He took a great interest in Cindy after the day she skated over to us and tearfully asked him: "'Is there a good luck charm for Russians as one of the Russian girls fell very badly this morning, and I want to give her something." Anatoly reached in his pocket and pulled out a tiny key. "Give her this."

"Thank you so much," she said as she kissed his cheek and skated off with the key.

The next morning, I went to breakfast later than Barnie, and I saw Anatoly at a corner table with some other Russians, or they looked like Russians. Big and burly and scary.

He looked up, beckoned me over, and introduced me.

They were, I realized later, some of the judges for the skating. One was from Czechoslovakia, one from the USSR, and one from East Germany. They seemed very afraid of him. *"Eto yeye mat*," he had said. I smiled and shook hands before I walked off. I went right back to my room to translate that phrase as I didn't think it had my name in it.

It was: "This is her mother." He had been talking about Cindy, most likely about how she had been so thoughtful toward the Russian girl who had taken such a devastating fall.

I then researched Anatoly but could find nothing about him, not even about his excellent chess ability. He must be powerful to be here in Russia's name to plan for their next Olympics. I asked Barnie at lunch: "Do you think our friend Anatoly could be KGB, as there is nothing at all about him on the internet." He laughed at me: "Yes. I think it is very possible, Vera." I had to wonder if Anatoly was telling those judges to give her high scores, but I said nothing to anyone. But I watched their scoring closely, and they did give her very high scores.

Right after she won her bronze medal in the Olympics, she beamed, "I have done it! I have done it! I have become an Olympic medalist. Oh, I have done it. Thank you so much for being on my team all these years. I love you both so very much. I was so scared when I did my routine at the start, but then the music took over, and I just skated with joy." Needless to say, we celebrated with all the people from Ann Arbor who had come to Sarajevo to see their hometown girl in the Olympics. They had watched as Cindy had worked tirelessly for years. She really did it. Barnie and I were in a dream all that night and the days to come. As we were leaving to go home, Cindy came into our room very tentatively.

"Mom and Dad, I have won a medal, and all my years of work have paid off, but now I just want to go to college and make some friends and sleep in the mornings and eat cheeseburgers and fries and drink milkshakes and Cokes and not have a schedule I have to keep. I have loved this, but I really want to stop."

She was laughing and crying at the same time. Barnie and I had never pushed her. She had pushed herself her entire childhood.

So off she went the following year to the University of Michigan in Ann Arbor, where a new passion entered her life.

She auditioned for a play, *BAREFOOT IN THE PARK,* and got the part. Cindy was very famous. She was an Olympic medalist, so I imagine they wanted her to star as the audience would increase exponentially. Or maybe she had my genes!!

Well, Fate came in, and she played opposite a very handsome senior, and naturally, they fell in love. Not just in love, but insanely in love, so her new passion became him. Her first boyfriend. Barnie and I were happy as could be till she announced they were going to marry when he graduated in June. She was as focused on him as she had been on skating, so we knew it was her happiness and gulped at her age but gave them a gorgeous wedding on our lawn in June. She wore white again, and the very diamond twirl she wore in the Olympics held her hair back. They were almost comic in their insane love for one another but were good enough to see us a great deal. She gave up school for a year to be a wife working part-time while he had a job in advertising.

They were inseparable . . . until they weren't. They were the perfect couple until they weren't. They were full of happiness until they weren't.

Until she died.

CLEO 9

At precisely 8:00 p.m., punctual as always, I walk into Ecco. Louis, the maitre d', escorts me with a sly smile to a small room I have never seen. I have been in Ecco often, but I had no idea this lovely room existed; this room with a fire burning and a view of the mountains. The floor-to-ceiling windows are shuttered by thick brown velvet curtains. Sergei and I are having a rendezvous, and a secret one at that. His driver had picked me up to take me on the short drive from St. Moritz to Giardino Mountain, a luxury hotel whose Alpine façade houses Ecco.

There are bookcases filled with books by Russian authors and books about Faberge eggs and fascinating cemeteries. He had given me our conversation when we first met. I sit by the fire and open a book called *Little Known Cemeteries Around the World*. It is then that I notice the table is only set for one. I reread Sergei's text, and I realize that there's no mention of him joining me. Hmm. It is not long before I see what he has ordered for me.

The waiter brings out the first course. It's a bowl of lobster bisque. Aha, in all of the background that he has gathered about me, he missed the fact that I am allergic to shellfish . . . As I take my book to the table, I have great fun turning it back and explaining why to the waiter. *"En fait je suis allergique aux crustacés,"* I tell the waiter.

The kitchen is aware of my crustacean allergy and so I am surprised that Sergei wasn't told, but it does make me smile that he went to the trouble of arranging this perfect rendezvous for me with me.

I sip champagne from my father's vineyard—very clever of Sergei, indeed—and I glance down at the navy taffeta dress that I spent quite a bit of time choosing. I have on my new boots and think to myself about how excited I was to see him as I was dressing. Naturally, I am wearing the Fabergé Egg too. But I am laughing at his plan with this hidden room and choice of books and dinner for one. The rest of my dinner is perfect, a tiny filet mignon with a sauce so brilliant that I mix it into the *pommes de terres* and into my *haricot vert.* And best of all, chocolate souffle for dessert. My absolute favorite and the restaurant's specialty.

When he arranged this rather peculiar dinner for one, was he letting me know he was thinking about me, wanting to please me? The instructions he must have given for the menu included which books to put in the bookcase and to have my father's wines. How had he pulled all this off? Well, money can do anything. When I finish, I float out of my hidden dining room with my head in the clouds. A night to remember, indeed. The only thing missing was Sergei.

As I turn into the main dining room, I instantly find the love birds. There they are, just gazing at each other and laughing, and again, I wish Sergei had come.

I catch Ricky's eye, and he beckons me over.

"You forgot to mention that you'd be here too!" Ricky stands to greet me.

"Oh, it was very last minute," I smile, and my eyes drift to the empty chair at their table. "Did Jake not join you?"

"He's just in the loo," Julia looks up at me with twinkling brown eyes.

"Had to fix his make-up," Ricky smiles.

Julia looks over my shoulder. "Are you here with anyone?"

"No, it's just me. It's a bit of a long story. I won't bore you with the details."

"Oh, what a shame. I wish we'd known. You could have joined us. We would've been happy to treat you as a token of our appreciation for the reservation . . ."

"Cleo," Jake says my name from behind.

I spin to find Zelli's father strutting toward me in a dapper navy blazer that was tailored perfectly to fit his broad shoulders.

"Jake, it's good to see you out and about again," I smile as he puts one hand on the small of my back. "How are you feeling?"

"Good as new. Good as new," he smiles, that same smile that had completely unraveled me all those years ago in Honolulu. If Sergei hadn't walked into my life, would Jake's smile still have that effect? "Do you want to pull up a chair?"

"Oh, no, thank you. My driver is outside."

"Party pooper. I'll walk you out."

"Enjoy your dinner," I wave to Ricky and Julia.

"We will! Thanks again," they both say, staring after us.

"Ready for tomorrow?" I ask him as soon as we're out of his family's earshot.

"Girl, I was born ready."

Then we smile at each other, both just so pleased with what is in store for Ricky and Julia tomorrow.

As I walk out with him, I thank Louis, the maitre d'.

"That you?" Jake points to the dark blue Mercedes.

I nod, kiss Jake on the cheek, and then, as the driver opens the door, I climb into the Mercedes that Sergei must keep in

St. Moritz. The driver whisks me home as he whisked me here earlier for my dinner with me.

When I arrive back at the hotel, I stop in Zelli's room and kiss her sweet, innocent face again and again. I take one of her tiny stuffies as she calls them to go with me to sleep. This one is a small elephant with long gray ears and a very dear face. My phone buzzes, and it's Sergei.

"I just arrived," he tells me as soon as I answer his call.

"Sergei, I thought you couldn't fly into Samedan on a cloudy night like this?"

"You can't." And he says nothing more.

Yet again, he knocks the air out of me. I am off balance and love it. Everyone else is so predictable. "I suppose I am to thank you for my romantic dinner with myself at Ecco . . ."

His silence again fills the space and I decide to join him in that place. So we hold on, listening to one another's inhales and exhales.

Finally, I give in. "I hear you have a house here, Sergei?"

"I do, Cleopatra. And I would love you to come for breakfast tomorrow. Or you could come now and spend the night with me. . . ."

I go to the window and see his Mercedes parked out front. I start laughing. "I can't tonight. I promised Zelli's Nannie she could sleep in the morning. Zelli wakes at six, but breakfast tomorrow sounds terrific. As long as there is no lobster bisque."

His turn to laugh. "See you at eight-thirty at the top of the gondola."

CLEO 10

The following morning at eight-thirty, there he is at the top of the lift, and I fall in love all over again. His good looks are astonishing, to me at least. He takes off his sunglasses, and his black eyes make me want to fall down. That is the power this man has over me. The morning sun is beating down on us both, and, as if Sergei can read my mind, he unzips his navy parka. It's as if he's an actor in a commercial or a model on a runway, showing me his muscular body that is nearly bursting through his turtleneck. Navy must be today's theme; I, too, am wearing a navy ski suit with faux fur over my navy turtleneck.

For a moment, we simply just smile at each other with such joy in our hearts. He gives me a curt nod, and I know that he wants me to follow him. Does he know that I'd follow him to the ends of the earth? I nod back to him. He turns, and in a flash, he's gracefully skiing down the mountain. I follow him until he comes to a stop about a third of the way down by a grouping of snow-laden trees that are sheltering three breathtaking chalets. I survey all three, and right away, I know which one is his. It's the chalet covered in big white canvas tents. The tents, there must be ten of them, are affixed to the roof and cascade down like a waterfall of snowy white canvas. It is beautiful.

He offers me another smile, his signal that we've arrived. Neither of us uttered one single word to each other yet, but I love it. It feels exotic but in an erotic way, like a game of foreplay that I have never tried before. I am trusting Sergei totally. I smile back at him as we shed our skis and then our boots. He takes my hand to escort me inside. He holds the door open for me, and we enter into a cavernous white room with carved-out ceilings that are lit only around the edges. As we tread on the white tile floor in our socks, I can tell that it's heated. There are brightly covered, comfy sofas that make me feel safe as if I could crawl into them and spend the rest of my life swaddled in them. It is like a white cathedral but with books all around and music playing softly. I want to see the titles, but he takes my hand again.

Sergei and I walk down a long corridor lined with the great old masters, Rembrandt, Carravagio, and Titian, which are so different and such a surprise from his very modern architecture. He is full of contradictions.

"I am taking you to my screening room," Sergei says at last with a little squeeze of my hand as we enter yet another surprise. He looks at me, "*Ty takaya krasivaya*".

You are so beautiful! He says in Russian, and of course, I answer, "*Ty takoy krasivyy*".

You are so handsome.

His screening room has the typical gigantic screen, but the walls, covered with murals of Fabergé eggs, are anything but typical, more an homage to his Russian background.

"Tell me about the time you met a psychic," he asks me. I have no idea what he is talking about. I scroll through my mind for an answer to this bizarre question, but I come up blank. I shrug, "Psychic?"

He nods at the Fabergé egg around my neck, then at one of the murals. It's an enlarged copy of my egg.

"Are we to open it together today, Sergei?" I ask hopefully as I take the egg off my neck.

"Don't you think we should save it for a special occasion?"

"This isn't one?"

He doesn't answer me, only walking over to a grand piano. It is one of three pianos in this majestic room.

"I told you where I was going before the storm?"

"Moscow."

"Yes, for a meeting. And then I went to my home in Siberia where I have my offices. Do you know Lake Baikal?"

"I have never been. But I know it's one of the world's largest lakes that's iced over much of the year."

"It's where I grew up. Where we all played piano. Russia produced thousands of pianos in the 1800s before the revolution. Every Russian owned a piano if they could afford it. I still have the ones that we had growing up at my home in Lake Baikal. Since we were snowbound much of the year, music was integral to our lives. There is a dimension to Siberian winters that makes you feel like your days shouldn't be hurried."

"When I am with you, Sergei, I don't want my days or my nights or my moments to be hurried . . ." Then it hits me. The psychic. "Oh. I did meet a psychic, but it was a very long time ago."

He nods and smiles at me again.

"Tell me about her."

"The only time I have been involved in the 'occult,' as I guess you'd call it, is when I went to a seer at a tea room in New York. It was on the third floor of a rundown brownstone on Lexington Avenue at 53rd Street or maybe 54th. My sisters and I had heard from friends that this woman could read tea leaves with amazing results. We were in our very early twenties, and I remember how silly we felt doing this. Before we met the woman, my sisters and I giggled incessantly as we climbed the stairs. She opened the door wearing black clothes that matched her black hair. She escorted us over to her dining room table. She poured a cup of tea for each of us, and she read my sister Beebe's tea leaves first. The psychic began, 'Beebe, you will marry someone with the initials LLL.' I remember Beebe, who was very eager to find a husband, excitedly asked, 'When will I meet him?' The seer said, 'You have already met him.' We all looked at one another and tried to think about whom we knew with the initials LLL. Several months later, lo and behold, Beebe got engaged to Lord Lawrence Lancaster, who was a distant cousin of her father's. LLL."

Then, the seer told Tree, my other sister—"

"Wait a moment," Sergei laughs. "Your sister's names are Beebe and Tree?"

"Yes. You could say my mother, Sandrine, had quite a literal sense of humor. Ask my father about her one day. She conceived Tree in Woodstock at the bottom of a silver birch and Beebe in her father's garden as bees buzzed around them in England. As for me, I was conceived on my parents' honeymoon at Cleopatra's tomb in Egypt."

"How fitting."

"Well, the seer said to Tree, 'You will have children, but you won't marry a man.' I can still picture the seer's face after Tree asked her what she meant. She looked at Tree and said, 'You know what I mean.' My sister married a fabulous woman, Crystal, and they have two sons and lots of black Labs."

"Finally, the seer read my tea leaves and informed me that, 'One day, an egg will save your life.' As you can imagine, I was flabbergasted! She just nodded and I still remember her words, 'It's important you hold onto it. This egg will save you.'"

I laugh. I stop and look at him and hold out the Fabergé egg he gave me. "But somehow, you know all this. Why did you ask me about the psychic, Sergei? How did you know?"

He plays a searingly lovely melody without answering me. He doesn't say another word as he rises off of the piano and walks toward me. I start shaking as he comes near me with pure desire. Suddenly, his lips are on mine as he kisses me. He kisses me again and again. We kiss, and then we are on the floor. Even though we are in his impossibly glamorous chalet, we are kissing on the floor and not in his bed. Again, we could not waste any time getting to a bed. Instead of an icy mountain, this time, we are on a soft white rug on a heated tile floor. Like our lovemaking on the snowy mountain, once again, it is hurried and breathless. We are entwined in each other's souls, which sounds so silly, and yet it feels so real. And for the first time, we can see one another's bodies. On the mountain, it was dark, with torches that hid most of us.

Afterward, we just lie there looking at one another. "Polo," he says as I trace a scar on his side. "Do you have a gym in here, Sergei? As you are certainly in rather perfect shape." "Yes, and how do you keep in shape, Cleopatra?" he asks as his hands run down my body, exploring it in the light of day. "Krav maga twice or three times a week. It saved my life once, so I am never going to stop it, and it gives me a great high."

"I wondered when I gave you this Fabergé egg if you would remember that prophecy," he tells me while I am lying in his arms. "I love the idea of giving you something that might protect you."

"But how did you know about it?"

He smiles, and I know.

"My father. For a moment, I was worried that you were Rasputin and had psychic powers."

He laughs and takes my hand.

"Yes, thank God for that."

I stare at him for a moment. This is the most I have ever seen him speak before.

"You seem more talkative than I've ever seen you before."

His eyes widen ever so slightly and end up locking on to my face.

"For so many years, people have asked me to open up, and I never showed my hand to anybody. But when I am with you, I can't stop."

"Shall we have breakfast? It's well after eleven?"

I had completely lost track of the time. "Oh, dear. Yes, I have to meet Zelli back at the Badrutt tea room at one. I will text my father and ask if he can get there and tell them I will be late."

We turn right into a small, cozy room filled with orchids, all white orchids. There's a table looking out over the white mountain and a charming hand-painted buffet table nearby with eggs and French toast and cocoa and yogurt and fruit in exquisite silver tureens with royal crests on them.

"My forebear way back was one of the Decembrists," he said, pointing to the royal crests. "He was sent to Siberia as a punishment for being involved in the plot to overthrow the Tsar in 1825."

"I studied the Decembrists at the Sorbonne," I say as he hands me a plate.

He scoops French toast onto my plate and drowns it in maple syrup.

"How amazing to have a Decembrist in your family, Sergei! These tureens belonged to him?"

He nods. "He had been, as all the Decembrists were, a close friend of the Tsar with many very large estates in Ukraine and in Russia, but he was stripped of these. His family was able to retain them. Several of the Decembrists were hanged, but instead of hanging his closest friends, the Tsar sent them to Siberia. My ancestor was sent to work in a mine near Lake Baikal for ten years of hard labor. Many of the wives went to Siberia to be with their husbands, giving up their children and privileged lives. But my great-great-great-great-grandfather's wife chose to stay in Russia to keep all of their extensive estates and be with their children. She sent huge sums of money and jewelry, paintings, and books to him constantly so he could bribe the guards and have an easier time working in the mines. After the ten years of hard labor were up, he and the other Decembrists were allowed to move into a town near Lake Baikal, and that is where he met my great-great-great-great-grandmother Kira."

"The Decembrists—How wonderful to have that blood in your veins." I run my hand down the veins in his arm. "I knew the Tsar let his friends' families keep their estates all over Russia and the Ukraine."

"Yes, he did. They were all his schoolmates and had served in the military with him. My forebear, whose name was also Sergei, built a beautiful home in Lake Baikal for Kira, much like the one in *Dr. Zhivago*. His wife sent all the lovely things you see here to him. Some of the paintings she sent are in this house. At age seventy-five, he returned to Russia, but he kept sending gifts and money to his Kira. Pianos arrived. Imagine the journeys across Siberia in sleds to get the pianos over the Urals in the 1800s. My favorite of his gifts to Kira is the egg you are wearing, which was made in 1885 before the Hen egg."

I touch the egg gently. "I treasure it even more now that I know it was a gift from a Decembrist."

He kisses me as he hands me more French toast, licking the syrup off my lips. "I know you need to meet Zelli, but first, come see my bedroom where we can act like normal people in a bed for our next rendezvous," he whispers.

St. Moritz, 2016

JAKE, 8

I take Zelli's hand as we head to the tea room. *Zelli.* What an interesting name. Not that I'd ever expect a woman like Cleopatra Gallier to name her daughter with a simple and commonplace name like Jennifer or Alison. But I've never even heard of anyone named Zelli, and there's nothing but wacky, new-age names floating around these days—usually by people with money. A buddy of mine from St. David's just named their kid Amethyst, and I heard from a friend of a friend about a baby named Gravity. Wonder how much weed little Gravity's parents were toking on when they came up with that one.

All of these children will probably end up at Harvard Law one day, but the whole thing just seems like yet another dumb competition to outdo one another. But I do like the name Zelli. I hardly know her yet, and yet it seems to suit her. The only other name that sounds vaguely similar is Zelda. I wonder if it's Cleo's homage to Zelda Fitzgerald.

There are so many questions I have for Cleopatra. They're all questions I should know the answers to now, questions I've been too ashamed to ask. Questions that I might not even deserve to know the answers to. Looking down at Zelli now, her little doll's hand cradled in mine, ten new questions spring to mind.

145

My hope is the more time I spend with Zelli, the more questions I can answer on my own.

Zelli seems sophisticated for her age, which is likely due to her upbringing in Paris, Dubai, St. Moritz, Algeria, and Honolulu. Christ, she probably has more stamps in her passport than I do. Most American kids have their hands strapped to screens before their bodies can digest solid food. But not my Zelli. After lunch yesterday, Cleo confided that Zelli was consumed by every single detail, arranging the perfect table decor for our lunch. The balloons, the types of cookies and how many, and the color scheme of the paper plates, crowns, and napkins.

"Didi!" Zelli shrieks. She drops my hand like a bad habit, rushing over to her grandfather.

My stomach sinks. I'd planned to have a little alone time with Zelli before today's introductions. I make my way over to Didier, sitting at a round table with Lola.

"Isn't your daughter *hübsches kleines Mädchen?*" she coos over Zelli.

Lola is from Austria I learned and once again, she's rocking that fur hat. For an older woman, Lola looks pretty damn good. Once upon a time, a cocky Jake Regan might've approached her if I'd guzzled down enough vodka sodas.

Lola bends down so she's on Zelli's level. "Yes, I'm talking about you, Zelli! What a *schones kleid.* Do you think that kleid comes in my size?" She's touching Zelli's dress, so I am guessing a 'kleid' is a dress.

Zelli smiles and leans into Didier's leg.

"I am afraid she's inherited her mother's lavish taste," Didier pats his granddaughter's head.

I feel like an interloper. My daughter barely knows me from a hole in the wall, and my pseudo father-in-law hasn't exactly welcomed me with open arms. Didier is intensely protective of his only daughter, and I suspect it may take a while for me to get in Didier's good graces—even though I did save Cleopatra's life.

"Would you like some fondue, Zelli?" Lola asks.

Zelli nods. She spears a piece of bread and dips it in the warm cheese. "Cheese fondue is my favorite! Even more than chocolate!"

"Even more than chocolate?" I chime in, worming my way into the conversation.

Didier stands and takes a step toward me. "Do you prefer that we leave?"

I'm not sure what he means.

"For the surprise. Cleo said she was going to be late, so she asked if we would be here."

"Oh, Um . . ." When I look down at my daughter, her little hummingbird arms clinging onto her grandfather's legs for dear life, I realize it might be less jarring for her to have a few familiar faces around at first. "Sure, why don't you stay? That might be good for Zelli if you don't mind."

"Not at all," Didier smiles graciously. "I'd do anything for my granddaughter." And I think there's a shade of menace in his otherwise velvety smooth voice that borders on threatening.

So would I, bucko. But I just muster a smile and say, "Great, thank you."

I'm pulling out a chair when I spot my brother and Julia as they enter the tea room. Their eyes, filled with mild bewilderment, bounce around everyone at the table, trying to piece together a puzzle that doesn't exist.

"Hey!" I join Julia and Ricky at the door.

"Here we are," says Julia with her arms outstretched.

"Please tell me that the fraulein in the little fur chapeau is your surprise," Ricky whispers in my ear.

Julia cracks a smile before she cracks Ricky on the shoulder.

"What? The guy does have a certain taste for . . . dare I say, older women."

"Guess you'll have to come and find out," I shrug.

"Lead the way," says Julia gamely.

The three of us approach the elegant, more worldly Europeans as they sip their tea. It feels like everything is moving in slo-mo. One by one, they each turn toward us.

First Lola, then Didier, and finally, Zelli—after she's gracefully scooped a piece of bread covered in gooey cheese into her mouth.

"Didier, Lola . . . I'd love for you to meet my brother Ricky, and his wife, my sister-in-law, Julia," I beam with unexpected familial pride.

Zelli gasps. "You're Julia?!" Her blue eyes ricochet off Julia and me then back to Julia again. "Are you my daddy's sister, who is having a baby for me to play with?"

Julia and Ricky's eyes bulge to the size of salad bowls at those two syllables. Daddy.

Even in shock, Julia is poised. "I—why, yes. Hello there, I'm Julia." She glances at me, stunned.

Welp, it looks like the big Zelli reveal that I rehearsed seventeen times in my head has been usurped by Zelli herself. I turn to Ricky and Julia, offering them a big grin. "Surprise."

My brother can barely string together a sentence. "You're . . . Whoa. This is your . . . You're a . . ."

"Father," Julia thankfully finishes it for him.

I nod, "This is Zelli, my daughter." Familial pride hits me from all angles. I'm radiating. If someone flicked off the lights, my skin would glow in the dark.

I witness Ricky and Julia instantaneously click into another gear, unlocking the hidden, untouched, yet-to-be-test-driven parts of themselves. Meeting their niece is a live dress rehearsal for when their own little bundle of joy gets dropped off by a stork. They strap on their Mom-and-Pop costumes and take their places at center stage.

"Wow! Zelli, it's so lovely to meet you! I'm Julia, though I think you might already know that," she smiles. "It sounds like you are one smart cookie."

Zelli giggles. "Cookies aren't smart, they're yummy!"

"Well, that too! And what a cool name you have! Lucky girl, all my life, I've had two other Julias in my classes. But I bet you're the only Zelli. A cool girl for a cool name," Julia glows with maternal instinct. She's a natural.

Zelli just stares at her, and it hits me that my daughter might have inherited some of my new introverted genes. These days, I'd much rather curl up in bed with an HBO show versus some chick I picked up at the club, where I was miserable the whole time.

"Zelli," Didier chimes in smiling, "What do you say to Julia?"

"Thank you," Zelli mumbles.

Ricky steps up to the plate. "Hey, Zelli! I'm your Uncle Ricky, your dad's little brother. And you have no idea how excited I am to meet you!"

"Nice to meet you too," her voice is barely above a whisper.

"Please, sit," Didier stands and politely pulls over two chairs from the empty table next door. "After all, you are family."

"Oh, yeah?" Ricky says. The identity of my baby mama was unquestionably the first thing that flashed across his mind. Zelli is almost an exact replica of her mother, so I'm amazed he hasn't guessed yet.

Didier gestures for Julia to take a seat in the chair he's holding out. "I have the pleasure of being Zelli's grandfather. Jake tells me you both met my daughter several years ago in Honolulu. Cleopatra Gallier?"

A guttural laugh that I was not expecting spurts out of Julia's mouth. "Cleo! Of course." She turns to Zelli, "You look exactly like her. You even have her dimples."

"Well, that explains why we ran into her at the hair place," my brother smiles at Julia first, then at me.

"Now Zelli. Serious question. Your dress. Does it come in my size?"

"That's what I asked!" Lola laughs.

"I can see why. It's tres chic. Don't you think, Ricky?"

"Oh, yes. With a fashionable mom like yours, I bet your closet's full of Valentinos."

Zelli giggles. "What's that?"

"Wait a sec. Do *you* even know what a Valentino is?" Julia asks Ricky.

A collective chuckle ripples through all of the adults around the table. My daughter is a quick study; she takes a cue from the rest of us and then joins in on the merriment.

"Pay no mind to your wacky Aunt Julia, Zelli. She's always giving your Uncle Ricky a hard time."

It's cute. Julia and Ricky both vying for the affection and approval of a four year old.

"Oh, please!" Julia says, mock offended as she turns toward Zelli, playfully boxing Ricky out. "Us gals gotta stick together, don't we?"

Zelli smiles and nods.

"But of course. And, look, here comes another member of our tribe," Lola flicks her neck.

Cleopatra has entered the building. And she ain't alone. There's a tall, handsome man with dark wavy hair and piercing dark eyes standing beside her. Hot damn, even I wouldn't kick this guy out of bed.

"Maman!" Zelli squeals and runs over to her mother, where she's waiting with open arms. Cleo picks her up and lets Zelli whisper something in her ear.

Whatever she says makes Cleo smile. "I know. They are nice, aren't they?"

"There she is," Ricky rises up and off his chair.

"Cleo," Julia waves. "Otherwise known as our locked vault!"

Cleo laughs. "As if you and Ricky haven't had your fill of thrilling introductions for one day, I'd like you to meet my friend, Sergei Kominitz," she beams with pride.

"Hey, man, great to meet you. Ricky Regan," My brother shakes this Sergei character's hand.

Julia starts to get out of her chair when Sergei puts his hand out. "Please, please, sit. Cleo tells me you're having a cousin for Zelli." Sergei gives Julia a suave smile and a shake of the hand.

Cleo comes over to me. "I take it everything's going well so far?" she whispers in between kisses on each cheek.

"Shockingly well," I admit.

"I told you," she smirks.

"What's with the Russki?" I whisper.

She pulls away from me. *None of your damn business, that's what.*

Ricky comes over and gives Cleo a hug. "Hey, *Mom*! Good work keeping the surprise a secret. Damn."

"Thanks, *Uncle* Ricky. What do you think? Dare I say, not the surprise you were expecting?"

"Not by a mile," Ricky snickers. "I was more prepared for Jake to introduce me to the Knicks City Dancers than I was to his daughter."

"Nah. Sadly, I had to take them all off my speed dial," I say.

"But, for real. How did this happen? *When* did this happen? All the way back in Honolulu?"

My brother's voice drowns out when my eyes, dancing around the room to verify that everyone is enjoying themselves, happen to land on Julia. It looks like she's seen a ghost. I follow her line of vision and trace it back to the door. But there's no one there. I turn my focus back to her. I know that look. You don't date someone for three years without picking up on every single one of their looks and their hidden meanings. Even from across the room, I can tell that she's shaken up.

"I'll be back," is all I say, deciding against alerting Ricky to his wife's potential alarm. The Julia that I know would be mortified by causing a scene. Cleo and Ricky nod and off I go. I wander across the room, approaching Julia and trying to act casual. When I get to her chair, she looks up at me expectantly.

"You okay?" I ask through gritted teeth, drawing as little attention to myself as possible.

At first, the look in Julia's eyes is blank. She's either embarrassed that I'm calling her out, or she's deciding how to dodge the question. Or both. The comforting thing about knowing another person so well is the trade-off that they know you just as well. Julia hasn't forgotten how stubborn I can be, how I'm like a dog with a bone. So she just nods, at least acknowledging that my assessment of the look on her face was accurate.

However, before we can even get into it, the Russian is by my side. He sticks out his hand and says, "I didn't get your name when Cleo introduced us." He doesn't sound Russian, but his name is impossibly Russian. I heard him speaking French with Didier and Lola, and his English is perfect. He must be one of those people who have an ear for languages. I can't wait to look him up when I get back to my room. From the way they look at each other, this could be Zelli's stepfather.

"Hey, yeah. I'm Jake, Jake Regan," I shake his hand.

It takes him a second until he smiles. "Cleo tells me you're Zelli's father. Lucky man!"

SERGEI, 1

It was Jake Regan's father, Tripp, who was responsible thirty-two years ago for the drowning of my three-year-old son, Dimitri, in Lake Baikal. Tripp had come after we graduated from the University of Michigan Law School to visit us in Russia for a few weeks. He had been holding Dimitri's hand while we were all watching one of the ice fishermen reel in a Lenok. There was a shudder and a small crack in the ice. Tripp let go of Dimitri's hand, and my sweet son was taken under. It happened so fast. So fast that, at first, we didn't realize he was gone. The crack was right under him, and he was so small he went right in. God, we tried to smash the crack to get to him, but not in time. The fishermen came with their knives, but we never even found his body. I wake up all the time, seeing his face underwater and praying it was quick. The worst thought is that he was terrified, even for a moment. And then I had to tell his mother.

When I went in to tell her, Sophie was smiling while reading by the fire. The pain was so great that our Dimitri wasn't the only thing she lost that day. She also lost the baby she was carrying and, shortly thereafter, her mind too. No matter how many doctor's offices we visited and which medications they prescribed, Sophie has never recovered. Even today, over thirty years later, she refuses to leave our home where she lives with full-time nurses and a staff that are devoted to her. Physically, Sophie can do anything she'd like, but mentally, she's been gone since Dimitri was taken.

She has not recognized me in decades.

Inches from me now stands Tripp Regan's son, Jake, whom I believe is Tripp's eldest. He was the reason Miranda had not come with Tripp to Lake Baikal. She didn't want to be so far from her doctor at that point in her term. Ricky is the youngest, and if I recall from reading about Tripp in the Michigan Law School magazine, there is a midde son too.

By the time Jake was born, my friendship with Tripp was lost. It was too painful to see him. It wouldn't have occurred to me that Ricky was also Tripp's son based on his looks alone until he introduced himself. His eyes, while still blue, lack the same sparkle and shine as his father and older brother's. Perhaps the Regan genes diluted with every child. Jake's complexion, dark hair, and bone structure all belong to his father, uncannily so. When he first caught my eye, I was floored by the resemblance, but I didn't conceive he could actually, really, be Tripp's son. The odds against such a coincidence are too great, but the Regan name proves me wrong.

For now, I say nothing.

I am transported back thirty years, standing next to my old friend at a University of Michigan Law School function. Sophie, Dimitri, and I lived across the hall from Miranda and Tripp near the campus in an old, furnished colonial house. We met the first day we arrived when we were both moving in. Tripp and I helped each other lug suitcases up to floor two for them and floor three for us. I knew he was in the CIA as I had been forewarned by the KGB, and I am sure he was also warned.

For three years, Tripp and I were inseparable, as were our wives. They were involved in something called the Michigan Law School Wives Club, which, looking back today, sounds strangely archaic. But in the 1980s, it's where all the primarily young wives gathered every Tuesday and Thursday nights for art projects, book clubs, and basket weaving. At least, that's what Sophie and Miranda told us. Still, presumably, it was also an excuse for the women to devour chocolate chip cookies and coffee and to bond over the long absences of their stubbornly aggressive husbands who studied constantly.

Dimitri was born during that first year in law school. He was a happy baby but also a fussy one. For Sophie, the club provided her with a respite from our cluttered apartment with a screaming baby inside. Her Russian accent made it hard to communicate, but Dimitri brought friends to her. Miranda often regaled Tripp and me with tales about how adoring the other women were of little Dimitri. Knowing Miranda, she may have been exaggerating for the sake of making her friend feel more at ease, but it didn't matter. Because it worked. It made Sophie feel better about being the only woman to show up with an infant in her arms, who's crying and needs to be fed or burped or changed, often distracted from the female merriment. The club did wonders for Sophie's exhaustion, confidence, and general well-being. She often felt like an alien who'd temporarily been deposited by the mother ship in a foreign land known as "The Mitten State." But these women made Sophie and my little Dimitri feel welcome. And I'll forever be grateful to that club and Miranda for extending those kindnesses.

Since there was a lot of overlap in our course schedule, Tripp and I frequently pulled long hours together in the law library. But on Sundays, the four of us would hop on our bikes for rides into the nearby suburbs to see the trees changing colors. And when we could afford it, we'd spend the night in a tiny inn. Dimitri, my tiny son, was always with us. I can still picture the five of us snowshoeing for hours during the winter months. Dimitri perched on my shoulders or on Tripp's. Sophie was so happy as she slid through the snow with Miranda. Some of my fondest memories back then are watching Sophie silk screen our Christmas cards and make our Christmas gifts like all the other women who were part of the Michigan Law Wives Club. She and Miranda bought dozens of oranges at the market. They stuck cloves into their peels, wrapped them in green velvet ribbon, and hung them all around both apartments to discharge the smell of Christmas. There were oranges everywhere I looked—on nobs, hooks, posts—and I can still conjure up that aroma as well as picture the tiny wounds on Sophie's hands from the cloves.

SOPHIE AND MIRANDA ROTATED COOKING DUTIES, with Miranda chipping in more frequently, since Sophie often had her hands full with Dimitri. On the nights that Sophie didn't feed us with her Russian dishes, Miranda cooked up her chicken and tuna casseroles.

Tripp and I were mirror images on either side of the Cold War, and yet, we were like brothers. And now, thirty years later, after so much has happened to us both, perhaps we will meet again.

I overhear Jake regaling Lola about his near-death experience in the whiteout. It occurs to me how strange it is that he decided to risk it and ski down the mountain.

Lola takes the words right out of my mouth. "I am wondering, dear Jake. Why didn't you sit down at the top of the mountain?"

"Well, to put it simply, I think I might have overestimated my skiing skills," Jake laughs.

He doesn't want to answer her; we can both see that.

"You saw the security footage from the gondola, yes?" Didier asks.

Jake nods.

"Apparently, no one knows what happened to the man who was with you. Have you seen him again?"

Jake shakes his head. "No. We chatted a bit on the way up, but I never got his name." Didier and I exchange a look.

We both know Jake is not telling us something. Perhaps the man no one has seen again has something to do with the reason he chose to ski down.

DIDIER AND LOLA EXCUSE THEMSELVES to go and sit with Zelli to play her favorite game, tic tac toe. Seeing an opening, I wander over. "Jake, how is your father?"

Jake furrows his brow, and his blue eyes stare at me, entirely taken aback. I suppose I could have been more graceful with my non-sequitur. "Um. My father? He's fine . . . Why?"

"Your father is Tripp Regan? The Tripp Regan who went to law school at the University of Michigan?"

Jake is still dubious. "Yeah . . . Were you—You two knew each other?"

"If you can believe it, yes. Forgive me, but I just put it together now. Has anyone ever told you that you're a dead ringer for your father when he was your age?"

"All the time," Jake smiles, relaxing slightly. "I'm sorry, I just can't—I mean, talk about a small world."

"The truth is often stranger than fiction," I laugh. "We were actually quite close at Michigan. I was very fond of your mother as well."

"No way. Are you guys all still in contact?"

"Sadly, no. I moved back to Russia after law school, and we just lost touch," I tell Jake, leaving out the part about Dimitri.

"Got it," Jake nods.

"Any chance he and Miranda are joining all of you here? I would like to see them again."

"Nah, he's working a big case. Doubt the firm's letting him leave the office, let alone the city."

"I see," I say. "That's too bad."

"We could give him a call?" his face twists into a smile as he fishes his phone out of his pocket. "I think it's a little after eight in New York. He and my mom are probably just having breakfast."

Hearing Tripp Regan's voice again after so much time has gone by would be interesting. "Oh," I pause. "Yes, by all means."

"Yeah, let's give the old man a shock first thing, shall we?" Jake laughs. He dials and holds his phone up to his ear as it rings. "C'mon. Pick up, pick up."

And then Jake perks up.

"Dad! There you are." For now, I can only hear Jake's end of the conversation. "I'm fine, yeah," Jake nods. "Yup. Much better today," Jake nods again. "Sure did. I'm looking at him and Julia as we speak," Jake nods a third time. Then his eyes meet mine. "But that's actually not why I called. I have a surprise for you. I ran into an old friend of yours, and he's dying to say hello . . . Yup, he's right here. One sec."

Jake gives me an encouraging smile as he hands his phone over to me.

"Tripp?"

A pause. Then, "This is Tripp. Who is this?"

Hearing Tripp's voice is a trip. But something about it also makes me sad. Perhaps it is all of this lost time.

I pause. Then, "It's Sergei Kominitz."

A long silence. I can almost hear the thoughts hurtling through his mind. "Sergei?"

"Yes, Tripp. It's me."

"Sergei. Jesus. How are you? It's been so long. Too long. What are you doing in St. Moritz? And how the hell did you manage to run into my sons?"

"I have a home here, Tripp, and my great friend Didier Gallier is here with his daughter Cleo. We are all skiing Corviglia. She knows your family."

A shorter silence this time. "You're with Cleopatra Gallier, too?"

Hmm. "I am. You know Cleopatra?" I can feel Jake's eyes boring into me.

"Not too well, but yes, we all met when she was living in Honolulu."

I laugh. "Well, then. It really is a small world."

"I'll say. Miranda might not even believe me when I tell her that you ran into the boys!"

"I did a double take when I saw Jake. He looks exactly as you did at his age," I smile over at Jake.

"Yeah, we get that a lot," Tripp laughs.

"Wonderful to hear your voice after all these years, Tripp."

"Yours, too, Sergei. Christ, it's been forever. How are things with you and Sophie?"

"She's happy but sadly, very unwell. Her memory has been gone for decades. She is in Lake Baikal and never leaves."

"Jesus." Tripp pauses, and I can picture him scratching his cheek, his habit for whenever he is contemplative. "I don't—" he pauses again. "I'm so sorry to hear that."

I change the subject, not wanting to dwell on what the death of Dimitri did to Sophie. "What about Miranda? Still making those scrumptious tuna casseroles?"

"Oh, yeah," Tripp chuckles. "She's bummed Christmas is over. Christmas is Miranda's Super Bowl, if you can remember that far back. Her favorite pastime is decorating the house, spending way too much money on gifts for the kids, then spending too much time wrapping the gifts in the perfect paper and matching bows."

I laugh, once again imagining Sophie and Miranda hanging oranges. "Oh, yes. I remember that well . . ."

There's silence on both ends of the phone. Both of us remembering the good old days before tragedy snuck up on us without warning. "I should let you get your day started. It was fun catching up, Tripp. Even just this briefly."

"You, too, Sergei. Take care of yourself. And make sure my boys stay out of trouble over there," he laughs. "You never know with those two . . ."

"Consider it done," I smile. Perhaps Tripp doesn't grasp the irony.

Jake takes the phone back, and I'm back to only hearing his end of the conversation. "I know, crazy. You and Mom should come on over!" he laughs. "Yeah, yeah, yeah, I know." He pauses again. "What if I told you there's another surprise, an even bigger surprise that would turn your whole life upside down? No," Jake laughs. "Upside down in a good way." He glances over at me, and gestures with his finger that he'll just be a moment. He turns and wanders across the room to finish the conversation with his father. But I hear him ask as I head toward Cleo.

"Dad, tell me about Serge Kominitz,"

I only hear Jake's side, so I wander closer to him. He must still care about Cleo to want to learn about who she is now with.

"He is here with Cleo, and he's a good friend of her father, Didier Gallier." Silence, so Tripp must be giving him my resume. I am tempted to tap him and give it to him myself. "OK, so he's an extremely rich Russian oligarch. I got that." Again silence. "Yeah, he probably got rich during the chaotic privatization of the 1990s by acquiring state-owned assets for pennies on the dollar."

SERGEI, 1

I POINT AT ZELLI, who has walked over to me. No more eavesdropping. She takes my finger in hers, which is sticky with whatever she has been eating.

"Remember when you and your mother watched me play polo with the red ball a few days ago?" I bend down.

She nods. "Chuka, chuka, chuka!"

"Would you like to ride on one of my ponies?"

Zelli's whole face lights up like a diamond. "A pony?! Yay! I love ponies!"

Jake, off the phone, comes over and bends down so he's on the same level as us. "Who doesn't love ponies?!" He smiles at his daughter.

"Do you think your father will come, Jake?" I ask him. However, I also want to ask him if his dad told him that I own gold mines, airlines, and so on. It's interesting how Tripp knows about my life as an oligarch.

Jake shrugs. Zelli imitates him, shrugging her shoulders, which makes us both smile.

Tactfully leaving the father-daughter, I head to Cleo.

"I just got off the phone with Tripp Regan whom I went to Michigan Law School with and whom Jake was trying to entice to come over for the Zelli surprise."

"You knew my dad, Sergei?" Ricky looks over when he hears this. "Yes, we studied together, and he helped me with my English colloquialisms when we lived in the same house near our school. My English was very stilted when I arrived, and my wife never really caught on, but Miranda was lovely to her." Cleo is just staring at me.

TRIPP, 1

But why is Sergei in St. Moritz with my family? And Cleo. Like most men, he's probably fallen in love with her. I tried not to.

Cleo's daughter, Jake's daughter, must be with them, and I am sure that's the surprise that's waiting for me. Unbeknown to my son, I know all about Zelli. I even gave Cleo that name. There was a moment two years ago when I'd returned to Honolulu after a presumed dead former asset turned up very much alive and kicking. Following a very unfortunate accident that left me temporarily blind, Cleo visited me at the hospital and confided in me that she'd given birth to a little girl two years prior. She believed her to be my daughter, born out of an affair that had finally been consummated after fifteen years. However, before she realized that Jake was my son, Cleo also had quite a fling with him around that same time. So, there was some overlap, which left Zelli's paternity in question. Ah, the tangled webs we weave.

When Cleo eventually told me she got the DNA results back and that I was, in fact, not Zelli's father but instead her . . . drum roll, grandfather, I was admittedly relieved and disappointed at the same time. Unless I was in the mood to blow my entire life up, I knew I could never be the father Zelli deserved. But Jake can. And I can only hope that from now on, he will be.

I head to the kitchen, where I find my wife, Miranda, making me the same breakfast she prepares every morning. Yogurt, raspberries, and black coffee. Little does she know, my first stop after I walk out the front door is Viand, my favorite coffee shop on 61st and Madison, where I pick up a glazed donut and a cappuccino on my way to work.

I smile as I flashback to my first wife, Cindy, and her breakfasts. We only had fourteen short months together before she was killed, but we filled it with such intensity. Breakfast might be served in a child's yellow tent she put up in the living room of our tiny apartment. She would fill it with different colored scarves that she'd unfold only to reveal four bananas, two for her and two for me. Or hot fudge sundaes that she'd serve completely naked with whipped cream, the only thing that covered her body. The original whipped cream bikini. Needless to say, I was always late for work. But I didn't care about anything except being with her. We were young and frivolous and insanely in love. And now, I'm middle-aged and not so frivolous, but still very happy for more than three decades with Miranda. I'd be lying if I said I never wondered how my life would have turned out had Cindy lived. Her death propelled me into a deep, deep depression that I only pulled out of when I joined the CIA.

"Jake just called," I say to Miranda as I reach for Mr. Coffee. "And you'll never guess who he's with . . ."

"So, tell me," she smiles and hands me my favorite mug. It has a photo of our three sons at Disney World from when they were still boys.

"Sergei . . . Kominitz."

Miranda nearly drops the bowl of raspberries onto the floor. "Sergei, Sergei?!"

I nod, sharing in her surprise.

"Heavens," she sets the bowl down. "I—what a coincidence. He's with Jake? In St. Moritz?"

I nod again.

"How is he? How did he sound?"

"Good. He sounded good. The same, I guess. But also, somehow, totally different. If that makes any sense," I laugh.

Miranda and I sit at the kitchen table. "How did he and Jake even make the connection? They'd have to cover quite a lot of ground."

"Well," I sip my coffee. "If you thought the world was small thirty seconds ago . . . Sergei was with Cleo Gallier."

Miranda just laughs. It's pretty unbelievable. But then, something dawns on her. "Wait a second. Jake didn't go to St. Moritz to see Cleo, did he? I thought—"

I shake my head. "No, no. Course not."

Miranda looks relieved. If she only knew . . .

"But Jake did say he has a surprise for us there . . ." I can't even look at her. If I do, I'm worried Jake's secret will somehow come spilling out of me.

"Oh? What kind of surprise?"

"Said he wants us to come see it for ourselves."

"To St. Moritz?"

"That's what he said . . ."

Again, she just laughs. It's as if I have just asked her to take an afternoon picnic to prison.

"Would be nice to see Sergei after all these years." I look at her now.

"Yes, of course. I wonder how everything is going for him in Russia." Miranda smiles, "And how Sophie is. Did he say?"

"Not well, sadly. Apparently, her memory's totally shot."

She cups her hand to her mouth. "Oh, no. Oh, how awful. Poor Sophie," Miranda looks off, thinking about her old friend.

"I know. It sounds like she hasn't set foot outside Lake Baikal in years."

Miranda switches gears. "Gosh, I'd love to see Sergei, especially after all this time. But . . . all that travel and the time changes. And with such short notice. I think it's just way too much for me.

I nod. I had a feeling that'd be her response.

"Did he say what the surprise was?"

I shake my head. Technically, he didn't.

I STEP INTO MY HOME OFFICE and call Jake back. "Hey, bud. So, I spoke to your mother, and it looks like we won't be able to make it."

Jake doesn't say anything. This is his way of telling me he's pissed.

"I'm really busy with the Colby case, and your mother wants to stay here with me. She's obsessed with getting the baby room ready for Julia and Ricky's baby. And her friend Lia is giving her a birthday party at the Colony Club. Remember her birthday is in two days.

But please tell Sergei I'll be in touch. It's been way too long."

Jake is still silent.

"Jake? You there?"

"Yup," he grumbles.

"I'm sorry. Can you just tell us what the surprise is? Your mother's dying to know. You know her."

"No can do. You gotta see it to believe it."

I roll my eyes. My oldest is as stubborn as me.

"Jake—"

"By the way, Cleo and your friend Sergei seem quite cozy . . ."

He's trying to bait his old man.

Nice try, Buster. "Really? Your mother and I are having dinner with Matt tonight. I bet he'll be delighted to hear that you and Ricky ran into Cleo."

"Perfect, tell Matt to come. He's obsessed with Cleo."

"Why don't you all just come home, Jake?"

JULIA, 4

My head feels light, and my belly is heavy. I glance over at Ricky, who's feeling quite cozy with the Gallier squad. The fact that Jake Regan had a child before me is, well, what's the opposite of poetic? Prosaic, maybe. And who he had said child with is next level. I couldn't be more thrilled for Jake and Cleo, but putting up a convincing poker face has never been one of my strengths. I was gobsmacked. God, I hope I wasn't rude. The last thing I want to seem is anything less than over-joyed at the risk of looking jealous. I count my lucky stars every other day that Ricky is the Regan brother I ended up with and that in three short months, we'll be parents to a beautiful baby.

Speaking of, I feel a kick. Ow! I clutch my belly and glance over at Ricky. I flutter my fingers to try to get his attention, but he's too enthralled by the Europeans.

Screw this. I sigh, and I get up from my chair.

"Need a hand?"

I look up and see Sergei with an outstretched hand. At least someone around here is still a gentleman. "Oh, thank you," I smile. "Do you happen to know where the ladies' room is?"

"I believe it's just across the lobby to the right," Sergei points out.

"Thank you," I smile again and glimpse Ricky as I cross the room. His arms are flailing around, no doubt regaling the Galliers with the greatest hits. Stories from when he and Jake were Zelli's age or one of the many tales about how Jake, drunk on older brother power, got his rocks off by locking Ricky in the basement.

My husband happens to look over, midstory. I gesture to the door and mouth: *bathroom*. He nods and gives me a thumbs-up. Excellent.

I continue to the door. My right hand reflexively rests on my belly as I enter the grand lobby. Lady with a baby is coming through. Before I was among their ranks, I hated that silly gesture where pregnant women felt a persistent need to announce to the world that, no, they had, in fact, not gained weight. They're just eating for two. But now that I'm one of them, I'm realizing that the hand on the belly has little to do with vanity and much more with motherly instinct. I haven't even met the little tyke, but I'd stand in front of a bus if it meant defending my baby.

"*Salle de bains?*" I say to the man behind the front desk and point across the lobby.

"*Oui*," the man smiles back at me. "*A droite au bout du couloir.*"

"*Merci*," I walk past him toward the hall and follow it down until I come to a door with 'Femmes' subtly written across a gold plate.

When I push open the door, it's large and elegant, and I remind myself that I'm in a palace. The crisp white walls match the tiles, the towels have a thin red stripe, and the fixtures have a shiny gold texture. A woman with red braided hair is washing her hands at the long vanity. We trade friendly smiles in the mirror as I walk behind her and into the second of six stalls.

I let out a big breath, perhaps relieved to finally be alone. I unzip my hip AG maternity jeans and sit down at the same time the red-haired woman turns off the faucet. I wait to pee until the woman's heels clack across the tile floor and swing open the door. My lungs release another breath, truly alone now.

But not for long. Mere seconds after the door closes, it breezes open and a new set of shoes clatter across the tile. This woman's walk is slower, softer, more deliberate. They say that curiosity killed the cat, but I hate cats. I crane my neck to try and check out this mystery person's shoes. My mother always said you can tell a lot about someone from their footwear, and I've found that advice to be disturbingly accurate. Once, I cut a date short because he showed up wearing Tevas with a little sun insignia.

Wait, where did the shoes go? I glance to my left, then to my right. That's odd. Maybe they changed their mind. I lean back, and I'm about to finally relieve myself when, suddenly, I hear those same slow, soft, deliberate steps. Only this time, they're next to me. I gasp, spying a pair of shiny Belgian loafers with the left bow missing, poking out from the stall next door. I cover my mouth with both hands to keep me from screaming.

It's him. The dog walker in NYC and the bellhop in Paris. I hold my breath, waiting for him to make the first move. My eyes peek over at his shoes again. He doesn't make a sound.

No rustling of his pants against his skin. No ceramic rattle as he sits on the toilet. No unfastening of his zipper. He's just standing there, silently. Terrifyingly silent. Like a total fucking lunatic. The thought of him scaling the stall wall and crashing down onto me flashes across my mind. And then I picture him crouching and crawling into my stall from underneath. I'm not sure which is worse.

My motherly instincts go into overdrive. I can't wait for this freak to make the first move. I have to act before him, or the only way I'm getting out of this glamorous bathroom is in a body bag. I start to take a breath to calm my nerves, but there's no time for that. I stand as quietly as I can and lurch forward to unlock the stall door, praying that a saintly maintenance worker has recently popped in with some WD-40. The door opens quickly and without a hitch. Thank you, thank you, thank you.

It swings against the other stalls, causing them to reverberate. I zip my fly as my Allbirds carry me across the tile floor as swiftly as they can. My right hand protects my belly, and I don't even dare look over my shoulder to see if the man in the Belgian loafers is chasing after me. I'm almost at the door. Five steps, four steps, three, two, one. I grab the golden handle and yank it toward me with all of my might.

I sprint down the hallway, hoping I'll see a kind soul, but there's no one. It's only me. All I can think about are Ricky's arms. Running into them, wrapped around my body, protecting me and the baby. At the end of the lobby, I turn left.

"Madame?" the man behind the front desk asks me.

But I'm in the zone. I don't even look his way. I need to get to Ricky in the tea room. I need to get the hell out of here.

I breeze through the double doors, and my eyes dart around in search of my husband. I hear him before I see him. Zelli's gleeful squeal precipitates Ricky's deep, throaty laugh. I can always pick his laugh out of a crowd. I whip my head around and find everyone clustered by a club chair in the corner. Cleo, Jake, Didier, Lola, and Sergei are watching Ricky as he bounces Zelli on his lap. He's humming a Western song as if Zelli were a cowgirl and his leg was a buckin' bronco.

"Ricky," I say breathlessly as I come up to him.

Everyone turns to me. This is what I was afraid of. I was hoping I'd be able to just dip back in and dip back out. But no, my husband has turned into Mr. Fucking Rogers. All he needs now is a zip-up cardigan.

"Jules? Are you okay? Here, Zelli. I'm going to put you down for a second," and he does.

"I'm fine," I clutch my belly so Ricky will take a hint. "I think I just might need to lie down for a little bit."

Jake puts his hand on my shoulder. "Sure you're good? You look a little . . ."

Yeah, Jake. Thanks. I'm sure I look terrible. That's not really my top concern at the moment, I think. But I just smile like a good little girl and say, "I'm good, thanks. Just tired," I rub my belly again.

"Would you like my driver to take you to your hotel?" Sergei cuts in.

It's amazing the power you can wield when you have a baby on board. I'm shocked more women don't stuff fake pillows under their dresses to elicit sympathy, free rides, empty chairs, and on and on.

"Um," I turn to Ricky. "No, that's alright. We can just get a cab."

"Nonsense, I insist. " Sergei takes out his phone and dials. He rattles off a few words in Russian and hangs up.

In under a minute, Ricky and I are sitting in the back seat of a black Maserati Quattroporte that's worth more than our apartment.

Ricky puts a comforting hand on my thigh. "What's going on?"

I shake my head and gesture to the driver. I don't trust anyone at this point.

He lowers his voice. "Seriously?"

"Seriously."

We sat in silence for the rest of the car ride. I was running over how to best present this whole situation to my poor husband, who is already quite concerned. He's been giving me that look ever since I came back from the bathroom. Even now, I can tell that those puppy dog eyes are boring into the back of my head, anxious for whatever might come spilling out my mouth as I walk past him into our room.

"Okay, what's going on, Jules?"

I take my time answering that. I sit on the bed. My eyes still don't meet his, afraid that I'll turn into a pile of mush. I glance across the room, over at the chess board, and—Oh, you've got to be kidding me. The white queen, she's in the wrong place again. Instead of presiding over her rightful throne to the left of the king, she's toppled over in the middle of the board. Before I know it, I'm off my feet. "Did you do that?" I point.

Ricky's eyes ricochet off of me and onto the chess board. "Huh? Do what, Jules?"

"This!" I pick up the white queen and shake it at Ricky. "She's in the wrong square again. Did you do that?"

There's that look again. "Her? No."

"Are you sure?!" My voice is more shrill than I'd intended.

"Jules, calm down. Let's just, here, take a seat," he puts his hand on the small of my back.

In the history of mankind, has commanding someone to calm down ever actually worked? "Dammit, Ricky! Don't tell me to calm down!"

I turn back to the chess board, wind my right arm back, and then follow through like I'm about to knock one out of the park, swatting the ever-loving shit out of the chess board. Pieces go flying every which way and the board lands on the oak with a loud thud that startles Ricky.

My husband just stands there. Shook. "Julia! What the—what the hell's wrong with you?! Jesus!"

That look in his eyes is killing me. But it's no longer one of concern, he's blown right past disturbed and panicked, and now he's petrified. Petrified of me, wondering what I did with his sweet, reserved, polite, goodie-goodie wife. "I'm sorry," I put a gentle hand on his forearm, trying to prove that she's still here. I'm still here.

"Are you—I mean, is it the hormones?" he asks as delicately as he can.

I roll my eyes. "No, Ricky. Jesus. It's not the hormones. Not everything is about hormones."

"I know that. Sorry, I just wanted to make sure." He reaches into our minibar, pulls out a water bottle, and unscrews the cap before handing it to me. "Let's . . . just . . . sit," Ricky puts one hand on the small of my back and guides me to the foot of the bed.

I let him take the lead. I sit next to him and sip from the water bottle. "I'm okay. I'm sorry for . . ." I gesture toward the chess pieces scattered around the floor.

He puts a hand on my thigh. "It's alright. Just tell me what's going on. Please."

"God, I don't even know where to start," I force a laugh, going for levity.

"How 'bout the beginning?" Ricky smiles. And it's exactly the smile I need.

"Remember that night at The Spaniard when I thought we were being followed?"

He nods uneasily.

And then I tell him everything, starting with the dog walker in NYC, sparing no details. I describe the bellhop, how I saw him again on my way to breakfast with Jules, then again in our very hotel's lobby here, and finally, his black Belgian shoes with the missing bow in the bathroom at The Badrutt Palace less than thirty minutes ago. He listens intently, his head nodding along the whole time.

"Do you want to go back to New York, Jules?" he asks me finally. "Because you just say the word, and we're on the next flight home."

"I just don't know what good that'll do. This whole thing started in the city. How do we know he won't be waiting for me when we get back?"

"We don't. But maybe you'll feel better at home?" Ricky puts an arm around me and brings me in for a half-hug.

My breath catches. "You think I'm crazy, don't you?"

"No," he looks me in the eye. "No way, babe. Unequivocally no. You're not crazy. I just want to make sure I'm doing whatever I can to keep you safe. I will always protect you, m'lady."

That makes me smile.

He starts to rub my back, and I admit that I do feel remarkably safer in his arms, but still. Not safe enough. "I hope you know . . . I mean it, Julia. You can tell me anything. It makes me sad to think about you going through all this by yourself."

I give his arm a squeeze. "I know. I'm sorry."

"Even if it's the most batshit thing you can think of. Literally. Even if you're suddenly convinced Beyonce is your long-lost mother, you can tell me." He smiles, "You can always tell your boy."

He's right. I don't know what I was so afraid of. I should've told him from the start. I was just so worried he'd think I was crazy. So, instead, I just let myself suffer in silence. I take a deep breath, "Promise."

"Good," he leans in and gives me a kiss. "You psycho."

I laugh and swat him on the bicep. "Asshole."

He laughs with me, gets up off the bed, and walks over to the minibar.

"You know, it's funny. When you said Belgian loafers, the first thing that popped into my head was my dad. He's the only person I know who wears those doofy things," he smiles crookedly.

"Smart minds think alike . . ."

There's a bang on our door, springing Ricky and me off the bed and out of our skin.

"What the hell?!" I shriek.

"Jake. It's just Jake, remember? He said he'd pick us up before dinner as we left." Ricky puts a comforting arm around me, and we both catch our breath.

"Well, he scared the shit out of me."

"Welcome to my world," Ricky smirks. "You good?"

Another bang on the door.

"Dude! We're coming!" Ricky calls out as he goes over to the door to let his brother in.

"Finally," Jake scoffs as he enters and looks right at me. "Is everything okay? Jules, when you left, you just seemed . . . I don't know. Spooked."

My husband and I lock eyes. He flicks his neck, encouraging me that it's safe to tell Jake.

"Um. Yeah. Well, we don't know . . ." I trail off. And we really don't.

"Okay, well, that sounds cryptic as hell," Jake snorts.

"I think we just tell Jake, Jules."

Jake turns to me again. "Tell Jake what, Jules?"

And then we tell Jake everything. Ricky mercifully takes the wheel, masterfully retaining the vast majority of what I just described. Every now and then, I jump in with an assist to fill in some of the finer details.

Jake is silent for several moments.

"Will you guys excuse me for a second?"

Ricky and I just look at him.

"I just need to make a quick phone call. To someone who might be able to help. And let's pass on dinner."

NEW YORK CITY, 2016

TRIPP, 2

I swivel my chair away from the door so that I'm facing the window.

"I think someone's after Julia," Jake tells me.

My brow furrows, and I ball my left hand into a tight fist. "What do you mean, *after?*"

"She's all worked up about some guy she thinks has been following her. Says she first spotted him in the city a few weeks ago, then again in Paris, and just a few hours ago here."

Rain starts pattering against my office window, slowly at first, then all at once. "Her story sound plausible?"

"What do you mean? It's Julia, Dad."

"I know. I'm only clarifying if it sounds like someone might actually be targeting her versus a case of coincidence or mistaken identity," I stand up from my chair. It's impossible for me to stay seated when I'm on the phone.

"Hard to say. She can't say 100 percent whether or not it was the same guy as he always looked different, but she was pretty adamant." Jake takes a breath, "She's really shaken up . . ."

Ah ha. I know what he's up to. Jake is all too aware of my soft spot for Julia. The daughter I never had.

179

"Between the guy in the whiteout and now this, I don't know. I just have a bad feeling . . ."

Damn him. I peer out my window and down at passersby, ducking for cover from the rain. The streets and everyone who forgot to check the weather today are already sopping wet.

"I'll be on the next flight."

Click.

JAKE, 9

I highly doubt that Sergei has anything to do with The Man in The White Ski Suit. Sergei is a few inches too tall anyway. But if Cleo's going to be spending a lot of time with him in the future, I have to do my due diligence for the sake of her and Zelli.

I grab my coat from the top of a pile of clothes off the leather chair. By the time I return, everything will be hung up and folded, even pressed if need be, by magical elves who snuck into my room while I was gone. "Hey," I say into my work phone to Fieldie, who is the mainstay of our intel, "Will you run a check for me?"

"Name?"

By force of habit, I lower my voice even though it's just me, myself, and my anxiety in my room. "Sergei Kominitz. Russian."

I can hear her fingers tapping across her keyboard. "Okay . . . Sergei Kominitz. Born in Lake Baikal in 1966. Only son of Katya and Igor Kominitz. Married Sophie Petrov in 1986. Son Dimitri, deceased 1990. Made his fortune in gold, cable, and shipping. Gorbachev named him an oligarch at the end of his reign in ninety-one. Owns properties all over the world in St. Petersburg, Paris, St. Moritz, London, Lake Baikal, Cap Ferrat, and a ranch in Argentina. Major on the equestrian circuit. Decorated polo player and also owns and breeds polo ponies.

His record looks squeaky clean."

I glance down at my watch. Shit. It's already eleven fifteen. I gotta move if I want to catch Zelli's ski lesson. I put one hand on the door handle but wait to open it until I ask, "Ties with Putin?"

"No. Looks like Kominitz has kept his distance."

I enter the hall. Glance to my left, then to my right. The coast is clear. "What about Rustikoff?"

Another pause as her fingers dance across the keyboard. "Rustikoff. Who is this Kominitz guy anyway?"

"Long story, Fieldie. Just someone I met on vacation."

I PRESS THE ELEVATOR CALL BUTTON. "Just doing my due dill. He knew my father back in the day from law school."

"Okay, I'm not seeing any links to Rustikoff either. Kominitz seems like a model, commie bastard citizen."

As I step into the elevator, relief washes over me. I had to be sure. Historically, Cleo and I haven't been the best judges of character, especially of those characters who are right under our noses. She let an international terrorist live on her property for two years, and my own mentor in the CIA was committing treason. On the bright side, at least Cleo and I made them both pay a steep price for their disloyalty.

Ten minutes later, I'm almost blinded by the sun. I shield my eyes as I step out onto the outer deck at the lodge. There are chairs on the deck with perfect 360 views of the bunny slope, which I'm guessing was designed so helicopter parents can keep a watchful eye on their children's ski school all while they are sipping hot toddies. I fish out my sunglasses from my pocket, double-checking that my phone is safe and sound.

A smile stretches across my face at the sight of my daughter. There she is, my sweet girl, in her little purple ski suit, the miniature version of her mom's, whose hand she's holding. Cleo chats with some cute young thang in a blood-red instructor's parka. I glance around for an empty chair until I find one next to three chicks that I certainly wouldn't kick out of bed. One is blond, one's brunette, and the third is a redhead. Something for everybody. "May I?" I point to the chair.

All three of them happily nod and toss sexy little smiles my way. Watch out, ladies. There's a new DILF in town. Their trio reminds me of Paulette, Claudette, and Laurette from *The Beauty & The Beast*, who followed Gaston around the whole time.

When I turn back to the bunny slope, I see Cleo waving goodbye to Zelli as she skies off. I wave, trying to get my daughter's attention, but she doesn't notice.

"Does she belong to you?" The brunette asks me with an Italiano accent. Let's call her Cindy, like Crawford.

I'm not sure who she means. Cleo, Zelli, or her ski instructor.

"The little girl," she smiles again, clocking the confusion on my face. "In the lavender."

"Oh! Yes, sorry. She's mine."

"She's adorable," says the blond in a German accent. We'll call her Claudia. Duh, after Claudia Schiffer.

"Thank you," I smile back.

"How old?" the American redhead chimes in. I'm naming her Angie, as in Angie Everhart.

"Four." Then, suddenly, it occurs to me that I don't even know Zelli's birthday. I do quick math. If my affair with Cleo was at the end of December, that means Zelli must've been born sometime in late September or early October. I say a silent prayer, hoping that this gorgeous trio of supermodels from the 1990s do not ask me her birthday or, God forbid, her sign.

"That's a great age," Angie dazzles.

"It is." Not that I have the first clue how particularly great this year is compared to the first three.

I turn my attention back to Zelli and her lesson. Another instructor, a guy in the classic ski instructor uniform, red jacket, and black pants, is talking to the girl instructor. The girl who Cleo hired waves at Zelli and skis off. Weird.

I turn back to the supermodels. "Is that normal, do you know? Switching out the ski instructor like that?"

"Aw. The protective daddy. So cute," coos Cindy the Italian.

Cindy is a certified twenty, but I don't have time for this. "Seriously," I say in a stern tone. "Is it?"

"Honestly, I don't know. It's never happened to my kids, but I'm sure it's nothing," Angie taps my arm. "Maybe the other one had a family emergency or something?"

The instructor looked like she didn't have a care in the world when she skied off. But I just nod, wary of being that kooky, over-protective girl dad my first week on the job. I lean forward in my chair, lasered in on this unexpected switcheroo. He points up to the chair lift as he removes his black sunglasses and cleans them with the cuff of his sleeve. Something about the way he moves is vaguely familiar. As he slides his sunglasses back on his face, they catch the sun's glare, and I'm nearly blinded again. Then, it hits me. The sunglasses. Bvlgari sunglasses. I can't see the label all the way from here, but it doesn't matter. The sunglasses trigger me into remembering where I know him from.

In my mind, I swap the red coat for a white one and the bunny slope with the gondola.

I quickly jump out of my chair and hustle across the porch and down the stairs. I click my boots into my skis, grab my poles, and glide over to the man and Zelli.

Zelli sees me first and smiles. "Daddy!"

"Hi, sweetheart," I take her hand in mine. "I'm sorry, but your lesson is over."

Her smile disappears. "But why?"

"Promise I'll tell you later, okay?"

"No, Daddy," she pouts. "Tell me now! I want to ski!"

"Later, okay?" I tell her, hoping to sound like the perfect combination of loving but firm. "I promise we'll ski as much as your little heart desires later on, okay?"

Zelli doesn't say anything. She looks down at her skis and keeps up her best pout. If I'm going to be a good father, sooner rather than later, I'll have to get used to that delightful look on her face every time I'm forced to disappoint her with the word "no." No time like the present.

I point to the women on the porch, who are all watching me in daddy mode. "See those three very nice ladies over there?" They take my cue and wave back.

Zelli nods.

"I want you to go over to them, tell them I sent you, and wait for Daddy just a minute while I talk to your instructor. Can you do that for me?"

Zelli makes me wait until she reluctantly nods.

"Perfect, off you go," I let go of her hand and give her a little nudge. I watch as she skis in the direction of the porch. She clicks her boots out of her skis before toddling up the wooden steps. She hesitates but does what I said and approaches the supermodel gang, who welcome her with open arms.

And now that I know my daughter is safe, for the first time I look up at her instructor. The expression on his face is utter bewilderment.

"Remember me?"

Now, he's even more confused. "Excuse me?" Different accent than on the gondola where he was Austrian. Now, he sounds British.

"We were in the gondola together right before the whiteout. You offered to help me down the mountain," I pause. "Before you disappeared and left me for dead."

"I—I'm sorry, sir. But I think you have me mistaken for someone else. I just got back to St. Moritz yesterday from my holiday with my family in London." The accent is different, but his voice sounds the same.

My eyes drift back over to the porch, double-checking that Zelli is still safe with our new friends. Everyone appreciates beauty, even little girls who have yet to learn what true power it wields. Zelli is smiling up at Cindy, Claudia, and Angie in such awe as they admire her purple ski suit.

I turn back to him. "I don't think so, pal. It was you. Oh, and I'd love my phone back anytime you're ready."

"Sir," he puts up his hand. "I don't know who you think I am, but I can assure you that I'm not who you suggest I am. I think you scared your daughter, and, well, I can understand why."

I step closer to him. *"There's a fruit store on our street, it's run by a Greek . . ."*

He freezes, but only for a second. Blink, and you missed it. "I beg your pardon?" he laughs, erasing all vestiges of the fear in his eyes from moments ago.

I take another step closer. *"And he keeps good things to eat . . ."* And I skip forward to, *"He tells you, "yes, we have no bananas, we have a no-bananas today."*

This time, the man doesn't react. His face is totally blank, betraying no emotions. But that's a tell in itself. They taught us that in week one of training at CIA University. If the song meant squat to him, he'd presumably acknowledge how absurd I am singing a song to him in the middle of the day on the bunny slope of a ski resort.

Instead, he remains calm, cool, and collected. "Your daughter is waving to you," he says with a blank tone.

When I turn toward Zelli, the bastard grabs my poles and takes off toward the chair lift.

"Mother fu—I knew it!" I scream at his back as he leaves me in his dust. I fucking knew it.

All I want to do is blast off after him, but I can't. My head whips back over to Zelli, who's sitting pretty in Claudia's lap. I'm about to ski back over to the lodge when a woman in a bright yellow parka and a fur hat skis up to me. Oh, happy day. It's Lola.

"Hey, Jake! What are you—?"

I cut her off. There's no time for that. "Lola! Zelli—she's up there," I point up to the porch. "See? With the women? Will you please go and keep an eye on her? I have to—it's a long story. I have to get to the gondola now or—I'll explain everything later, okay?!"

Lola doesn't miss a beat. She hands me her poles, "Here, take these. Bit short for you but better than none."

"Thank you!" I take them.

She starts toward the lodge and then turns back. "How long will you be gone? I have an appointment in an hour and a half. Should I call Cleo?"

"No, I'll be back way before that. Thank you, Lola!" I wave to her, and I'm off like a rocket.

The wind is at my back, my body is in the zone, and for the first time in days, I'm back in the game. I bob and weave in between children and their parents, racing over to the gondola as fast as my skis take me. Like a heat-seeking missile, my eyes stay fixated on the artist formerly known as White Ski Suit.

I watch him push to the front of the chair lift line and haphazardly hop onto the first empty one. Not so smooth now that I can keep you in my sights, are you, shithead . . .

Since I can't advertise my actual employer, especially in a foreign land, I fudge the truth. *"Police! La policia!"* I scream when I make it to the gondola about four minutes after Red Ski Suit boarded his chairlift. The gondola is twice the speed, so I'll be able to make up time. All eyes are on me, politely stepping aside as I ski to the front of the line. I step inside the gondola along with three other people around my age, two bleached blonds and a guy in a bright orange hat.

"Hi there," smiles one of the blonds.

Ah, fellow Americans. My comrades. "How's it going?"

"Pretty good, pretty good," the guy answers in a distinctly California drawl. I can't tell if he's annoyed that I crashed their menage a trois.

I toss them a smile before pressing my face against the glass. I scan each of the chair lifts before us to see if I can spot the red coat. Black, black, black, navy, hot pink, bright yellow, black, black. Red! There he is! I gotcha, you sick son of a bitch. I count. He's one, two, three, four, five, six, seven, eight chairs ahead of my gondola. But I'm gaining on him, and I'm gaining on him fast.

"Come on, come on," I say under my breath. My eyes glare at his red coat as I will the gondola into catching up to him. And it starts to work. We overtake the first chairlift. One down. Then the second, two down. Then the third and fourth, only four more to go. "Come on, buddy," I encourage the gondola as if we are in actual cahoots. We overtake the fifth gondola. Okay, only three more to go. I keep glaring at his stupid red coat as we inch closer and closer. He doesn't even have a clue. For all he knows, my ass stayed up on the bunny slope with my daughter.

But then, as if he can sense my presence, his head whips around seconds before my gondola catches up to his dinky little chairlift. Our eyes meet through the glass. Chills tingle up and down my entire body. My face twists into a smile, and my right hand waves at him tauntingly. As Dave Chapelle would say, *gotcha bitch.*

He freezes. He knows I have him beat, that I'll be waiting for him to step into my trap at the top of the mountain. He's out of clever options, and he must humbly accept his fate as the loser to my triumphant winner. He has no other choice.

Except that. As my gondola passes his chair, my mocking smile leaps off my face and lands onto his.

"No!" I pound my fist on the glass. "God dammit! Don't you dare!"

But it's too late. He's already doing it, and there's nothing I can do to stop him. The bastard grins at me, lifting the protective bar over his head. He peers down at the mountain below, calculating the best moment for his jump. And then, poof. He does it. He's gone.

"God fucking dammit! No!" I bang my fists again. I turn and sprint to the back of the gondola, pressing my face against the glass. I scan the white vastness until I find a flash of bright red.

The man is down, but not out. I'm suddenly reminded of a recent article I read in *Backcountry* about K-points, which is basically a perfect landing spot beyond the steepest part of the slope where the hill begins to flatten. It's a term used for traditional ski jumping, not out-of-chair lifts, but the same logic must still apply. And the man formerly known as White Ski Suit has found his K-point.

Skiers in other chairlifts suspended above him point down at him in awe. And in my gondola, they are shouting in total disbelief too.

"Whoa! Did you see that?!" asks one of the blonds.

"Yeah, that guy, he just did it!" says Orange Hat.

"That was crazy! I hope he's okay! How's he not dead?!" says the other blond.

"That's the Chowtel! Haven't you guys heard of that?" Orange Hat asks.

I sure as hell haven't. I turn to them.

"Chowtel? What is that?"

"Pretty sure it's illegal," blond number one scoffs.

"It's the jump at stanchion 32. By the really steep rocky precipices?" says blond number two.

"You're obviously not supposed to do it, but some of the really chill skiers jump off the chairlift there. Sort of a got-to-do-it thing. Apparently, they've been doing it for years, like some old-school urban legend. This is the first time I've seen it though," Orange Hat chimes in.

I look down at the man one last time. He looks up at me and gives me a thumbs-up. Then he turns and starts skiing backward down the mountain as if nothing ever happened. Backward.

And here I am. Stuck up here like a chump, resigned to watching helplessly as my enemy escapes my clutches—once again, down a mountain in St. Moritz.

DIDIER, 2

When you get to be my age, it's tiring keeping up with the others, so I've been skiing solo part of each day. The line to the chairlift is unusually long for this time of year. Christmas vacation is over, so a majority of skiers should have left. But instead, I am behind at least thirty people.

I have a pass to get ahead of the lines, and as I am making my way up to the preferred line, I see Lola ahead of me. While I could call out to her, I think I might prefer quiet on the chairlift up.

As she gets on the lift, a man joins her on her chair, and they are headed to the top of the mountain. I am four chairs behind her and happily seated, marveling at the view, which never gets old.

I reach into my pocket to get my phone and text Lola.

"Would you care to join me at the Evergreen for lunch in an hour?"

While I can't see much from this distance, I do see her take out her phone in response to me texting her a message. She then puts it right back in her bright yellow parka.

As we're going around a bend I catch a glimpse into her chair. I look down at my phone again.

No response. Odd. Or is it?

I send her another message.

"Fondue at Evergreen in an hour?"

She puts her hand on her parka where her phone is, there is no way she did not feel the vibration from my message. But she doesn't answer. I watch her from my vantage point four lifts back, get off the lift, and gracefully ski toward her house. The man with her heads down the mountain.

Not answering my text is so interesting that I decided to see who she was with on the chairlift. I head right into the restaurant near the chairlift and go directly into the security office on the right to see the tape.

"Buona giornata, Didier,"

One of the guards calls out to me in Italian as I approach. They know me well. I'm hit with a waft of Parisienne. They offer me one which I take and we all smoke as I ask them about the footage for Lola's chair.

"Numero 342, per favore."

It was only seconds until we looked at it.

Lola, in her bright yellow parka, was talking, facing straight ahead. I couldn't see him. He was so bundled up. But when he got off the chairlift, his hat must have gotten caught, and it pulled his scarf off. I got a good look at him as he grimaced.

Something stirred in me, some recognition. Why? It's killing me. I know that Sergei's facial recognition is astounding. I am better at recognizing a spy's walk and voices, especially from behind.

It wasn't much of a hassle convincing the security officers to give me the tape, and we made a date to ski next week on their day off.

They hand me the tape, and I leave the lodge. It's practically muscle memory for me as I ski right down to Sergei's house, a path I know very well.

Sergei's house is right near Lola's. Interesting. Regardless, this just means that I'm following right in her tracks.

The door to his house is unlocked, which means he's home. I ring the bell and wander right inside to his office, a familiar place.

Sergei is wearing ski pants, black socks, and a black turtleneck. We exchange a look as I pull the tape that security gave me out of my parka and fumble with it for a minute. We've known each other so long that we don't even need to say a word for him to know it's important. He takes it out of my hand and inserts it into one of the many screens on his desk.

Sergei then turns and looks at the screen. I have him fast-forward it to the part right before the man's scarf is pulled off and he presses play. It doesn't take long for Sergei's eyes to light up. The man on the tape grimaces as he quickly tries to cover his face again. Sergei presses pause on the player and continues to stare for a few moments at the somewhat blurry frame of the man.

He stands up, absolutely dumbstruck. "I know him. I was at his funeral. Full military funeral over two years ago. He was one of Anatoly Rustikoff's closest friends, Fyodor Akapov. He was also in Putin's inner circle. I am sure it's Akapov as I recognize his teeth. They were always oddly gray. He had a beautiful wife, who, now that I think of it . . ." he pauses.

". . . was—*is* Lola."

We both smile.

CLEO 11

"Jake is picking Zelli up from ski school at noon. And then he's taking her skiing on the bunny slope and on to lunch." I am smiling as I tell this to my father, Jay, Heidi, Lady Eleanor, and Maya. I already told Sergei between kisses on the chair lift. We are acting like teenagers who can't get enough of one another.

"What a nice father-daughter day," Heidi chirps. Eleanor adds, "Chuka chuka chuka."

We are at my father's table at the Evergreen Club, having a late lunch of our favorite cheese souffle while sitting happily under black-and-white photos of beautiful people who have come here over the decades. There is one of my mother and father that I pointed out to Sergei as we walked in.

He laughed and said, "Ah, The Pilgrimage of Ashes. Did she have you leave some of her ashes here too?"

"She didn't, and I have to wonder why." I am still smiling so broadly because he remembers everything I told him the night we met.

He's sitting so close to me, our elbows pressing against one another as we share a cheese fondue and a carafe of chardonnay. His elbow brushes up against my breast quite often, and I put my hand on his lap quite often. No more skiing for today, but we had a lovely morning. The sun was out, the sky was blue, and the snow was fluff. And I am so in love. All I really want is to go back to Sergei's chalet and make love all afternoon.

My phone vibrates, and I glance at the number.

"Sorry," I apologize to the table as I step outside, "It's Jake."

"Jake? Everything okay?"

"Hey, can you meet me at the lodge? Don't worry, Zelli's fine."

Except something about Jake's tone seems off. "What do you mean? Is everything alright?"

"Yeah, but I need to talk to you one-on-one in person. I just dropped Zelli with Nannie at the Badrutt."

Everything definitely does not seem alright. "Now?"

"Now."

I check the time. Two fifteen.

"Okay, give me twenty minutes. I'm having lunch at the Evergreen Club. I'll ski down and meet you."

He hangs up without another word.

I walk back in. Sergei looks the question by raising his eyebrows. He's sipping our chardonnay.

"I'm not sure. Jake has something important to tell me."

"Oh?"

"I think it concerns Zelli. I hope it is not some 'I am a new dad thing' where he says her skiing isn't proficient or her boots don't fit. But I better leave you all and find out."

I stand and pull up my lavender ski suit, fastening the pink belt. I unzipped it to the waist as it gets toasty here near the fire.

Sergei goes with me outside. As I step into my skis, he bends down and whispers, "I love you." He reaches for my hand and then heads back into the club to join our friends, laughing at me, "Now I get all the cheese fondue and all the wine." He shakes his head at how turned on he is, and so am I.

I feel like I am floating down the mountain. Sergei loves me, I know. But the way he said it just now and the amethyst ring he slyly slipped on my finger makes it perfect.

Jake waits in the lodge, drumming his fingers on the table absentmindedly. He looks up from his phone and stands when he sees me coming.

"Sorry to pull you away."

"It's alright. What's happened?" I sit.

He takes a breath. "Okay, you know how there was another guy on the mountain with me during the whiteout? The one who disappeared, like, halfway down?"

"Yes . . ." I say impatiently. I wish Jake would hurry up and get to the point.

"Well . . . I just saw him again. He was Zelli's ski instructor."

My eyebrows furrow. "No, Jake. Zelli's instructor is a girl named Jesse. I dropped Zelli off with her."

"I know. I saw you, I was on the porch. I tried waving when you were leaving—anyway, it's not important. What's important is this guy skied up to her instructor, who then skied off, and took over the lesson. I got a weird feeling, and I've learned to trust my weird feelings. So I went over to them and stopped the lesson," he pauses. "It's definitely him. The same guy who left me on the mountain in the whiteout."

"How do you know? I thought you didn't get a good look at his face?"

"His voice is the same—different accent, but anyone can change an accent. I just know, okay. And then . . ." Jake trails off.

"What? And then what?" My anxiety is growing by the second.

Jake just looks at me. "And then . . . I sang him this song."

"I beg your pardon?"

Jake takes a deep breath. "When he led me down the moun-tain, he was singing this song, *Yes We Have No Bananas*, so I could follow the sound of his voice down the mountain. But he stopped singing, and that's when I lost him. It was a song my father sang to us every night at bedtime when he was home."

I am really at a loss now. "Alright. What did he say when you sang it to him?"

"Nothing. But there was this split second. This split second when there was a look on his face. It was brief, but it was there, and I saw it."

Jake went on, "Cleo, Lola came by and I asked her to watch Zelli. Then I chased him. I was in the gondola but lost him when he jumped out of his chair lift and did the Chowtel. Backward."

My concern must be all over my face because Jake reaches across the table and puts his hand over mine.

"I know it all sounds crazy, but you'll just have to trust me, Cleo."

"I do. You say he skied backward down the Chowtel? Well then, I met him on the mountain a few days ago, Jake. He skied backward on the Flotsy Run too."

"You met him?" I nod, but I can only think of my daughter. "Zelli must have been so confused, Jake. Thank God Lola was able to look after her."

"I know. But . . ." Jake pauses. "I hope you know I wouldn't have just abandoned Zelli if Lola wasn't there. You know that, right?"

I meet Jake's gaze, and I nod. I do know that. At least I hope I do.

"Zelli's fine, I promise. She was a little upset that I cut her lesson short, but we skied several runs together before lunch to calm her down. She's a good little skier, by the way," Jake cracks a smile. "Great hockey stop."

I ignore his compliments. "We need to go to the ski school and find out what happened."

He's already on his feet. "I went. But I wasn't in their system, so they wouldn't give out any information. Which I found ironic."

I stand. "Now you have me, and they'll have to tell us."

"Have you ever heard of the Chowtel?" Jake asks me, holding open the door.

"Yes, it's the jump at Stanchion 32. I did it often when I was younger." I turn to Jake as he holds open the door for me. "Why?"

He shrugs. "These people on the gondola mentioned it after he jumped. I'd never heard of it."

Hopefully, this is all just one big misunderstanding.

Was the man trying to kidnap Zelli? I push down that thought as we walk over to the ski school.

"Ms. Gallier," says Gabi, the head instructor. *"Vous êtes ravissante dans cette couleur."*

It's so obvious what he's doing. He's usually a rather aloof man, but he knows they made a mistake, and he's trying to win me over with flattery.

"Merci, Gabi. Mais. Please speak in English for Mr. Regan, who is Zelli's father," I glance over at Jake. "Mr. Regan said he saw another instructor take over Zelli's lesson from Jesse?"

Gabi sighs. "Yes, he said that earlier," he replies with a hint of frustration in his tone. "And as I told Mr. Regan, we didn't call in for any change in instructors."

"Then why, Gabi, was there another ski instructor with her? Answer me that. Where is Jesse? We need to understand. Please get her here now."

Gabi puts his hands up in defense mode. "Please, Ms. Gallier, we're just as concerned as you—"

"Do you have any idea who he was?" I raise my voice.

Gabi sighs again, louder this time. "Not yet, Ms. Gallier. But we're doing everything we can to locate this man."

"Like what?" Jake chimes in. He is looking at Gabi with a completely blank look. All business.

"We have alerted the ski patrol, and they are searching the mountain for him using the description that you, er, exuberantly provided."

"Have they had any luck?" Jake asks. Still all business.

Gabi has the audacity to sigh for a fourth time as if we are bothering him with our silly questions related to our only daughter. "Not yet, I am afraid."

"He could have kidnapped my daughter," I blurt. "Do you understand that? How could someone who isn't one of your employees have taken over my daughter's lesson?"

Gabi motions to someone behind me. "Hans?" he gestures. "*S'il vous plait va chercher* Jesse." "Jake, he is sending Hans to get Jesse," I explain.

I TURN AROUND TO GET A LOOK AT HANS. He has sandy blond hair and a muscular frame, but there is a sheepish look on his face. "*Quand je suis arrivé au travail, il manquait ma veste rouge.*"

"Jake, Hans said his red instructor's jacket was missing when he got to work."

"Missing?" Jake asks.

"*J'ai dû emprunter*, Jacques," he says looking at Gabi. "How could someone walk in and take a jacket?" I ask Gabi, who points to the locker room out back.

Just then, my father walks in. My protector has arrived. "Daddy! Oh, thank heaven you are here."

"Mon chaton," my father wraps his arms around me. "What's going on?"

I look at Jake over my father's shoulder, signaling to him that I am handing this mission off to him. After all of this time, Jake still knows my signals. You never forget the signals of an old lover.

"That's what we're trying to figure out," Jake turns to my father. "Long story short, someone who wasn't an employee of the mountain took over Zelli's ski lesson. So, we're trying to get to the bottom of why."

"And how!" I blurt out again. I think I am too emotional. All I want is to be with Zelli.

"Cleo, do you maybe want to—"

I cut Jake off. "Yes, I am going back to The Badrutt. I need to see her."

Before I know it, I push open the wooden door and find myself back in the snow. Then I immediately text Sergei: *Someone tried to kidnap Zelli.*

If this is how I feel after a foiled kidnapping attempt on my daughter, I can't even imagine what he went through after his son drowned. My legs are like jelly, and my stomach feels sick. Nothing has ever struck this much fear in me. I had no qualms about killing a deadly terrorist, and I didn't blink as I outfoxed a shooter who was hunting me. But this is somehow worse. Much, much worse. I have to get to her.

I don't even remember getting to The Badrutt or up to our room. All I know is that when I see Zelli I almost burst into tears. But for her sake, I must pretend all is well. "Let's play with all the Hazels, shall we?"

Zelli runs to get all six Hazels and splays them out on the floor. "Mommy, let's ask them things like you told me you did on TV."

"Good idea, Zelli! You ask the first one."

"No, Maman, you," my four-year-old pouts. "I don't know how."

I smile and pick up the Hazel doll that's closest to me. "Hazel doll number one. How do you like your name?"

Zelli claps and says, "Hazel doll number two, how do—what do I ask her again?"

"How she likes her name."

And now Zelli gets it. She continues down the row of Hazels, asking, one by one, if they like their name. When she's done, she starts all over again until each of the dolls has been asked the same question multiple times. Nannie, to whom I gave the Cliff Notes of the whole ordeal in the kitchen, ordered milk and tiny tea sandwiches from room service. The three of us happily gulp them down while I think up a new question for the Hazel dolls.

That is until Zelli says, "Mommy, did I tell you? This nice man today said he had a new Hazel doll for me."

I can't breathe. I look over at Nannie who is already staring at me with horror in her dark brown eyes. "Really? Do you know who this nice man is, Zelli?" I force a smile.

Zelli looks away from me and down at Hazel number four. She starts to slowly brush her hair. "My new ski teacher, I guess," she shrugs. "I miss JoJo."

I choke out the words: "JoJo had to go back home, so we got Jesse."

"Do you remember your new ski teacher's name?"

Zelli thinks. "I don't think I remember, Maman. But he never gave me a new Hazel because Daddy came and he took me away. I've only been on the baby chair lift. When Daddy came, I never got to go on the grown-up chair lift with the new ski teacher."

Nannie and I are both smiling at Zelli, or at least I am trying to, hiding the fear of what could've happened to my only child. "He was going to take you on the grown-up chair lift?"

I jump when the door opens. To my great relief, it's my father and Sergei.

I urge Zelli to tell them all about the "nice man" who was her teacher. When she does, for once, my father is not his cool self. He usually doesn't smoke near Zelli, but he does now and quickly lights one of his Gitanes.

Sergei catches my eye and gestures for me to follow him out to the hall. I do, and there I fall into his arms.

"Are you alright?" Sergei whispers into my ear. He is literally holding me up.

I look up at him.

"No."

"Have you ever heard that famous line of the Samurai warriors?"

"Which one?"

"'I am already dead.'" He pauses. "Is that how you feel, Cleo?"

"Yes. Exactly how I am feeling, Sergei."

"It's how I spent years. After Dimitri, nothing scared me because I was already dead. There is a motorcycle gang in America called The Sons of Silence who use those words as their motto. Cleopatra, I am trying to distract you. Thank God she is safe."

I hold his hand so tightly as we walk back into the living room, where Zelli is sitting on my father's lap.

Sergei is smiling down at her. "Qui sont ces jolies poupées, Zelli."

She jumps down off of her grandfather's lap, takes Sergie's hand, and has him sit with her on the floor as she introduces them all to him one by one in French. When that's finally over, Zelli asks Sergei: *"Demander les poupees une question*, Sergei." I think she is happy speaking French again and having Sergei ask her dolls questions.

HE SMILES AND GRACIOUSLY ASKS EACH ONE: *"Hazel, combien aimes-tu ta maman*, Zelli?" How much do the dolls love their Mother, Zelli? Not a fraction of how much I love her.

He is doing a fabulous job distracting her so she doesn't pick up on our fears. And she seems to enjoy him.

"Since the 'instructor' skied Chowtel, he knows his way around," my father says. "I agree. He must be a professional skier. Jake said he was skiing it backward. There was a man on the slopes with me a few days ago who acknowledged me, then used his ski pole on a snow bank to make a crown in the snow. Then he skied down the black diamond run backward. The next day, Zelli and I were sent slippers with the same crown."

"Yes, and every morning, Zelli gets one in her cocoa," Nannie adds.

"Crowns, Hmmm. Why crowns? Queens?" Didier muses.

I walk over to the chessboard where I saw the raised Queen earlier. I bring my father the gold Franc coin with the crown imagery.

My father nods as he continues: "We met with Jesse. The poor girl is very sweet and very scared as she is new and is sure she will lose her job. We made sure she won't."

"What did the would-be instructor say to her?" I ask.

My father shrugs, "I am to take over this lesson, and you will get the rest of the hour off. Just enough time for a few good runs. She said she thanked him and took off for a few runs. He had on the red jacket, so it never dawned on her to question him."

Sergei looks up from Hazel's World across the living room floor and says, "We have a new question for the Hazels. 'Do they like cocoa?'" Which may be a not-too-subtle hint?"

2016

VERA, 4

"You're going to think I'm Inspector Gadget once you hear about this. It was a trivial task getting into Jake's room using a keycard spoofing device. Then, once I was in the room, I opted to use my nifty Killswitch to break into and make a hard copy of nearly everything important on Jake's personal laptop. Good thing it wasn't a Mac.

"Now, here's the kicker. He had his father's plane flight on his calendar. His father is flying across the ocean to St. Moritz right now. He rented a private plane from Zurich to St. Moritz."

"Oh dear, thank you, Kasparov. The king and I haven't spoken in over two years, though part of me wants to call him a 'friendly' call out of the blue right now. Though then I'd be in the front of his mind, and that would be dangerous, but oh, it is so tempting."

"You would be flying too close to the sun if you did that, Vera." He hung up.

My nights are still mine and filled with plans to scare him, not badly but enough so he suffers. I leave my answering machine on. I still have a landline in case of emergency. On September 11th, hardly anyone in the tri-state area could use their cell phones after the towers went down. It is my extra insurance.

"Hello, it's Vera. Thank you for calling, but I am not at home, so please leave your name and number, and I will call you back." My friends must wonder where I am and with whom, but they are far too polite to ask. They will wonder if I have a date, which is rather ironic since, in reality, I am out with my anger. I have a date with my fury. He deserted us.

"Vera, it's Magnus. I have been identified, so I am driving to the Geneva airport. They will be looking at Zurich. I was doing a scare on Jake, and he caught me. I got away, but I need to leave. I put the Blackphone in Kasparov's digs. The good news is Kasparov is fine."

"Thank you, Magnus. Come see me when you get home."

"Kasparov, it's me again. We need to stop for a while with the king arriving there now and with Magnus found out. Please keep me in the loop about what they are doing. Call me with information, especially about the man. But no scares. I want it quiet so they relax. One place to find them is the lunch club halfway down the mountain. Go at twelve thirty. It is a private club called the Evergreen. I will ensure you get in. Use the name Leo Carnegie and go every day."

TRIPP, 3

We're approaching our final descent. Instead of hopping on a three-hour train ride after the eight-hour flight, I opted to book a small charter plane from Zurich to St. Moritz. No snow storms, so we take right off. If I've learned one thing in all my years, it's when you can, throw money at the problem. It'll save you a headache, keep you in a good mood, and rid you of a helluva lot of hassle.

Miranda chooses to stay home, where she is being given a birthday party at the Colony Club by her friend Lia, who is the charming lovely Pearl Mesta of our day. She's also hard at work in the "baby's room" for what she presumes is her very first grandchild. Soon, however, she'll learn that a little girl named Zelli, who lives halfway around the world, beat Julia and Ricky's future progeny by about four years. Even if they don't realize it yet, soon Julia and Ricky will see just how much having in-laws who are only a short cab ride away comes in handy. Miranda is going to spoil this poor child rotten until his or her little teeth fall out. And I can't wait. Miranda has been looking forward to being a grandmother since before the boys even had braces.

To my great surprise, Matt came along—he hates the snow but was ultimately convinced when I told him that Cleopatra was there.

In his Carhartt's and lace-up boots, Matt looks more like my gardener than my son. When he hasn't been sleeping, Matt has been shockingly chipper, which is never a guarantee with him. His autism can often put him in a distant mood where he prefers to be alone. Or with his plants, hence the gardener motif. Among his shrubs, weeds, and seeds is my middle son's happy place.

My sons. My sweet, beautiful, often infuriating children. Who'd want to come after them? Beside me and their mother after they've frayed our very last nerve. And Julia too. Poor Julia, who's probably held funerals for flies after she's accidentally killed them with her windshield. The devil wears Belgian shoes, in Julia's case. And so do I. For most of my adult life, Belgians are the only shoes I have ever put on my feet unless I'm exercising, on the beach, or just getting out of bed. Something about the piano wood sole flawlessly molds to my wide feet and hammer toes. Strangely, I had a pair of black Belgian shoes missing a bow when I was doing *BAREFOOT IN THE PARK* with Cindy. That with the Banana song is too close for comfort. Is someone warning me off?

Their flagship store is on 54th and Park. Whenever I run a pair into the ground—on average, every four to six months—I give Marie a call and put in an order of three new pairs, which lasts me for the year. If nothing else, I'm a creature of habit. An old dog doesn't learn new tricks. The boys used to make fun of them because they thought the tiny bows were "for girls." But who's laughing now because years later, all three of them each have a pair. They only wear them on special occasions, and I don't think Matt has ever worn his, but still. They're not as wholly original now as they once were—today, they come in every color of the rainbow and have styles for women and babies too. If Julia wasn't so spooked by them, I'd be tempted to put in an order with Marie for Baby Regan.

Matt looks over and throws me a lopsided grin after he stirs from his fifth slumber. He turns and looks out the small, egg-shaped window. "Are we there yet?"

"Just about, bud," I pat Matt on his knee, forgetting, as I often do, that he hates to be touched. "Good sleep?" He moves my hand aside and nods, captivated by the mountains as we sink lower and closer to them. I find this particularly interesting, seeing as Matt has detested the snow and, ergo, skiing all of his life. But if there's one consistency with Matt, it's that the boy is full of surprises. "Do you think Cleopatra will remember me?"

That makes me laugh. Oh, Matt. Like I said, full of surprises. "You? How could Cleo possibly forget a guy like you?"

A relieved smile forms on his anxious face. "Okay, phew. I'll call her as soon as we land so that she isn't worried about me."

I give him a wink. "Good idea."

Then, without any warning from the pilot, our plane bumps onto the runway.

"Ah!" Matt squeals, surprised by the sudden jolt.

"We're alright, bud. We're fine. Perfectly normal landing," I assure him as the pilot puts on the brakes, and we eventually come to a stop.

I fish my phone out of my pocket, turn it on, and wait for it to whir to life.

"That was . . . jarring," Matt mumbles to himself. Now that the plane is taxiing, he looks more relaxed.

"Can't disagree with you there."

My voicemail notification on my phone dings. It's from Jake. I click the icon and hold my phone to my ear as I listen.

"Dad," Jake says breathlessly. I sit up straight in my seat, sensing by that one syllable something's wrong. Something has happened. "This call went straight to voicemail, which I'm assuming means you're in the air again. Just, uh, call me when you land. Everything's fine now, but just call me, okay?"

Of my three sons, Jake is the most like me. He's, by far, the most calm under fire. That doesn't mean his cage doesn't get rattled every now and then. This is one of those times. I dial Jake.

Half a ring later, he answers. "Dad? Are you here?"

"Just landed. What's going on?" I ask with a slight edge to my otherwise even tone.

"You know what, I'll tell you when I see you," he says, all business. "I decided to just come to the airport and pick you up myself. When are you getting off?"

I look over Matt's shoulder out the window. "We're pulling the stairs down now. Should be disembarking any minute."

"K, I'm here. Meet you outside," Jake says.

"Alright," I don't push him. "See you soon."

"Was that Jake?" Matt asks.

"It sure was. He can't wait to see you," I force a smile while I run through the worst possible scenarios.

"Yeah, Dad. I've always been Jake's favorite brother. Duh," Matt tells me with his infamous poker face.

Less than three minutes later, Matt and I are deplaning. Yet again, I'm reminded that you really can't put a price on the efficiency that comes with throwing money at a problem.

"Matt, where's your bag?" I ask when I notice his empty hands.

"Oh," he remembers. I back up a few steps to allow him the space to turn around and retrieve his bag from the overhead bin.

Ten seconds later, Matt and I are on terra firma. I shield my eyes from the sun as we walk down the narrow metal staircase and head toward the private terminal. I spot Jake striding toward us in his usual clipped, intentional gait.

"There's Jake," Matt points. "Yikes, look how dirty his coat is. Maybe they don't have dry cleaners in St. Moritz."

I chuckle at Matt's unintended joke. If you want an honest take, Matt's your guy. "Bud, I think your brother's had a lot going on the past few days."

Jake's taut expression twists into a smile as he gets closer. He goes to me first, wrapping his sturdy arms around my torso for a tighter hug than I'd anticipated.

"You okay?" I whisper into Jake's ear so that his younger brother doesn't overhear.

Jake just nods. He's not going to tell me more until Matt takes a hike. "Thanks for coming all this way. I—you have no idea, Dad. I really appreciate it."

I give him a good fatherly pat on the back. "'Course. Anytime."

Jake lets go of me and plasters on an exuberant smile for his brother. He's much better at remembering Matt's aversion to physical touch. "Bud! You made it! You're in Switzerland! Isn't that wild?"

"Not really, Jake. You invited me," says Matt flatly.

Jake and I both laugh. "Shall we?"

THE THREE OF US PILE into Jake's Audi A4 rental. The black paint is speckled with white salt, which almost makes the vehicle look like a reverse Dalmatian.

"Your car is as dirty as your coat, Jake," Matt declares from the back seat as we peel out of Samedan airport.

"Thanks, bro!"

For the majority of the eleven-minute car ride to The Badrutt Palace Hotel, we mainly make small talk.

"How's Julia feeling?" I ask.

"She's okay." But his pointed look tells a different story. He taps his fingers against the steering wheel, and even though I have no clue what the speed limit is around these parts, Jake is certainly not abiding by it.

"Did you tell Cleopatra that I'm coming, Jake? She's not answering my calls," Matt chimes in again.

"I did. I think Cleo might just be a little tied up at the moment, bud, but I'm sure she'll give you a call back as soon as she can," Jake says before he slams on the brakes at a red light. We all pitch forward, not expecting the sudden jolt.

"Sorry about that. I thought I could make it."

"It's alright," I tap him on the knee. "We're almost there."

"Busy with what?" Matt asks, not reading the room.

My eyes scan Jake's reaction. Something tells me the thing Jake has to tell me is related to Cleo somehow.

"It's a surprise! You'll just have to wait and see," Jake forces a smile as he takes on a turn a little too quickly.

I hold onto the door handle for support. "Easy, Jake."

"You know I hate surprises, Jake . . ."

Jake and I trade looks again. If I didn't already know what it was, I'd be tempted to goad Jake about the surprise too. But my eldest's patience is running thin.

"Well, too bad, bud."

And that makes Matt shut his yap for the remainder of the drive.

But not when we arrive. "Wow, this is a really nice hotel. It looks like a castle," Matt comments as we pull into the entrance. "How much did it cost, Dad?"

"Oh, only half of your inheritance," I say.

"It really does look like a castle . . ."

"That's because it is one," I tell him, suddenly feeling like a peasant in Jake's dirty Audi as we pass what appears to be a showroom for Bentleys, Rolls Royces, and Aston Martins.

There are no tattered heirlooms in this palace. Everything is first class all the way, including the guests with luggage from Louis Vuitton, not like our Patagonia duffels as we go to check in. A short man in a black uniform smiles warmly at us as we approach his reception desk.

Two minutes later, after we're checked in, I hand Matt the key to his room. "Here you go, bud. I need to have a chat with your brother about something for a while. Why don't you go—"

But I might as well be speaking Urdu because Matt has just left our orbit and has once again found himself fully absorbed in his happy place, his world of plants. He's currently studying what looks like a palm tree.

"You'll be okay here, Matt?"

"Yup, fine. I can't believe these grow here in the winter," he rubs one of the palms between his fingers, totally enrapt.

"Okay, what's going on?" I turn to Jake when we're finally alone in the elevator.

He takes a deep breath, and his ice-blue eyes don't meet mine.

"Everything's fine now. We just had a bit of a . . ." he pauses. "Scare earlier."

"What kind of scare?"

"Cleo and I . . . We thought someone was trying to kidnap her daughter."

Here it is. Here's the moment where, after four long years, my son is going to finally reveal that he and my long-ago flame, Cleopatra, have a love child together. But Jake still can't look at me.

I wait another moment for his confession which doesn't come. So, all I say is: "Jesus. Who?"

He tenses. "Cleopatra's daughter. Zelli."

"No, who do you think kidnapped her?"

He looks at me now. "Oh. Right." He takes another breath. "We think it was that same guy who was in the whiteout with me."

"You're sure?"

Jake nods. "Yeah, he tried to take Zelli during her ski lesson . . ."

And then, in Jake's room, he recounts the full story of what happened to Zelli on the mountain earlier today. If my son hadn't been there, trusted those legendary Regan instincts, and lept into action, there's no telling what could've happened to that little girl. I look over at Jake, sitting on the king-sized bed, and I tell him just that.

He nods, taking that in. "There's one other thing."

I nod, bracing myself. "Okay . . ."

"Zelli . . . She, um. She's actually my daughter too."

I make my eyes get wide. "Oh. Oh, wow," I say in the shocked and yet delighted tone that I'd rehearsed on the flight over. Jake and I just look at each other, measuring each other's reaction. I know that he suspects I also have a past with the mother of his child. He may not have any idea about the actual nature of my relationship with Cleo, and God willing, he never will, but Jake undoubtedly suspects we're more than mere acquaintances. "You have a daughter? You and Cleo have a daughter? Together?"

He just nods.

"Wow," I smile. "That's . . . wow, Jake!" I'm really leaning into the surprised half of my reaction.

"I know," he manages a laugh. "Surprise," he shrugs.

"I'll say," I smile. "So, this is 'the' surprise, yes?"

"Yeah, Dad. This is it," he laughs again.

I get to my feet and stick out my hand. "Congratulations, son," I say sternly.

Jake shakes my hand and matches my serious tone. "Thanks, Dad."

"Guess you're really a man now," I bring some much-needed levity into the room.

Jake laughs. "Finally."

"A father . . ." I smile again. This time, I am thinking of the look on Miranda's face when she finds out about having a grandchild—especially when she hears the good news that it's a girl. Understandably, Miranda assumed that Jake's little 'surprise' was, indeed, of the female variety. But in the girlfriend or even fiance category. "So, who does she look like?"

"She has my eyes, but you'll meet her soon enough."

Now is not the time to press him about why he's been keeping this a secret for the past few years. I think I already know why anyway.

ST. MORITZ, 2016

JAKE, 10

"You and Cleo have a baby together?" Matt asks evenly.

"Well, she's not really a baby anymore," I smile. "But, yeah! What do you think about that, bud?"

Matt casts his eyes down at the snow and digs one of his boots into a well-worn footprint. "What's her name?"

I watch my brother slide his boot in and out of the footprint, enlarging it with every stroke. "Zelli."

"Like Hazel?"

"A little. It was Cleo's idea. Kind of funky, right?"

Matt nods. "Maybe Cleo named your daughter after the Italian shoe company. They make really nice leather shoes from crocodiles, pythons, and lizards. And Cleo loves fancy things, so I bet that's why she named her that."

I laugh. Only Matt. I've stopped wondering how he even comes up with this stuff or where he gets his research. "You should ask her! We'll see them in a little bit."

Matt just shrugs. As usual, he's thoroughly unimpressed by anything that isn't green and rooted into the ground.

217

I look across the snowy lawn at my dad on the phone with my mother. We just relayed the good news to her, and so right about now, Mom is plying my father with a gazillion follow-up questions.

"Why didn't you tell us sooner, Jake?"

I turn back to Matt. There it is. Shit. I had a hunch this question was coming. It was just a matter of who'd do the asking. It's probably the exact question my mother and father are hashing out at this very moment. "Oh, I don't know, bud. It's kind of a long story, I guess."

"Well, I'm not going anywhere," Matt says without any emotion. "I have time."

Seeing as he just flew halfway around the world at my beck and call, I suppose I owe him an explanation. "Well, honestly—"

"So?" I jump to find my dad approaching us from behind. "What do you think, Matt? You're an uncle!"

Finally, Matt smiles. It's the smallest of smiles, but it's something. "Well, Dad, I was already going to be an uncle when Julia and Ricky had their baby. But I'm glad Jake had a baby first. He is the oldest. And now Cleo is part of my family."

My father and I laugh. Classic Matt. He loves it when things are in order, even, and symmetrical. "The man does have a point," Tripp claps me on the shoulder.

"Oh, yeah. You heard it here first, folks."

"Hey, bud," my father turns to Matt. "Will you be okay out here for a little while? I have to go over a few things with your brother."

"Is Jake in trouble, Dad? He and Cleo aren't even married, you know."

We laugh again. "No, of course not. I just need to offer him some fatherly advice. We'll be in my room if you need us, though."

"Maybe I'll go back into the lobby and see the palm trees . . ."

"ARE YOU SURE there wasn't anything on there?"

"On my phone?"

He nods.

"I mean, I basically only use my personal phone for Instagram, texts, ESPN updates, and the occasional dating app," I tell him.

"Email?"

"Sure, but it's all, like, Paperless Posts and order confirmations. Both email accounts on that phone are really just dumb, personal shit."

"How do you know this isn't personal?"

I lean back in my chair. "I don't. With how this is going, this feels more personal than having anything to do with the agency. But unless this mastermind is trying to hack into my Hinge account or my weird browser history, then I suspect he's not going to come up with anything particularly groundbreaking."

"S'up, grandpa!" my youngest brother's ever-exuberant voice bounces around the huge suite sitting room.

We both turn to find Ricky entering Dad's room, hand-in-hand with Julia. The expression on her face is pure relief. With her own father living six time zones away and having lost her mother when she was only a kid, my dad, who was only blessed with sons, has lovingly taken Julia under his wing. They met almost seven years ago when she and I were an item way back when and instantly forged what can't be described as anything other than a bond. Their senses of humor are similar, they both have an odd affinity for rom-coms, they share a bitter rivalry over *The New York Times* crossword, and Julia has tapped in for my mother and competed in several marathons alongside my father—to Miranda's great relief. At their wedding, he was Ricky's Best Man (yours truly walked her down the aisle). To my dad, the idea of anything bad happening to his only daughter-in-law is just as horrific as if it was happening to his own sons.

"Tripp!" she smiles with her arms outstretched. "What a surprise!"

He jokingly shoves Ricky out of the way to get to Julia. "Ah, you know me . . . I can't resist a family get-together."

"Bullshit," Ricky laughs.

"What size fruit this week?" my father asks, wrapping his arms around his daughter-in-law.

"An ear of corn," Julia beams.

I look over at my brother, not having the foggiest idea what the fuck these two are talking about. Ricky pats his belly, implying that it's baby-related.

"And who the hell doesn't love corn?" Tripp chuckles.

Julia possesses a borderline spooky supernatural talent for bringing out my father's lighter, goofier side. Not that he has a stick up his ass the rest of the time, but—and I think I can speak for my brothers here—Tripp Regan is not exactly the jolly, jovial, joking-around type. I hope his first granddaughter will have a similar effect.

I glance over at Ricky again. He lovingly rolls his eyes at their jawboning.

"Hey, Dad. Yoo hoo. Remember me?" Ricky taps him on the shoulder.

"Who are you again?" Tripp jokes before bringing his youngest in for a man hug.

Enough of the schmaltz. I clear my throat and motion toward the sitting room. "Shall we?"

The mood suddenly switches from light to dark as we all take our seats. The concierge had sent up tea and goodies for our meeting in Dad's sitting room. He went for the suite for a good reason. Privacy. And it has the added benefit of gorgeous views. There are thick red curtains, an Oriental rug, and chairs for us all. All quite luxurious.

MY FATHER TURNS TO JULIA. "Okay, so, Jules. Jake gave me very broad strokes, but can you tell me in your own words what's been going on?"

And she does. Julia spares no detail, and my father certainly doesn't go easy on the follow-up questions. If I didn't already know who my father really worked for, I might tell him that he shouldn't quit his day job as an attorney.

"The Belgians are an interesting wrinkle," my father strokes his chin like he were Dr. Evil.

"Dad," I smirk. "I hate to break it to you, but you're not as original with those things as you think. Half the guys in my office wear them."

"I know that. It could be nothing, but compounded with the song 'Yes We Have No Bananas,' it's curious."

"He's got a point, Jake," Ricky agrees.

"And one more thing we've noticed is the Queen piece on our chess board is always toppled when we come back to the room."

"That's odd, I wonder what that means. Who's the Queen? Julia? And you haven't reported this?" Tripp's eyes volley back and forth between Julia and Ricky.

"Not yet," says Julia. "Suppose I just thought without any 'evidence' or whatever that they'd just laugh me out of the station."

Tripp puts a comforting arm on Julia's shoulder. "Nobody's laughing you out of anywhere as long as I'm around."

There he goes again.

"So, what's our move then?" Ricky asks. "I'd say leave it alone and just get the hell outta here, but since she first saw him in New York . . ."

"Sorry, Tripp," Julia smiles. "I'm sure you didn't come all this way to hear about the illusions of a crazy pregnant woman! Don't you want to go skiing or see—"

"Nonsense, I'll get out there tomorrow. Between this and," Tripp turns to me, "my new granddaughter, you guys are my first priority."

"Well, you're very kind," Julia smiles. "It sure is nice having a lawyer in the family!"

"Speaking of which, you and Cleo reported Zelli's incident, right?" Ricky asks.

"The mountain is aware, yes. But we haven't reported it officially. Not yet, at least," I tell him.

"Why not?"

"Well, primarily because she wasn't actually taken, so no crime—other than posing as a ski instructor—was actually committed."

Julia and Ricky trade looks. "True," she says. "But maybe it's good that the police have it on record just in case something else happens."

"It won't," Tripp says firmly.

VERA, 5

I nearly jump out of my skin when my cell phone starts to ring. I look down at my phone on the kitchen counter. My friend Meg is calling. I wonder what she wants. I haven't been out of the house in several days, Not since the King landed and Carlson was spotted, so maybe she is calling to check up on me. Meg was such a good friend after Barnie died. Always calling, always bringing piles of homemade food over, always inviting me out to dinner, and picking me up for parties.

I answer. "Hi, Meg."

"Vera? Are you on your way?" She's whispering.

"On my way where?"

"Vera!" she's no longer whispering. "We're all waiting for you at the first tee!"

I'd completely forgotten about the interclub golf match between my club, Barton Hills Country Club in Ann Arbor, where they held both the Women's Amateur in 1998 and the Women's Mid Amateur in 2008, and Oakland Hills Country Club in Bloomfield Hills, where they have held the U.S. Open more than once.

"Vera? Where are you? This is so unlike you . . . Is everything alright?"

I can't tell her the truth. I have to lie. So I put on a feeble voice. "Meg, I am so sorry. I must've fallen asleep. I am really not feeling well."

Her voice softens. "Oh, you poor thing. You are never sick. Never. Maybe I can get Betty to fill in," she sighs. "I know she is here as her car was here when I pulled in—Oh I see her. Hold on. Betty," she yells.

"Meg, I'm so sorry. I should've—"

"It's alright. You're sick. Is your help there?"

"No, I told them to go home. I didn't want them to catch whatever this is. And I already know what you're thinking, Meg. Don't you come and—"

"Don't be ridiculous, Vera. I'll bring over your favorite dinner. Turkey, stuffing, gravy, cranberry sauce, and popovers too. Doesn't that sound nice? And Betty will fill in."

"You better go, Meg. I don't want our opponents to wait any longer. Please apologize on my behalf."

I hang up. Take a deep breath. I am getting hungry . . . I haven't eaten all day as I am so involved in my chess duel. Waiting for information from Kasparov on what has been happening since HE arrived.

Several hours later, I hear the doorbell ring. I check my reflection in the mirror before I head downstairs to answer it. Earlier, I'd applied white concealer onto my cheeks and forehead, hoping that it'll achieve a sickly, pale look.

"Goodness! You look terrible!" Meg gasps. She barges in, delicious smells trailing her.

Well, that backfired.

I was hoping she might just hand over the goods and be on her merry way. I'm in no mood for the third degree. It's my home, but she's the one who leads me into the kitchen. She sets down two large platters on the counter and gestures to the table.

"Sit." Suddenly, I feel like I am back in my mother's kitchen.

"Gosh, Meg. This is too much. I really wish you didn't go to all of this trouble. Really, I'm fine."

"Okay, Vera, all your friends at the club are worried about you. Missing a tournament and forgetting our golf date is so unlike you. And you missed the LaMotte's dinner party in their gorgeous new house. It is just a perfect house, but of course, she does everything perfectly." She changes her voice to a scolding one. "You haven't seen Dr. Roberts, have you?"

Under different circumstances, I'd lie to Meg and say that I had. But we go to the same doctor whom I, of course, haven't seen. I pour her fabulous homemade gravy over the white turkey, stuffing, and popovers. She's watching me intently.

"Well, at least your appetite is alive and well," she laughs.

I want to distract her from my health. "How was the golf?"

"Oh, it was fabulous. We won. Betty ended up playing so well, and I got a hole-in-one on the ninth hole!" She is laughing so happily.

"Meg! Good for you! Didn't your ball go in the water on the ninth the last time we played?"

The broad smile that was on my sweet friend Meg's face only moments ago evaporates. Her body language shifts. I was only teasing her. "Meg, I was teasing."

THE NEXT NIGHT, MY FRIEND MEG and her lovely daughter Piper came over with more food. And again, it was things I loved, this time cornbread and ham with baked beans and pineapple.

"Vera, I know you don't like to admit you are sick, but I want you to see our doctor." "No, no, Meg, I am all better and plan to play golf tomorrow."

I was enjoying staying home and talking to my Kasparov whenever he called, but the next morning, I hopped in my golf cart after putting my clubs in the back, and headed over for the Women's Nine-Hole Tournament at Barton Hills. It is a Donald Ross golf course that Barnie and I joined decades ago. I will do my best to win so everyone will stop worrying about me. I had my hair done this morning and put on makeup too. I have an eight handicap and have had three holes in one and won the Club Championship five years in a row several decades ago.

As we were playing along, for some reason, I flashback to Anatoly telling me it was Tripp who didn't warn the people on the boat the boom was coming around. The boom which killed his wife, my daughter Cindy. I got such an adrenaline rush that I hit an insanely straight 225-yard drive. It's my best shot of the day, maybe even of my life. I chip up the fairway, and the ball settles a little over a foot away from the hole, and then it starts to move and drops in the cup. An eagle!!

I will win this. Yes, I will.

As our foursome heads to lunch at the golf house, we discuss my 225-yard drive on the eighth hole. It is nice being normal again. "Vera," Christabel smiles at me, "when that ball started rolling, I figured it was Barnie giving you an eagle." I smile so hard at that idea.

Eating lunch, I realize how ravenous I still am. My good friend Betty grins at me, "You have lost far too much weight. I think I need that virus you had." I probably lost ten pounds which I didn't need to do.

Betty, my only actress friend, is still working at our ripe old age. She just returned from a national tour all over the country. She is a real star, and we love to reminisce about acting school when we were at RADA together back in the day.

"Betty," I lean over my potato salad. "Remember a lifetime ago when you wanted to meet someone like my Barnie?"

"Feels like yesterday," she dabs at her mouth with a napkin.

"And so, Barnie asked a very good looking friend of his to have dinner with us right here in this dining room?"

"Oh, God," Betty hangs her beautiful head. She looks back up at me and laughs. "Don't remind me!"

I laugh along with her. "God, you really were so gorgeous. "Were?" she growls. "Oh right, you still are. Sorry. His friend Ted couldn't believe his good luck when you swooped in!"

"Unfortunately for Ted," Betty swallows her Caesar salad. "His luck ran out."

"Did it ever! Two hours later, you were up on the table, showing us how to lasso a steer. And Ted was so goddamn uptight, you pretended to lasso him back in as he was walking out!"

"Poor Ted . . . We were so young and carefree then, weren't we?"

I nod. Tears are running down our faces as we remember the things we did back then that were so ridiculous.

"Remember our vacation to that spa in Arizona?" Betty asks me.

"Of course," I crack a smile as I take a big sip of my iced tea. "It was a thousand degrees, and on the plane home, it was even hotter. No wonder that man collapsed!"

Betty laughs, "I can't believe you told the stewardess you were a doctor!"

"No, that was you! When no real doctor came forward, you, my friend, suggested I tell the stewardess that I wasn't an actual doctor, but I played one on stage so I could maybe at the very least comfort him with the right words . . ."

Betty laughs again. "Oh, God. I think you're right! You held his hand and talked to him about his pulse and blood pressure and his heart rhythms."

"Scalpel and aorta!" I laugh.

"But I bet your pulse was just as high," she elbows me. "He was quite good-looking and very much your type. Tall, blond, and preppy. Like Barnie."

"He asked me out three months later. Did I tell you this?"

"Yes, often Vera." Meg is smiling at me as she sees I am all better, and I feel so happy. I think I should stop this scare right now.

SERGEI, 2

After today's chaos, Didier and I agreed that a change in scenery might be in order to calm all of our nerves. Nannie was given a well-deserved few hours off while Didier, Cleo, and I got in the back of my car. Zelli enjoys sitting in the front with my driver, Vitya, who covertly feeds her candy, which we pretend not to see. Off we went to Gonolezza, one of my favorite restaurants in St. Moritz.

The atmosphere, a wooden cable car that overlooks the Alps, is casual, and the food is good. We all finally relax over raclette, and Aperol spritzes in our fur-covered seats. Didier ensured the bodyguard he hired for Zelli was at the restaurant. He is eating at a table nearby. His name is Bruno, and he constantly surveys the room surreptitiously.

I hope Cleo will keep the merriment when we're back at the hotel. More than anyone in her life, I understand how even a soft murmur about tragedy befalling your child consumes your entire being. Paralyzing, acute anguish that knocks you down to your knees. For me, however, the murmur became a living nightmare.

As Vitya pulled into The Badrutt, I could feel Cleo tense up all over again. She held her breath as if bracing herself for something terrible.

"Matt?" says Cleo in a rather shocked manner, her voice barely above a whisper as the bodyguard holds the door open for us to walk in.

I follow her line of sight until it lands on a young man across the lobby admiring a potted palm tree. He mustn't have heard Cleo because he doesn't turn in our direction.

I'm struck by how little Matt resembles his taller, darker brothers. With his red hair and light skin, the middle Regan son most clearly takes after his mother. I smile to myself, remembering Miranda and how tremendously she enjoyed her cheeseburgers. "Matt Regan?" I whisper to Cleo.

Cleo smiles and nods.

"Does he . . ." I gesture to Zelli.

"Yes, Jake told him a little while ago." She leans down to Zelli. "See that man over there, mon chaton?"

Zelli nods.

"That's Maman's good friend, Matt," Cleo grins. "And he's a very special friend because Matt is also your father's brother." She measures Zelli's reaction.

"I have another uncle besides Uncle Ricky? Is Sergei my uncle too?"

"No, not Sergei," Cleo laughs as she looks up at me. "But you do get Uncle Ricky and Uncle Matt. Should we go say 'hi' to Uncle Matt?"

Zelli nods again. "Yeah!"

"Just remember," Cleo glances up at me. "Matt doesn't like it when other people touch him, so just give him a nice little wave, and that's all. He'll love it."

Zelli and Sergei both nod.

"Is that my favorite Regan brother I see?" Cleo calls out to him.

Matt is already wearing a warm smile when he turns around. "Cleo!"

Cleo opens her arms expectantly. "Just kidding, Matt," she laughs as she puts her arms down.

But Matt is too mesmerized by the little lady whose hand is latched onto her mother's. "Are you . . ."

"Matt, I'd love for you to meet your niece, Zelli Gallier."

Matt can't stop staring. "Hello."

How interesting. Matt is shy. So unlike his brothers.

Zelli can't stop staring at him either, suddenly bashful. "Bonjour," Zelli mumbles. She's clinging onto her mother's leg now.

Cleo and I smile at the sweet moment. She turns to me, "And this is Sergei Kominitz, Matt. Sergei knew your mother and father before you were even born."

The Regan boy looks at me skeptically, like he may not even believe Cleo. "You know my parents?"

I nod, resisting the inclination to shake Matt's hand. "Yes, a very, very long time ago," I smile.

"What are my parents' names?" He challenges me. His eyes are avoiding mine, and his pale face divulges nothing.

I don't miss a beat. "Miranda and Tripp."

An awkward silence envelops us all.

"Do you remember telling me this plant reminded you of me, Matt?" Cleo wisely changes the subject. She lifts an exotic plant from a stand behind her.

Matt smiles at the plant as if it was an old friend. "Yep. It was at the outdoor lunch at our hotel in Honolulu. It was the second time I met you, and you were wearing purple earrings and a purple bathing suit to match your eyes," he says in a robotic tone.

Matt's distaste of touch, avoidance of eye contact, blunt communication style, and attention to small details are obviously high on the spectrum. Earlier, Cleo mentioned that Matt was "different" from his brothers, but she failed to go into any further detail. She's far too kind.

Cleo beams, "That's right. Every day, I laugh to myself and think of you as I walk by the Venus fly trap. And now you're here too! In the flesh!"

"And so is Dionaea muscipula," he nods.

"Maybe you should tell your niece about it?"

Zelli clutches Matt's hand, forgetting her shyness as well as her mother's instructions from thirty seconds before. But, strangely, Matt looks unaffected. He peers down at their interlaced fingers, but he allows it nonetheless as they go and sit in two red upholstered chairs just off the lobby with the Venus flytrap.

Cleo interlocks her arm with mine, and we follow them into the living room, as does Zelli's bodyguard.

"Bien différent de ses frères? hmmm?"

I nod. "Very different from his brothers."

Beneath Zelli and Matt's chairs, elegant dhurrie carpets cover the polished marble floor. The living room is a place where you want to read, talk, or just watch the world coming and going. The chair Zelli is sitting in is so huge compared to her tiny body that the cushions nearly gobble her whole.

Keeping watch from the doorway, Cleo and I laugh as Zelli sinks further into the softness. Cleo's smile fades as her daughter struggles to worm her way out from under a pillow. Cleo takes a step forward, at the ready, but I gently tug at her arm.

"She's okay," I reassure Cleo. "Let her be."

Zelli manages to wiggle out, propelling herself out of the chair and onto the carpet. For a moment, she just sits there in stunned silence. Again, Cleo steps forward, and I tug at her arm.

"I'm just . . . after today . . . I can't bear to . . ."

"Of course. I understand. But look, she's fine."

Zelli looks up at Matt. "Uncle Matt?"

Matt climbs out of his chair to join her on the floor. "I'm here, Zelli. You're okay."

"See," I smile.

Cleo nods, takes a breath, and looks back at her daughter.

"I love plants, Zelli," Matt tells his niece. He's still holding onto the plant that Cleo handed to him. "And this plant is called a Venus Fly Trap. Can you say that?"

She nods but doesn't attempt to.

Matt continues, "This plant reminds me of your mother. Insects and arachnids are drawn to the Venus Fly Trap because it's so lovely, the same way people are attracted to your mother's beauty."

"And you're a little Cleo," Matt says.

Zelli screams with joy. "Me too, me too! I am a . . ." she stops and peers at Matt before gathering herself. "What am I again?" She yawns.

Her head leans against Matt's arm until her eyes flutter and close, exhausted from a long and eventful day. Matt is trapped by a baby Venus Fly Trap. This time, I don't stop Cleo when she goes to her daughter.

"She already adores you, Matt," Cleo whispers, prying Zelli off of him. Cleo waves goodbye, and he looks devastated to see Zelli go. I am sure Matt gets along better with children than adults his own age. The bodyguard hustles past us and pushes the button for the elevator.

"I'll be in touch after Zelli is tucked in," Cleo whispers to me. "Nannie and the bodyguard will be with her, too, but after today, I may not want to leave her side."

I put my hand in hers. "I'm going for a nightcap at King's, so why don't you just text me how you're feeling after Zelli is asleep."

She dazzles me with that magical smile. I pull her close to me, and we kiss as though we are parting forever. But no, I shall never leave her. "Goodbye, my Venus fly trap."

SERGEI, 2

MY ORANGE DRINK SWIRLS inside the heavy rocks glass. It's listed on the cocktail menu at King's Social House as a Naked & Famous. I set it back down on the regal, emerald colored bar and take in my surroundings. King's Social House, part of Badrutt's, is considered by many to be the oldest nightclub in all of Switzerland. Luckily, King's does not turn into a late-night spot for another three hours. I am hardly up for loud music and a swelling crowd.

I take one last sip before I ask to sign the bill. Living on the mountain allows me to sign anywhere in St. Moritz.

"C'est déjà payé," the bartender, Simone, shakes her head.

Ah, apparently, someone has already paid for my drink.

Simone gestures to her left. I look to my right. Our eyes meet. But of course. It's my old friend, Tripp Regan, perched at the far end of the long bar. After three decades apart, we're both stunned by the sight of the other. For some, thirty years is a lifetime, well more than my beloved Dimitri was afforded, and Tripp and I had a tragic end to our time together. For several seconds, we simply stare at each other, summing one another up. I nod, and he nods back at me.

We are two bullfighters from different nations, both heroes in our own lands, electric at the chance to stand face-to-face with another warrior. We have each reached an age where we can enjoy our careers and what we did on our journey.

But personally, our lives turned out so differently from each other. His three sons have surrounded Tripp and Miranda with noise and life. My wife's memory loss, the loss of our son, and our unborn baby are all tied to this man sitting no more than three meters away.

Tripp raises his beer mug. I raise my rocks glass before I give him a parting look and rise out of my seat.

The elevator doors hum open just as I set foot back into Badrutt's marble lobby. And looking as if she were a princess in my own fairy tale, she arrives in a gold satin full-skirted dress with gold sandals and a white fur wrap. It's quite a transformation from thirty minutes ago. Perhaps our kiss inspired this look. At midnight, that dress will be off her. Cleopatra runs to me, throws herself into my arms, and kisses me deeply. I am sure Tripp is witness to this moment. I very much hope he is.

"Are you coming back with me?" I smile down at her.

She smiles back, and off we go to my heated car.

"Sergei, I love you," Cleo says as soon as the car door is shut by Vatya as if she couldn't wait a moment longer to tell me. Her head nuzzles into the crook of my neck, and she rubs her body against mine. "I think what happened today makes me want you. One of my closest friends told me the night her father died she conceived her first child. Life and death"

I feel the same way. "*Vatya, pozhaluysta, voz'mi vykhodnoy.*"

Vatya nods, puts the car in park, and disappears into the night without a word.

We get as far as the end of the parking lot. I stop my car, relieved that the Maserati has such dark windows and wide seats. I pull her dress lower as I slowly unzip it to see what I need to see—her incredible body. My hands are all over her, beginning with her neck. I kiss each part of her as the dress falls off, and she is naked. She pulls my clothes off and kisses every part of me.

And once again, we are in an uncomfortable place—this time in the front seat of my car; too turned on to care about anything except being with each other.

She takes my face in her hands. "Thank you for helping me today, Sergei. No one can understand like you. Especially for what you had to relive . . ." She looks down. "I—I really just can't imagine."

I stroke her arm with my fingertips. "Cleopatra, there is something about my life that you should know."

She sits up in the seat next to mine. "Yes."

"That day," I pause. "I also lost my unborn child. And . . . my wife."

Her lips part, but no words come out of them.

"Well, her mind at least. Sophie still lives in Russia but she doesn't recognize me. She hasn't for almost thirty years." I pause again, allowing space for Cleo to interrupt me. But she doesn't.

"Sophie smiles at me as if I were a guest in my own home. She roams from room to room, her fingers grazing each chair, table, lamp, and vase of flowers. She does this, trailed by her dutiful nurse, thirty or more times a day on repeat every day of the week as if she were a record that keeps spinning the same songs forever."

Again, I wait to see if Cleopatra would like to say anything. But she remains silent, breathing in my words. She nods for me to continue.

"In one day, the life I knew evaporated before my very eyes. But unlike the Samurai, I am no longer already dead. You have rescued me and brought me back to life with a furious vengeance. I am alive again because of you."

Finally, Cleopatra shows me something. A sad smile washes across her face.

"And I must thank you for always wearing my Fabergé egg and the ring," my fingers rub the gold chain dangling from her swan-like neck. "Nothing gets by me, Cleopatra. To my foes in the boardroom or on the polo field, I never let on that I catch every little thing, every innuendo. But to you, the woman I love, I will let on."

That same sad smile again. Cleo sets her hand on my thigh. "Oh, Sergei . . . the pain you live with every day."

I shrug. This moment was never meant to be woe is me or even about my tragedies, but to share them so that I can grow even closer to her.

"And your poor, poor wife. To lose two children in one day . . . My heart breaks for her."

I put my hand on top of Cleo's. "She's alright now. Or, as alright as she can be. She is happy only in Lake Baikal. After I took her to every specialist on just about every continent, I had to accept fate. I see her whenever I go to Russia, though she has no idea who I am."

"Your loyalty to her is wonderful, Sergei." Her fingers nuzzle mine. She gives me the softness and the strength that I have been yearning for. Other women—ah, well, they weren't Cleopatra.

We sit in silence; our hands are held tight. "I am so sorry for her, Sergei. For both of you."

"Don't be, Cleopatra. Please don't cry for me. I just couldn't go on any longer without telling you all of it. There is one more piece I need to tell you about. The man who let go of Dimitri's hand. I saw him in the bar tonight, and we raised our glasses to each other. So maybe it's best if you go to Zelli, and I go home alone tonight."

"Who is the man who raised his glass to you? Did you know he would be here?" I just shake my head that I did know he would be here.

"I will go back to Zelli now—do you really want to be alone? I don't want to be selfish."

"We can all meet for lunch tomorrow," I kiss her on that perfect cheek. "And you are never selfish—well, except for when you eat all of the cheese fondue and drink all of the champagne."

We both smile. After we make ourselves presentable, I turn the car around and deposit her back at the front door of Badrutt's. I open the door for her, and she gets out and tips me. She's genuinely amusing, which is one of my favorite qualities about her. So, I play into the joke.

SERGEI, 2

I bow, "You already tipped me handsomely, Madam."
"It wasn't enough, Monsieur. Your driving is so titillating."
She laughs, and I laugh.
The miracle of love.

DIDIER, 3

An American, a Russian, and a Frenchman are about to go skiing. Three former spies. The Russian, however, is running unusually late.

"Tripp Regan," the American says, offering his hand with a polite smile. "Great to finally meet you, Didier. I've heard stories about you."

"I'm sure they fall short and I have heard stories about you," I respond, taking Tripp Regan's outstretched hand in a firm handshake.

A knowing glimpse briefly passes between us. In one breath, Tripp appears to be stunned by my comment but also as if he were expecting it. "Cleopatra and I might have our secrets, but we know when to reveal them," I whisper, my eyes lingering on Tripp just a moment too long.

Tripp grimaces. "Indeed," he says, his eyes holding mine just a moment too long. "But actually, I was referring to . . . your work."

"Ah, my work," I say with a measured smile, my eyes holding a poker face of their own. "The next time you find yourself in Algeria, you must come and pay my vineyards a visit. I tend to keep some very interesting company that you might enjoy."

Tripp returns my smile, his eyes searching mine for any sign of weakness. "Consider it done."

"Excellent. A meeting of the finest, most venerated grandfathers in their homelands," I add.

Tripp laughs with a slight tinge, deciphering my code.

And thus, that is how it goes in the intricate play between us. Tripp's agency might adhere to its own rules, but The Business? We stand apart. Our ranks are filled with those who've carved their own destinies—be it through lineage, wealth, or sheer brilliance. Using our network of connections to get the job done is one of our greatest strengths.

While we don't have to report to anyone, we chase a common goal: a brighter world, however trite that may sound. Publicly, I may be a respected aristocrat with vineyards in Algeria and Paris, but behind the scenes, the game of espionage is my true calling.

Now that I'm in my midseventies, I watch as, day by day, the sun slowly sets on my career.

"Have you been to St. Moritz before, Tripp? We will ski and then have lunch at my club, The Evergreen, where you will finally meet Zelli. She's the joy of my life."

"Thanks so much, I'm really looking forward to meeting her. Hard to believe we're old enough to be grandfathers," he laughs, revealing two rows of straight, white teeth.

"I like to think there's a certain dignity in being the elder of your tribe."

As Tripp knows, our granddaughter is currently on the bunny slope with her uncles, aunt, and the bodyguard I used since the kidnapping event, who will keep his distance but miss nothing.

"I was sorry to hear that your wife, Miranda, couldn't accompany you."

"Yeah, next time. When you meet her one day, you'll see that she's not big on spontaneity. I think this was just a bridge too far, but she sends all of her love."

Something tells me dear Miranda does not have a clue about my daughter's past with her husband. In fact, it wouldn't surprise me to learn that Miranda believes her husband to be a full-time attorney. "Well, Cleo had lovely things to say about her. It sounds as if she will be a wonderful grandmother to our Zelli."

"Yeah, of course. When I called to tell her the good news about Zelli, she totally flipped out. Now she's devastated that she's not here."

"WELL, WE'LL HAVE TO FIND TIME for Miranda to meet her. Zelli hasn't been to the mainland yet, only Hawaii," I tell Tripp. "She goes to school in Paris, so perhaps Miranda would enjoy a visit to the City of Love."

"Oh, yeah. Miranda is already on my case to learn some French," Tripp laughs.

"Cleo also tells me that you suffered a most unfortunate accident a few years ago in Honolulu . . ."

Tripp gives me a funny look, and I cannot discern whether he's surprised that this episode was on my radar or if he is unsure which episode I'm referring to.

"You were blinded for months, isn't that right?"

"Oh, yeah. Just over two years ago. I've tried to block it out."

"How frightening. Have you been skiing since?"

He shakes his head and laughs. "No, this will be interesting. It's been about five years . . ."

"Ah, with an athlete like you . . . it should be like riding a bicycle, as you Americans say."

"Let's hope." He glances down at his watch. "Where is Sergei, anyway?"

"Good question. Let's give him a few more minutes, and then I will call."

Tripp nods. He takes a step closer to me, his voice dropping to a hushed tone. "Any more insight about yesterday? I want to catch that damn bastard," he says through gritted teeth.

"As do I. No leads as of yet, but rest assured, I have alerted my contacts. They are aware that this is of the utmost importance, but you and I know that whoever he is, he is long gone."

Tripp nods.

"May I ask you something?"

"Shoot."

"I've been running through each scenario . . . is there any possibility of an unresolved issue from your undercover days? You know, old enemies resurfacing or something like that?"

"I thought of that. But, as far as I know, *they're* all long gone. Dead." he smirks.

I nod. I hope he's right.

"My guys have been monitoring the airports and train stations," Tripp continues. "In total, I think they pulled aside twelve different suspects who matched his description. But then, after reviewing their phone records and which towers they dinged, none put them at Corviglia."

"Jake says he'd recognize him in a line-up."

"Right, but getting to the line-up's the challenge."

I nod. "Between your connections and mine, we'll get to the bottom of this." At least that is what I must keep telling myself and Cleopatra, but I'd be surprised if he was even in our time zone anymore.

My network stretches past every corner, and there's no stone or pebble that I won't turn over until the man who put his hands on my granddaughter is punished. I always get my target.

Just ask the man who tried to assassinate my friend, Joaquin Balaguer, the president of the Dominican Republic.

At the very beginning of my career, many of Rafael Trujillo's supporters were incensed when Joaquin appointed General Antonio Imbert Barrera as his Defense Minister. Considering that Imbert had Trujillo assassinated, the outrage was perhaps justified. Several years later, I found myself visiting political friends in Casa de Campo when I started to hear rumblings about a possible attempt on Joaquin's life. Beyond the typical scuttlebutt, he was mainly unaware of the threats, but since I was nearby anyway, Joaquin asked me to look into it.

It didn't take me long. Once I effectively identified an extremist group of local Trujillo supporters, the threat was neutralized, and the entire gang was disbanded. To this day, none of them have been able to return home to the Caribbean.

My reward for tracking down Joaquin's would-be assassins was eighteen holes at the finest course in all of the Dominican Republic, Teeth of the Dog, with my friend Roman. We were all alone—the course was ours! The only pursuit that I enjoy as much as a morning on the mountain is a late afternoon on the greens.

It may sound trite, but the greatest lesson I have learned is to expect the unexpected. Eight years ago, Cleopatra sought refuge at my home in Dubai for nearly two years to get over her wounds in the wake of her heartbreak over Danny (a.k.a. Tripp Regan). If someone had told me that one day, I would share a granddaughter with this man . . . Quite frankly, I would have suggested that they get their head examined. But, here we are . . .

I hear the crunch of snow drawing near. Tripp senses it, too, because we both turn at the same moment to find Sergei in his black ski suit on the approach. I smile, "He hath risen!"

"He hath," Sergei shrugs and puts his skis down to slip into them.

I am trying to read his expression, a mission impossible if there ever was one.

Sergei Kominitz has a world-class poker face, and I should know, with my experience working alongside heads of state, business leaders, and politicians who were all brilliant at not showing their hands. It appears as if Sergei has only been looking at me then, finally, Sergei turns to Tripp.

"Sorry to be late. I haven't been checking in with my office lately and needed to tie up a few dealings. I apologize."

Yet another cliche lesson that I have learned along the way, the world is a much smaller place than you think. And the older you get, it only gets smaller. What fun it is that in another lifetime, Sergei and Tripp studied the law inside a cold University of Michigan library. And now, here we all are, thirty years later—two former spies, the same two of us grandfathers to the most marvelous little girl, and one in a romance with her mother. I know Sergei never worked in the spy world after law school. Instead, he made a fortune and used that to stay away from the field of intelligence and Putin.

When Sergei finally turns to Tripp, they end up sharing a deafening moment of silence. I know what that's all about. Sergei seemingly struggles to remove his hand from his ski glove, then stretches his arm outward.

"It's good to see you, Tripp," says the Russian.

"You too," says the American. "You too."

"Shall we?"

Considering that Tripp is long out of practice, I decided to ease us into the day with gentle runs. How I yearn for the days when my knees did not creak, and my joints did not ache. When you're young and take a break from skiing, your body can quickly recover, like a yoyo. But as you reach your seventies, it's a very different story.

As the three of us go up and away in the gondola, I point out Stanchion 32. "There's the Chowtel. See?"

"The what-tel?" Tripp crinkles his brow as he peers down below.

I laugh. "It's what they call the jump when you leap out of the chairlift onto that treacherous slope."

"Shall we give it a go on the next run?" Sergei asks with that legendary straight face.

Tripp looks stunned.

"Uh . . . maybe in our law school days, bucko . . . I'd probably pop a disc if I did it now," Tripp says and claps Sergei on the back.

"I'm afraid Tripp's right. And now we have a granddaughter to think about."

"A convenient excuse," Sergei smiles.

"Hey, by all means, old sport. If you're still up for it . . ." Tripp gestures to the mountain.

"Yes, we'd be happy to escort you on the chairlift."

Sergei glances down at the fall line, and his face twists. "We'll see . . . I did it several times before Christmas,"

"Of course . . ." Tripp peers down at the mountain again. "I don't know. If we were in our prime . . ."

"Oh, yes. *Un jeu d'enfant*," I say.

"*Dazhe yozhik ponimayet*," adds Sergei.

"Piece of cake," Tripp agrees.

Once we have completed a trifecta of platitudes, we share a laugh.

We glide off the gondola, into our skis, and onto the powder. We each take a moment before putting our sunglasses on to absorb the sunlight reflecting off the bright snow.

"Helluva day," exhales Tripp as he takes in the three-hundred-and-sixty-degree views.

"Bluebird," Sergei nods.

"I read somewhere that in Iroquois culture, the call of the bluebird is believed to ward off Sawiskera, the spirit of winter,"

I impart my enlightened wisdom onto Sergei and Tripp. And by "read somewhere," what I really mean is an asset told me that while I was undercover in Montreal.

My old friend and my new friend feign interest, not quite as enthralled with fun facts about the spirit world as my daughter.

Sergei flicks his head, and off he goes like a rocket. In seconds, his body is a black blur.

Tripp looks over at me and nods.

"After you."

Seconds later, I glance over my shoulder and find that Tripp is in my wake. And this is how it went for three invigorating runs: Sergei, our fearless leader, followed by me, with Tripp taking up the rear. As most field agents are, Tripp is remarkably dexterous with lightning-quick reflexes, but he's the one to tire first. Understandable, given how out of practice he is, especially when compared to Sergei and me, though I am a good twenty years older than both of them.

Halfway through our fourth run, Tripp stops and turns to us. "Time for lunch, gents?" he cracks a smile, his voice breathless.

"Of course. The Evergreen is just a bit further down. Follow me," I say, and off we go again.

We walk into the club. Sergei and I wave hello to a group of our friends, each with a drink in hand, lounging about in cozy, cushy armchairs and wooden benches adorned with crimson and chocolate brown pillows. For a group of only six, I detect at least three different languages—French, Italian, and German.

"*Jour parfait!*" Camille raises her glass.

I bring my fingers to my lips, miming a chef's kiss. "*Magnifique. Je suis resté debout tout le temps!*"

"*Moi aussi!*" Sergei chimes in.

My friends laugh, I introduce them to Tripp, and after pleasantries are exchanged, we continue on our way toward my table across the room by the imposing bay windows that offer some of the best views on the mountain. Tripp glances around at the black-and-white photos of snow scenes, skiers sitting on the terrace, and gorgeous women on the walls, all in ski clothes.

"Would you like a drink, Tripp? I usually have a hot toddy the moment I come in."

He doesn't answer. His eyes are lost in a photo directly in front of him.

"God," Tripp gasps. "I forgot how beautiful she was."

JULIA, 5

I take in the stunning views for the last time and feel pangs of guilt. The Swiss Alps in wintertime are heart-stopping. But even beauty can be impossible to relish with the threat of danger lurking behind every door and between each corridor. Unless you're Michael Douglas in an erotic thriller from the 1990s where being bad with the hot yet deadly femme fatale never felt so goddamn good. But I'm no Sharon Stone, and sadly, I forgot my ice pick at home.

If only I could enjoy my last twenty-four hours on a holiday we can hardly afford in a winter wonderland for rich people way out of our league.

"Hurry up, Auntie Julia!" Zelli giggles back at me as she pizzas down the bunny slope again.

I stick my poles into the snow and thrust off of them for speed. "Coming!"

As he's been all morning, Matt is dutifully by his niece's side, rendering the "bodyguard" that Didier brought in completely unnecessary. I glance to my right and force a smile at Bruno or whatever his name is. He looks like a linebacker with his height and broad shoulders. By all accounts, Bruno should put my mind at ease—his imposing stature striking fear in the eyes of my pesky stalker and maybe even scaring him off entirely. But it doesn't. Even though Bruno has been paid a pretty penny to follow us around, now he just feels like one more stalker I've got to shake.

I've already gained one in my husband since I finally came clean about the man in the Belgian loafers. Talk about following me around . . . It's sweet, of course. How Ricky will hardly let me out of his sight for half a second.

The four of us—excuse me, five, including our new friend, Bruno—are gathered at the bottom of the slope, our little post-run ritual of the morning.

"One more!" Zelli shrieks, lifting both poles in the air.

"Yeah, one more!" Matt gleefully agrees. It's fantastic seeing him getting along with a living thing that doesn't have petals or roots.

Ricky looks at me, then down at his Tag Heuer. "I'm sorry, guys, but I don't think we have time. We're supposed to meet the fam for lunch in ten minutes, and it'll take that long to get up there."

Matt always hated skiing, but it seems like Zelli has transformed him into a total ski freak.

"We'll be quick, Ricky," Matt smiles.

Damn. Zelli has wrapped Matt around her tiny, little finger.

"Dude, I think Dad's pretty anxious to meet Zelli."

"Please, please, pretty please," Zelli begs, old enough to understand the effectiveness of puppy-dog eyes.

Ricky and I trade looks again. I love how he always makes me feel part of his team.

"I'll handle your dad," I smile at Ricky, then turn to Tweedle Dee and Tweedle Dum. "Okay, one more, but let's be quick like bunnies!"

The four of us, sorry, five, glide over to the chairlift and get in the line, which is, mercifully, very short.

Having Tripp in St. Moritz has been moderately comforting, but not so much that I'm able to kick my shoes off and let my hair down. He's like a father who gasses you up before a field hockey game you have no chance of winning. You feel momentarily hopeful, inspired even, but then reality comes flooding over you once the bigger, stronger, angrier foes step onto the field, and a bitter reality sets in. And now that the cat's out of the bag and purred a hello to most of the Regan family, I feel like Mia Farrow in *Rosemary's Baby.*

Ricky, Jake, and Tripp are all entertaining my bizarre, perhaps even paranoid suspicions—for now. And they say they'll do whatever they can to help find this creepy stalker man, but for all I know, the whole lot of them are just being polite. To my face, they're killing me with kindness, all the while having secret side conversations about how pregnant ol' Jules has really lost her marbles this time.

It's moments like these that make me wish my mother was here. It's every moment, really, but especially the lonelier ones where I feel adrift even from a loving family that's not really my own—not the way she was. She'd know just what to say. She always knew just what to say.

"This thing makes me chafe like a mother fucker," my very own Shakespeare of a husband says, tugging at the crotch of his Gore-Tex suit.

"I'm so sorry to hear that, babe," I say as we ski toward The Evergreen Club after our extra run.

Zelli and Matt are several paces ahead of us, trailed a few feet behind by the ever-present Bruno.

"Not as much as I am," he laughs and points to a large wooden structure about one hundred yards away. "I think that's it, over there."

"Oh, how pretty," I say. "It looks like a cabin you'd see on a postcard."

"Greetings from St. Moritz, an icy playground for people with way more money than you," jokes Ricky as we ski up to the club.

Zelli, Matt, and Bruno are apparently too busy to give us so much as a wave before they hurry inside.

"Do you think Matt will like our kid as much as he's obsessed with Zelli?" I laugh as Ricky and I kick off our skis.

"Doubt it."

"Damn."

We stick our poles in the snow and are about to head in when the most delightful sleigh pulls up to the club. Sadly, no red-nosed reindeers in sight, but there is a pretty white horse that matches the snow. I'm absolute shit with horses, so I couldn't tell you if it's an Arabian, a Clydesdale, or a Pomeranian. It's pretty, and it's a horse. The elderly man steps out of the sleigh first, then stretches out one hand to assist his lady companion.

"Oh!" she squeals as her foot catches on the lip of the sleigh. The elderly woman topples over and lands in the snow with a thump.

"Oh, no! Are you okay?" Ricky hurries over to the couple and helps the poor woman get on her feet.

She brushes the snow off of her clothes and smiles. "Well, I believe that's all the excitement I need for one day!"

"Are you alright, my dear? I'm so sorry, I tried to catch you, but it all happened so fast!" the man asks in a very posh English accent, grabbing onto her hand.

She nods and turns to Ricky. "Thank you, young man. Goodness, I'm quite embarrassed."

"Oh, don't be," I chime in. "He's seen me take far more humiliating tumbles than that."

"It's true," Ricky laughs.

The woman's eyes volley off of Ricky and back to me. "What a lovely couple you make."

"Oh, yes," her husband agrees without making eye contact.

"Are you in St. Moritz long?" the woman asks, whose name we haven't caught.

"Just until tomorrow, actually," I say.

"Oh, what a shame. Well, don't let us keep you. Enjoy your last day!" she says.

"Thank you," I grin, turning to go inside. I'd rather not be any later than we already are.

"Be careful," Ricky smiles back at the woman as he opens the door for me.

"Who did he remind you of?" I ask Ricky once we're inside The Evergreen Club.

"Uh . . ."

I try to think of it. "I think he's a mix of Burt Reynolds and Gene Hackman . . ."

"What a combo!"

TRIPP, 4

I stumble, moving closer for a better look.

"Friend of yours?"

My brain registers that Didier has just asked me a simple question, but it's all white noise. The entire room blurs and fades. The only thing that remains in focus is Cindy's face. Cindy's gorgeous, perfect face before her life was destroyed. All I can think about is ripping the frame off the wall and bringing it back home.

"Tripp? Are you alright?"

"Sorry," I mumble as I come out of my trance. "I, um. Wow. Blast from the past."

"Who is she?" Sergei asks.

I take another step closer to the photo, more to ensure that I'm not hallucinating. I hold my breath. It's really her. How young she looks. This photo was taken before we even met. She always reminded me of Grace Kelly. It's Cindy Lowe in her Olympic skating outfit, holding her bronze medal.

"You look like you've seen a ghost," Didier smiles.

Interesting choice of words. I have. I point at the photo, "That's Cindy. My first wife."

An ironic moment of silence.

"She's lovely, Tripp. Just as you described," Sergei adds.

"Cindy died about a year after we got married," I say to Didier. "It was a horrible boating accident."

I can't tear my eyes away from her.

"I'm sorry," Didier says finally.

"I remember you telling me about her when we were young. It's funny how time heals all wounds until it doesn't, and one tiny little thing transports you back into a memory," says my old friend.

"Yeah, I just . . ." I pause. "I'm embarrassed by how much this little photo has knocked me off my game."

"Why don't we sit and have a drink?" Didier asks.

I nod warily before the three of us take a seat at Didier's table.

"Did she—your wife—come to St. Moritz often?" Didier asks me, maybe just trying to fill the silence.

"Yeah, well, probably as a little girl. But I can't imagine she would with all the training she did for the Olympics. One fall and she'd be out . . ." I trail off.

"Remind me of her name, Tripp," Sergei asks.

"Cindy Regan—well, she would've been Cindy Lowe back then."

"Cindy Lowe . . ." Didier thinks. "Doesn't ring any bells. "But . . ." something over my shoulder grabs his attention. "Ah, Cleo and Lola have arrived. Lola knows absolutely everyone; let's ask her."

"No, Didier, that's alright. We don't have to make a big thing of it," I insist. The last thing I need is a table full of near strangers chatting about my dead wife.

Except I'm not sure Didier and Sergei got the message. Sergei lights up, and he's already out of his seat as if Cleo has a gravitational pull over him. And Didier might be distracted by the colorful feathers on the woman I assume is his friend Lola's sweater, as she and Cleo move over to us.

"How was the skiing? We found new snow in the back bowls," Cleo smiles at Sergei.

"Wonderful. I only wish I was there with you," he smiles back. "And you know Tripp Regan, don't you?"

"Tripp," Cleo shines her light in my direction, and we hug. In an undercover life, Cleo and I fell in love. In this one, she's the mother of my first grandchild. Ain't life funny. "Great to see you, Cleo. You look exactly the same. One of these days, you'll have to spread the love and tell us your secret."

She pecks her father on the cheeks before Didier turns back to me. "Oh, and Tripp. This is my friend, Lola de la Falaise, the one I was telling you about."

"Ah, mon amour, Didier," Lola kisses him as she turns my way in a fur-trimmed tan ski suit. A matching fur hat covers her graying blond hair. She takes it off, and her hair tumbles out in perfect waves.

"Pleasure to meet you, Lola. Tripp Regan," I shake her hand.

"And you, Tripp Regan," Lola dazzles.

Didier clears his throat. "Lola, my dear, Tripp and I were wondering if you happen to know this woman?" he points to the framed photo of Cindy on the wall.

This is precisely what I wanted to avoid.

"Her maiden name was Cindy Lowe," I force a smile.

Lola waltzes over to the wall and takes a closer look. "Cindy Lowe . . ." she repeats. "Oh, yes. But I knew her parents better. Such a pretty girl." Then Lola turns back to me. "It was such a shame what happened to her."

Here we go.

"Yeah, it was," I nod, hoping to leave it at that.

"Were you and Cindy . . ." Lola lowers her voice and stares with menace at me. I must be mistaken, but.

"She was my wife."

"Oh, you poor thing. I'm so sorry to hear that. How dreadful that must have been for you," Lola pouts. No menace at all.

The waiter mercifully comes to our table and takes our drink orders, giving us a brief respite from this god-awful conversation. I'm in desperate need of a large stiff scotch.

"Tripp," Cleo calls to me from across the round wooden table. "Did you say you knew one of the women in the photos?"

Jesus. Where's an ejection button when you need it? All eyes are on me. "Yeah. Cindy. She was my first wife. We got married right out of college," I pause. "But, a little over a year later, there was an accident on a boat."

Everyone is still staring at me.

"The boom hit her head, and then . . . yeah. That was it."

Lola adds without hesitation: "I read her father's obituary recently. When was the funeral? I'm sure you were there for her mother. She had no one but her daughter who died so tragically." And I see menace again.

"Were you, Tripp?" Cleo asks me. "Of course, you were."

I don't answer. I can't answer. I wasn't there.

THE FULL STORY IS THIS. One day, Cindy and I were out sailing on Lake Michigan with our large, fun-loving group of friends from college. The sun was shining, the wind was howling, and the wine was flowing. It was a perfect day on the water. Everyone was having a blast, laughing nonstop. We were so young then. Our biggest concern was what we were going to eat for dinner that night.

But then, in an instant, all the laughter stopped. I was the captain that day. I was supposed to alert everyone on board that I was tacking the sail from starboard to port. But the mood was loose, and so, in my moderately inebriated mind, I forgot to. Minutes earlier, Cindy had gone below to use the bathroom and grab some more ice. As soon as I released the boom, a bad feeling came over me. I will never forget the sound. The sound of the boom hitting Cindy in the back of her head. We called for help, and she went to the hospital, but she was brain-dead. That was well over thirty years ago, and I haven't been in a sailboat since. Doubt I ever will.

"Her mother was lovely too. She was an actress," Lola says, thankfully shifting the subject slightly.

I nod, "That's right."

"Years and years ago, I saw her as Ophelia in London. She was spectacular. I remember we had dinner afterward at Boulestin; she had just gotten engaged. She was contemplating whether or not she would leave the stage because she didn't want it to steal her away from her future husband and children every night and weekend."

I'm about to respond to Lola when I feel a light tug on my pants pocket. I smile at what I find down there. She's the cutest, most radiant little thing that I've ever seen. And my God, is she the spitting image of her mother.

Zelli has inherited Cleo's hair, dimples, and smile, but she has Jake's blue eyes. My blue eyes.

"Do you know who that is, Zelli?" Cleo asks her.

Zelli nods, and a small smile widens across her cherubic face. Oh, those dimples . . .

"That's your other grandfather," Cleo comes over and kneels next to Zelli.

"Your new favorite grandfather . . ." I nudge Didier.

"It's so nice to meet you, Zelli," I stick my hand out even though I'm not sure four year olds even do that yet.

Zelli takes my hand in hers, and I suddenly feel like a giant compared to her tiny, delicate features. Fee-fi-fo-fum.

"I'm so glad to be your grandfather, Zelli," I smile again.

"Thank you," says her tiny voice. She moves away and tries to coax Matt outside.

"Please can we go, Matt! I want to throw snowballs with you," she smiles.

"Can I also throw some with you, Zelli?"

Zelli gives me a shy smile. "*Mais oui*, but you must be on your own team so Matt and I can throw snowballs at you. Then we will win!"

And off we go.

VERA, 6

The pawn calls me at a strange time, much earlier than usual. "Yes, is anything wrong?"

"As you suggested, I improvised, which, of course, I have been doing all along. You were right to tell us to trust our instincts. So this time, I called a friend in Winterthur outside of Zurich and asked her to join me for a few days in St. Moritz and pretend to be my wife. She was there in a flash as I had her fly private with the money you gave me. We took a sleigh to lunch at the Evergreen Club. She tripped getting out of the sleigh, but a nice man helped her up. He was with his wife, and they are leaving soon. His wife is the woman I have been stalking. She didn't recognize me as I am now dressed like an elderly bookwormish man.

I didn't say much and my partner, Fischer, I dubbed her for the famous chess player Bobby Fischer, caught on and did the talking. When we entered the Evergreen, it was as if I walked onto your chess board. We got the table close to them, which you had told the club to give me, so we were privy to their conversations. They had a photo of your daughter holding her Olympic medal. One of them said she had known you when you were doing Ophelia in London, so your name was mentioned. That is why I am calling you to let you know you are now in their minds. And to tell you how upset he was by seeing the photo of your lovely child."

"Not upset enough."

I think I am insane.

But, if you think that, you are not insane.

What am I doing?

I am rich and still look and feel surprisingly well for my octogenarian age. I am healthy and intelligent and well-liked and athletic.

What am I doing?

I lost my husband, but so have many women. I lost my only child, which, fortunately, other women have not had to do. But there is so much pain and hunger and suffering in this world. Why am I adding to that?

I am insane, but what fun this insanity is. How dare I have caused pain to his family. He alone deserves the pain. Dear God, I miscalculated. I went after his innocent family. He thought I was insignificant so he could disregard me, and I would fade away. I was asserting my presence through these scares as I didn't want to be dismissed. I want revenge, and it is addictive because it allows me to see I still have an impact on life.

I AM GOING TO CALL ANATOLY on my Blackphone. Fortunately, Barnie gave him one years ago. Anatoly is the one who came here and told me Tripp Regan, Cindy's beloved husband, was the reason for her death. He had written statements from everyone on the boat. Others before had tried to tell me who was responsible, but I had refused to listen.

JAKE, 11

I'm doin' it, baby. I need a release. Ever since I saw him take the plunge, the Chowtel's been calling my name. And now, my friend, the time has come.

ALL OF THE ADRENALINE AND ANXIETY from yesterday's nightmare just keeps bouncing around my body, ricocheting from organ to organ. The tension needs out. And of all my old vices that come to mind, of which—trust me—there are several, the Chowtel is by far the healthiest option.

MY SKIS KNOCK TOGETHER while I peer down at the mountain below, giving myself a Vince Lombardi-style pep talk as I sit alone on the chair lift. Doubt suddenly washes over me like an unexpected avalanche that starts barreling down the mountain on an otherwise sunny day. But this is what I love, I remind myself. This is the type of daredevil shit I was born to do. Punching the clock at The CIA has never been for the faint of heart. No, it's for the brave ones, the show-offs, and the pistols who grab life by the balls and put their lives on the line every chance they get. What defines someone who's brave isn't that they simply aren't afraid of the boogeyman. It's that they can look the boogeyman directly in those ugly-ass demon eyes and tell him to take a hike.

I shut my eyes and take a big inhale—breathing positivity into my muscles and bones. And then I breathe out, letting go of my fears, doubts, and all of my negativity. When I open my eyes again, I look down at the mountain one last time as the chairlift approaches stanchion 32. I slide forward, lift my poles, pull up the guard rail, and bend my knees.

And then I jump.

I'm flying. The cold wind slaps me across the face and smacks through every nook and cranny in my suit, goggles, and hat. It's a bizarre sensation but an exhilarating one. And it goes by way too fast. Before I know it, my skis crash onto the hard ground. There's nothing that can prepare you for that moment. Either you land on your feet, or you don't. And by the grace of whoever's upstairs, I do. Well, I sort of do. It ain't graceful, but at least it's not a dumpster fire. My neck snaps back, and I let out the loudest groan as I try to regain control of my haphazard limbs as they bob up and down.

I hear sprinklings of scattered applause. My head bobbles from one side to another, and it takes me a second to realize that the person they're all cheering on is yours truly. Looks like we've got a bunch of lawbreakers in our midst because, technically, doing the Chowtel is illegal due to the severe risk to life. Laws, schmaws.

Who gives a rat's ass when the adrenaline is this damn good.

I'm euphoric. I've been on runner's high and surf stoke zillions of times, but what I'm enjoying right now doesn't even compare. I feel like Tom Brady in Super Bowl LI after he crawled out of a 28–3 hole to come back and beat the Falcons late in the fourth quarter. Or Tiger Woods when he won his first Masters at the ripe old age of twenty-one. Or Jackie Robinson when he broke the—okay, now I'm getting carried away. I laugh out loud at my own hubris. As the run starts to flatten out near the bottom, I crane my neck and look at the sky through the trees.

Against the white snow, right away, the red catches my eye. I'd recognize my ski poles anywhere too. I veer to my left and see for myself. No. It can't be.

There, hanging on my navy and gold poles, is a red ski coat. I recognize the St. Moritz Ski Patrol patch on the right sleeve first.

"What the fuck," I mumble to myself.

I yank the coat off my poles and check the pockets. Holy shit, my phone. What else does he have in there? I fish around some more and feel something. A folded piece of paper:

Jake,

Congratulations on surviving the Chowtel. I am even more impressed now than when you made it out of the whiteout. But I was with you all the way that day. Seemed like you felt my presence!! It's over now.

Checkmate.

I repeat, "What the fuck?"

A chill runs up and down my body, and it's not because of the frosty air. I look over my right shoulder, then my left. He's long gone. How could his coat and my poles have been here since yesterday? Wouldn't someone have seen them? Maybe not, unless dozens of other people with death wishes suddenly had an inkling to jump out of the chair lift. I didn't see another soul as I came down.

My vibrating phone makes me jump. I reach into my pocket to find a new text from Ricky. *Hey. We're all at lunch. You coming?* Shit, I glance at the time and realize that I've totally lost track of it. I'm already ten minutes late. My cold fingers fly across the keyboard. *Yup, be there in twenty.* I shove White Ski Suit's creepy note into my pocket along with my other phone and head to a ski lift where I can leave the red coat and get to lunch.

Ever since Prince Harry was photographed with his flavor of the week stumbling out of The Evergreen Club back in college, I knew that I had to go one day. And now, because of my daughter, of all people, I finally have that golden ticket.

"Jake! Behind you!" My youngest brother calls my name.

I whip my head around to find both of my brothers, my father, sister-in-law, Didier, Sergei, Lola, Cleo, and my daughter all seated around a large, circular table made of oak that has hot toddies and mugs of hot cocoa scattered all over it. The whole damn gang. We all say our hellos and I take a seat in the empty chair in between my father and Ricky.

"Get some good runs in?" Dad asks.

I slide my father the note under the table. It seems like everyone's in pretty good spirits, and I don't want to send them all into a tizzy before I have to.

My father gives me a look before he unfolds the note. He reads it once, twice, then looks over at me again. "Is that him?" he whispers.

I whisper back. "Who else?"

"Checkmate?" "It's all over now"?

I shrug. "That struck me as kind of odd too. Well, the whole thing is fucking weird, but that part in particular."

"What's going on?" Ricky nudges me from my other side.

Before I can show my brother the note, a man in a waiter's uniform stops by our table. "Nico wanted me to give these to you," he says. The waiter is about to hand what looks like a small stack of photos to Sergei, but Sergei points to my father, and the waiter turns to hand them to him instead.

"*Spasiba*," Sergei smiles. "Merci. Sometimes, my Russian comes out first. Speaking of Russia, I gather Fyodor Akapov, who has been dead for two years, was on the chairlift yesterday. I went to his funeral in Moscow. He was a great friend of Putin and most likely here as a ghost. He was adept at poisoning his enemies. I wonder who he was here to kill." Didier looks at Lola, who has gone white, and gives her the Russian "OK" sign. She gets up, and Didier puts his hand out.

"Lola, my dear, I'll walk you to the door as you tell me who you were spying on, Sergei or me? And who was your husband here to kill? I know he is/was a friend of Putins and Anatoly Rustikoff."

I can hear him, as I imagine I am supposed to.

She leans over Didier, brushes his cheek with her lips, and responds in Russian, a language I know well.

"Neither of you, my dear. You see, you're not on this board. I truly enjoyed being with you, as I hope you did me. This was a favor for a very good friend. And now it's nearly over. Checkmate."

What the hell is with the Checkmates?

Lola puts a hand in her parka, taking out a tiny chess piece of a queen. She puts it on the table facing my father. She blows a kiss to Zelli, and then elegantly leaves us. Is the poison for my father?

Sergei and Didier look at each other and exchange a smile. Dad is too engrossed with his pictures to even understand the weight of what has just happened. But I certainly know something big's gone down. Lots of chess analogies and a queen piece Lola aimed at my father.

Dad's just leafing through four or five old monochrome photos that look like they were taken here at Evergreen a million years ago. It takes me a minute to snap out of Lola's grand departure and realize that the same blond woman is in every photo. It takes me another moment until I recognize her.

"Wait, is that . . . ?"

My father nods without looking up from the photos.

"Holy shit. Is that Cindy?" asks Ricky from over my shoulder.

He never talks about Cindy. But he had to tell his sons that she existed when we were all in high school. One Saturday morning, when Matt was feeling particularly restless, he found himself holed up in the basement sorting through old boxes. At which point, he stumbled upon a wedding album starring my dad as the proud groom and another woman who was definitely not our mother as the blushing bride. I'll never forget the look on Matt's face when he and Ricky stormed into my room as if they'd just seen dead people. I quickly stuffed my Playboy under a pillow and saw what all the fuss was about.

Matt peers down at one of the photos from over Dad's shoulder. "She looks like Cleo with blond hair."

How ironic. I never made that connection before, but now that I'm looking at photos of Cindy after all this time, I catch Matt's drift. Just then, the waiter appears at my side. "Anything to drink, sir?"

"Yes, I'd love a glass of Veuve Clicquot, please," I say to the waiter with a suggestive smile at my father.

"Oo, are we celebrating?" Julia chimes in.

"I wouldn't go that far. But I did manage to . . . do the Chowtel about an hour ago." I hold for applause.

Everyone looks over at me as if I've just told them I was nominated for an Oscar.

My father strikes first. "Really? You did that?"

Then Didier. "Splendid! Good for you, Jake. You have joined the Club with Sergei, Cleo, and me!"

Then Cleo. "Zelli, did you hear that? Your daddy did the Chowtel!"

RICKY. "SCREW YOU, DUDE," he laughs, the jealousy killing him.

And finally, Julia. "What the heck is the Chowtel?"

The whole table erupts into laughter. And throughout lunch, the Chowtel is all we talk about. It's a nice change of pace from kidnappers and stalkers. Everyone is having a great time together. It makes me wish I was a part of Zelli's life years ago, but at least we're all here now. But I wonder if the poisoner ghost is still here.

After my father excuses himself for the bathroom, Didier turns to me. "Does your father have any enemies?"

"Enemies?"

"Or, perhaps, there's someone at the CIA with a vendetta?"

I know why he's asking me this. I've already asked myself these questions twenty times. "Not that I know of. My father is shockingly well-liked."

"There just appears to be a strong revenge angle to the alleged targets, and they're all related to him. You, Julia, Zelli."

"True, except Julia and Zelli are also related to me. And more directly."

"So is it your instinct that this is about you, not your father? Certainly possible. Enemies?"

"Anatoly Rustikoff."

Didier looks at Sergei, who laughs softly. "I was warned off Didier by Anatoly, who lives near me at Lake Baikal. He told me I was 'dining with the spy of spies' when we were in Sochi several years ago. Didier thought he was flying under the radar, but Anatoly's radar is everywhere."

"Yes, he even sent me a canary in a cage when I was at a rendezvous in Hawaii after Dad recovered from his blindness. How he knew I was there was quite a surprise. So pulling these stunts is in keeping with that cage he sent me, but he is upping the fear." I glanced at Cleo as we were together when the cage and bird arrived two years ago. She is pretending she didn't hear me and is chatting with Zelli, who is sitting on her lap, feeding her popcorn one at a time.

Didier looks at me sharply and says, "I believe strongly in instinct. One single moment can sum up our whole life, and if we want to, we can see it. I can sense betrayal before the betrayer knows what he will do, and instinctively, I know who isn't trustworthy. Lola. But I needed to know what she was after and why she was always so conveniently there for me. No one wants to see what is right there before them. Jake, if your instinct is that this is about you, then who else but Anatoly would be after you?"

"No one. My work is all about him. I think he may be trying to scare me off, and if so, he is doing a good job. He seems to be up to something in Lake Baikal, Sergei, and maybe I am getting too close." My phone rings, and on it, I see a CANARY.

CLEO, 12

"Daddy, I think we need to find out what really happened the day Cindy died."

"I already know, Cleopatra. Tripp was the reason she died. He didn't call out that the boom was coming about. He was the captain that day."

"How do you know this?"

"Your mother told me years ago. She and Vera were quite close so your mother snooped around and found out what had happened though she never told Vera. Vera forbade anyone talking to her about the death of her daughter."

"He must feel so guilty."

"Not guilty enough."

"Did Sergei ever mention his son to you?"

"No, but I know how that happened as well, Cleopatra. Just like I know Danny was Tripp doing an undercover mission in Africa and how he fell in love with you but failed to mention he had children and a wife."

"I was so angry when I learned what Tripp Regan had done to me; I wanted to kill him. I told him my deepest secret. I told him how I was raped as a child, and he used that to make me fall in love with him. I never told anyone except you and Mother and then him. He betrayed me. But he destroyed Sergei's and Cindy's mother's lives far more tragically."

"Well, what do you think about the possibility of Cindy's mother being after him? Her husband just died. She must be alone."

Jake exclaims. My father turns to look at him.

"What is it, Jake?"

"A canary just appeared on my phone."

My father smiles at him and then speaks sotto voce to me.

"Remember how you told me Anatoly Rustikoff sent a canary to your hotel room where you were having a rendezvous with Jake? It's not unlike him to want to take credit for his actions. However, I still believe you are on to something. Don't you think the canary is too obvious? It came after Lola left and had time for a phone call. She and her husband are friends of Anatoly though how he is involved is what I need to know.

"Lola made a point of telling me she was doing a favor for a friend. Vera was definitely a friend. I think we may want to pay a visit to Cindy's mother at some point in the future."

ANN ARBOR, 2016

VERA, 7

I am seated at the Egyptian chessboard Ilse and Anatoly gave me when Cindy was killed. I smile up at him and gesture for him to sit opposite me. He takes a pawn and does the Queen's Gambit for his opening move. It's my favorite move.

"I am glad you came. Do the others have suspicions?"

"No, Vera. That has been taken care of by me, who meddled with the clues, tampered with the birdcage, so to speak."

"I find it a form of poetic justice that the chessboard you gave me when Cindy died was the stage for my revenge. Tripp will never know who was stalking his children, and he will always wonder who it was. It will niggle at him as he couldn't solve this one. He'll obviously think it was you, Anatoly, as you sent that photo of a canary. But I know him. He will soon see through your coverup and always wonder who, and why, and how, and again, *who*."

Anatoly looks at me.

"Just don't forget that it's not over yet. I still need my checkmate for Tripp stealing my Hawaiian garden. I haven't told you why I needed that garden, Vera. I will one day soon."

CLEO, 13

I met Anatoly Rustikoff in a doorway and told him in Russian that he "looked dangerous." There was silence until his men heard him laugh adding, "I am dangerous." A week later, he sent a canary to the hotel room where Jake and I were having a rendezvous in Honolulu.

We initially suspected he masterminded all the scary things in St. Moritz since a canary appeared on Jake's cell phone. But as always, there is more to it. That's why two years after the St. Moritz incident, Sergei, my father Didier, and I are on a trip to Ann Arbor, Michigan.

My hands are freezing as the chauffeur opens the door for me, and Sergei insists on helping me out.

Daddy is ringing a bell at the front door of our destination. I get a call on my cell phone. I hope it's Zelli telling me about her day at school. But no, it's Julia.

"Cleo! I had to call you and tell you I received the strangest text today! It says, 'The money deposited in your account is in reparation for hurting you, and it will allow you to have a nanny for as long as you and Ricky want.' I looked into my account, and there it was—God, Cleo, it will pay for our baby Constance's school as well. This is such a relief, but I have no idea who sent it. I don't believe Anatoly would have done this. What do you think, should I take it? I earned it! Ricky says I should think about it. But Jake got a windfall too."

"Julia, you certainly did earn it. It would make your life easier. And, speaking of babies, I have some news, too, and you're not going to believe it. I'm five months pregnant at age forty-five no less, and it's a boy!"

"What? What? That's amazing! Oh my god, Cleo! HOW?"

"It's called in vitro!"

"I don't know what to say! I bet you're thrilled, and Zelli must be thrilled, as for Sergei, to finally have a son again, Cleo, that makes me want to cry for him." Her enthusiasm bubbles over. "That's all true, Julia, and my father, who can't imagine he can love anyone as much as he loves Zelli, will find out he can. Oh dear, I have to go now. But take the money, Julia. I imagine Jake will."

Looking upward I see this rambling stone house. Orange and red trees dot the lawns.

We're still waiting for the maid to let us in.

We enter stage left. Vera is disheveled having just returned from a long hike. She laughs when we are introduced and engulfs us all while ordering lunch for us. My father seems entranced, as Vera is lovely and his age, and so normal in her windblown state. And like him, she has hearing aids. He knew her years ago. When she sits with us and starts to laugh happily again, I find I can't help laughing with her.

"I know why you are here, and I'm so happy you are." she says to us all.

"And we know why you did it, and we applaud you except Tripp's family isn't responsible for his sins. You were hurting Julia and Jake, and kidnapping *my* daughter."

"Heavens no, Cleo, that is the last thing I would do as the mother of a daughter. My pawn got carried away and I was furious when he told me what happened with Zelli. He had it all planned to take her up, give her a doll and even had a girl ski instructor lined up to take her down. But it went so wrong. I am so sorry and trying to make it up to everyone."

She turns to my father and smiles, "He did the Chowtel to get away. Didier, do you still do it? I must say it no longer beckons me."

"I did it last year, but it was my last hoorah."

They look at each other as they share the reality that means admitting your age and letting something you love go.

Vera has so many photos littered all around her living room. Everywhere you look, there are pictures of Cindy and a handsome, tall blond man that I'm sure was Vera's husband. One photo on the piano catches my eye, so I wander over to it. I see Lola, Vera, the same blond man, Anatoly, and a Russian-looking woman.

"Look at this picture," I bring it over to show everyone.

While everyone is staring at it, I turn to Vera and ask,

"How was Lola involved with you? What happened to her? She seemed to evaporate after she walked out of our lunch at Evergreen."

She laughs.

"Uh uh! Lola is a dear friend of mine, so I'm not telling you what happened to her or where she is. One clever thing Lola did for my "scares" was to move Cindy's photo to be right at your table so Tripp would see it. I imagine you noticed that Didier? I also gather you saw her husband so he wasn't able to administer a tiny touch of poison though I rather wish he had." She is musing. Then she turns to my father. "But, she told me how attractive you are these days, Didier. And I couldn't agree more. She was helping me punish Tripp, so it wasn't about either of you. As she told you, you weren't on this board."

He smiles. She's flirting with him, and he's enjoying it.

"And that's my husband, Barnie." She's pointing to him in the picture. "We were married for over fifty years."

My father pulls out his wallet and shows her a picture of him and my mother, Sandrine, in Algeria at his vineyard probably forty years ago.

Vera looks at Didier. "I miss her. She was a good friend."

"I'm enjoying this exchange between the two of you immensely, but how do you know Anatoly Rustikoff?" I interrupt.

"Anatoly and his wife Ilse are avid chess players like Barnie and I were. We played in tournaments against them all over the world. They won often, but not all the time."

She leans in slightly.

"I want to tell you a secret. Anatoly was very helpful when Cindy won her bronze medal. I really credit him with perhaps a bit too much influence on some of the judges." She laughs. "I never told anyone my suspicions. Not even Barnie. But Anatoly's 'friends' who were judges gave Cindy excellent marks. And when she died, Anatoly came right away to help us and hold us and grieve with us. He is a true friend. He loved Cindy. And he loved Barnie and me. Therefore the canary to take any suspicion away from me."

Before I could argue that point, a gong sounds announcing our lunch. Vera gathers us up to go into the dining room. My father walks next to her and slips his arm through hers. It saddens me to notice how he walks a step or two slower than he would have even a few years ago. But he seems relaxed to be with someone who, like him, has begun the aging process so gracefully.

I notice she is whispering to him.

VERA 8

"After lunch, Didier, I will be doing something very difficult and since you arrived providentially, I am asking you to be my witness. It will be shocking, and I must have been waiting for the right person, which seems to be you. It would help me to have you there."

"Yes, Vera, of course."

Lunch seems interminable to me, but I see the checkmate in my mind, so after lunch, I order coffee and dessert in the drawing room for the others and taking Didier's arm excuse ourselves for a short while.

Heading upstairs, I leave him in the hall as I get dressed for the moment in a mantilla, black dress, and heels. I put on makeup, fix my hair, and pick up an envelope.

"This is getting a bit suspenseful, Vera," he says as I walk back out to join him. I just smile tremulously.

We walk down the long hallway toward the room. I open the door, and a nurse comes over. I give her the envelope I've had ready for her, and she leaves, squeezing my hand.

Then I take Didier's hand and lead him into the room.

There is Cindy lying in a hospital-style bed with pumps and all the instruments that have kept her body alive, even though she has been brain-dead for over thirty years.

She looks beautiful lying there.

Her doctor walks in and looks at Didier quizzically.

"Are you ready, Vera?" he asks solemnly. I nod.

"Yes, I will leave everything else to you," I say as I walk over to her bed. I take off the small diamond earrings she wore when she won the Olympics and at her wedding and put them in my ears.

I kiss her goodbye and reach up to pull the plug before I can think. And then the doctor quickly goes to her bed and turns off all the monitors.

The silence is deafening.

"It is over." I stand there. Alone.

Didier comes to her bed and pulls the sheet up over her face. He takes my hand.

"No, Vera, It is beginning."